Crime Exposed

CRIME

EXPOSED

A BUCK TAYLOR NOVEL

BOOK 4

BY

CHUCK MORGAN

Printed in the United States of America

First printing 2019

ISBN 978-1-7337960-0-2...Paperback

ISBN 978-1-7337960-1-9...eBook

ISBN 978-1-7337960-7-1 Large Print

LIBRARY OF CONGRESS CONTROL NUMBER

2019904492

Contents

DEDICATION   viii

Chapter One   1
Chapter Two   9
Chapter Three   16
Chapter Four   25
Chapter Five   33
Chapter Six   41
Chapter Seven   49
Chapter Eight   57
Chapter Nine   66
Chapter Ten   75
Chapter Eleven   82
Chapter Twelve   89
Chapter Thirteen   97
Chapter Fourteen   105
Chapter Fifteen   114
Chapter Sixteen   120
Chapter Seventeen   131
Chapter Eighteen   136
Chapter Nineteen   143

Chapter Twenty   150

Chapter Twenty-One   156

Chapter Twenty-Two   162

Chapter Twenty-Three   171

Chapter Twenty-Four   177

Chapter Twenty-Five   184

Chapter Twenty-Six   190

Chapter Twenty-Seven   196

Chapter Twenty-Eight   203

Chapter Twenty-Nine   210

Chapter Thirty   216

Chapter Thirty-One   221

Chapter Thirty-Two   227

Chapter Thirty-Three   231

Chapter Thirty-Four   238

Chapter Thirty-Five   243

Chapter Thirty-Six   251

Chapter Thirty-Seven   255

Chapter Thirty-Eight   261

Chapter Thirty-Nine   269

Chapter Forty   275

Chapter Forty-One   283

Chapter Forty-Two   291

Chapter Forty-Three   299

Chapter Forty-Four   306

Chapter Forty-Five   313

Chapter Forty-Six   319

Chapter Forty-Seven   326

Epilogue   328

Acknowledgments   332

About the Author   333

Other Books by the Author   334

DEDICATION

Dedicated to everyone involved in battling sex trafficking and child pornography.

Chapter One

Jim McBride knew his wife was pissed; he just wasn't sure what had set her off this time. The sound of slamming doors that bombarded his ears indicated that whoever she was mad at would receive her full wrath. He was glad it wasn't him. It didn't even cross his mind that he would be the cause of all that racket. He wasn't even sure that she thought about him at all. She didn't seem to care enough about him to get mad at him. She had plenty of producers and cameramen and hapless assistants upon whom to vent her anger. Their relationship had been strained for several years, especially once the last of their children had left the house to pursue their own lives. But throughout their marriage, Jim had always accepted the mood swings. They seemed to be part of being married to a celebrity, or at least that's how it had been for as long as he could remember.

So, sitting in his office, he poured himself an after-dinner brandy and opened the *New York Times* website on his laptop. He settled into the big cushy leather chair that sat behind his desk and started to read about the day's events. It didn't take long before the warmth from the fire in the hearth, and the warmth from the brandy in his belly, worked their magic, and he drifted off to sleep.

Jim awoke with a start, and in his foggy mind, he realized two things that made him believe that this time Barb, his wife, was pissed at him. The first was when she threw open the glass panel door that closed him off from the world and three panes of glass shattered when the door hit the wall. The second indicator that he was in deep shit was the fire that raged in her eyes. He couldn't remember if he had ever seen her that angry, and he could feel the fear of what was about to happen well up inside him. The full glass of wine she threw at him was the cherry on top of all that anger.

The wineglass bounced off the back of the leather chair, spraying wine all over him and the desk, and continued until it met the river-rock fireplace and shattered against the stones, spilling what was left of the wine down the front of the hearth.

"What the hell, Barb?"

"Don't you what the hell Barb me, you son of a bitch. How dare you?" she yelled.

"How dare I what? Why don't you calm down and tell me what's going on?"

Jim knew before the words were out of his mouth that he'd made a huge mistake. He turned away from her and started to wipe the wine off his laptop screen.

Barb walked to the edge of his desk and threw a handful of papers across the desk.

"How dare you bring this filth into my house? Have you no shame?"

Jim picked up the papers and leafed through

them, and his eyes got as big as saucers. He could not believe what he was looking at. The papers were pictures of children, pornographic pictures of children, and it momentarily stunned him.

"Whe . . . Where did you get these? These are disgusting."

The warmth he had experienced earlier was gone, and all that was left was confusion.

"Someone emailed those to me. Probably one of your pervert friends. What the fuck is wrong with you. I'm right in the middle of an exposé on child porn, and you have the balls to be involved in something like this."

"I have no idea what these are. I would never be involved in something like this," he said.

Barb didn't seem convinced, and she threw down the last piece of paper she held in her hand. Jim picked up the picture and felt like he wanted to vomit. The picture was a young girl, no older than fourteen or fifteen, and she was sitting half-naked on his bed. Barb had recognized the picture on the wall over the bed.

Disgust and revulsion showed on his face and he raised his hand to his mouth. He didn't have a clue how to respond.

"I have never seen this girl before, and I have no idea how you got a picture of her sitting on my bed."

"You should be ashamed of yourself. You are a disgusting pig, and I want nothing else to do with you."

"Barb, I would never do something like this."

She stared at him with disgust and disbelief.

"I should call the sheriff right now and have you arrested, you pig. You and your friends are the lowest forms of humanity, and when I am finished investigating you, your pathetic life will be worthless."

Barb turned and walked out of his office, grabbed her coat off the hook in the hallway and picked up her overnight bag, which she had left at the foot of the stairs.

"I'm going to spend a couple nights at my sister's. I want you gone when I come back, or I swear to god, my first call will be to the sheriff."

"Barb, wait. Let's talk about this first. I am sure there's a reason for all this. We need . . ."

He heard the front door slam, and the sound reverberated through the house. He sat and leafed through the pictures on his desk. He had no idea who would have sent these or why. He had never seen Barb that angry and he wasn't sure what to do next. He poured himself another brandy, finished wiping the wine off his desk and sat back in his chair. He thought about going after her, but it was apparent she was not in a mood to talk. Maybe a few days at her sister's would be good.

Her car pulled out of the garage and he sensed the garage door closing, and then she was past the house and flying up the road towards the highway. He took a long drink, sat back and closed his eyes.

****

Barb had never felt so humiliated in her life. You would have thought after all those years of marriage you would know someone, but that was not the case, and she wasn't sure what she was going to do about it. She should call the sheriff and have Jim arrested. It wouldn't be a big loss since he was basically worthless anyway, but deep inside she still loved him, and she was having a hard time believing he would be involved in something like this. She would decide what to do once she had a chance to cool off and talk to her sister.

She threw her overnight bag in the trunk, slid into her car, started it and pulled out of the garage, pushing the button to close the door as she left. She drove past the house and then headed down the dirt road towards Highway 9.

As she approached the end of her road, she didn't see any oncoming lights, and she blasted onto the highway, fishtailing as she went. Light snow was beginning to fall, and she hoped she would be able to make the hour-and-a-half drive to Steamboat Springs before the roads got bad. She hated driving over Rabbit Ear's Pass in the snow, especially at night.

She had driven about five miles north of the ranch and was approaching the South Cow Creek campground at Green Mountain Reservoir when the lights in the car flickered, and the engine died, plunging her into complete darkness. She managed to steer the car over to the shoulder before she lost all her momentum.

"Shit. What now?" she said out loud.

She stepped on the brake and pushed the start button, and nothing happened.

"This is all I need," she thought to herself. "The damn car is only two years old. What the hell?"

She reached for her purse and pulled out her cell phone, but when she pushed the button to activate the screen, it also appeared dead. She felt alone on an empty stretch of highway, and the snow was getting worse. She considered her options, which were not good, but the best option was to walk back to the house. She hated that idea, and besides, she wasn't dressed for a long walk in the snow. She decided to wait it out and hope someone would come along.

She didn't have to wait long before her prayers were answered, and a pair of headlights pulled onto the shoulder behind her. Now, Barb was no dummy. She knew better than to open her door to just anyone, but opening the door was her only option as she had no power to the windows, so she waited until what she hoped was a Good Samaritan walked up to her door.

The man walked up and tapped on her window.

"Barb, are you all right?"

She was so relieved to see who it was that she set her phone down on the console and opened her door.

"Thank god. I'm not sure what happened. The car just died, and so did my phone. Can you give me a ride back to the house?"

"Sure can," he said. "See if it will start now. Maybe it needed to sit for a minute."

Barb stepped on the brake and pushed the start button, and the engine started right away.

"What the hell?" she said. "It was deader than a doornail."

She was about to thank the Good Samaritan when he reached a huge hand behind her head and in one swift move slammed her forehead into the steering wheel. The blow was so hard that it cracked the top of the steering wheel. It took two more blows to knock her out.

The Good Samaritan checked the highway in both directions and didn't see any lights coming from either direction. He reached across the unconscious Barb, picked up her cell phone and pulled her laptop out of her purse. He walked back and put them on the seat of his truck and then returned to the car. The car had stopped precisely where he wanted it to stop.

This section of Highway 9 skirted one of the finger inlets that made up the east side of the reservoir. The guardrail covered the area that was open to the lake below, and there was just enough room to roll the car past the guardrail, where it would plummet the forty feet into the reservoir below.

He put the car in gear and, checking once more up and down the highway, pushed the car past the end of the guardrail and stopped it at the edge of the drop-off. The reservoir was still frozen, but he hoped that enough of the thaw had occurred to make the ice thin enough so the car would crash right through it. He was confident that the snowfall that was under way would cover the hole in the ice.

With one last look up and down the empty

highway, he closed the door, walked behind the car and gave it a shove. With a grinding of metal against rock, the car bounced over the edge and rolled down the side of the reservoir, crashing into the ice with a loud bang, and after a second's hesitation, broke through the ice and disappeared beneath the surface. He stood on the shoulder of the road and watched until the taillights blinked off.

Comforted in knowing that Barb had not fallen out of the car or revived enough to swim out of it, he turned, walked back to his truck, did a U-turn and left the scene.

Chapter Two

Buck Taylor usually loved his job. He'd been with the Colorado Bureau of Investigation for almost eighteen years, and he enjoyed the variety of crimes he got to investigate. But there were two types of investigations he hated. One was when a child was involved: murder, abduction, abuse, or whatever. These types of crimes were devastating to everyone involved. The other type of investigation he dreaded was when a police officer was shot, or worse yet, murdered in the line of duty. Those types of crimes were fraught with drama and emotions always ran high.

As soon as CBI Director Kevin Jackson called that morning, three days ago, Buck knew this case was going to be bad. Whenever a law enforcement officer was murdered, the Colorado Bureau of Investigation got the call. Their forensics teams were top notch, and because of the emotional toll it took on the other officers and personnel in the department involved, CBI served as an outside investigator, keeping the investigation impartial. Buck had been involved in several "officer down" calls during his career, and they never got any easier, but everyone involved who knew Buck understood that if he was on the case, the investigation would be thorough, and justice would be swift.

That morning was no different except that emotions were already off the charts.

The last member of the Grand Junction Police Department to be killed in the line of duty was K9 Gero, whose end of watch came on May 5, 2004. He was shot while he and his handler covered the execution of a warrant, and his handler was able to kill the assailant. For the most part, Grand Junction was a small, peaceful city on the western slope of Colorado, a few miles from the Colorado-Utah border. The fact that nothing like this had happened in such a long time in the city made this early-morning call even harder.

Buck had arrived at the scene two hours after the bodies were discovered, and already the other officers in the police department were ready to round up every bad guy in Grand Junction and string them up. The police chief had his hands full trying to keep everyone from running off to track down suspects.

Sergeant Bill Smalley was a tall, thin officer with nineteen years on the force. He was one of the most well-respected officers in the city and had devoted his life to volunteering for any charity that needed help. The other officer on the scene was Rosy Trujillo, a three-year veteran of the force and the mother of a four-year-old named Anthony. She was married to her high-school sweetheart, and they had been talking about having another child.

Sergeant   Smalley   answered   the

possible burglary-in-progress call at 2:15 a.m. and headed for a small industrial park that sat along the Colorado River. Officer Trujillo took the call as backup, and they both arrived on the scene at almost the same time. The evidence would indicate that both officers opened the doors to their respective patrol cars and before they could even swing their legs out of the car, they were shot multiple times by one, possibly two unseen assailants. Both officers died lying on the ground next to their patrol cars.

Buck walked up and shook hands with Police Chief Mike Whitaker. "My condolences, Mike."

"Thanks, Buck. I'm glad you're here. Your forensics guys are already working on the car, and the doc released the bodies."

Buck saw the tears form in the chief's eyes. He reached out and took hold of the chief's arm. "It's okay, Mike. You go be with your people. We'll take care of your officers. Did you set up roadblocks?"

"Yeah, as soon as we found the bodies. I-70 in both directions, 50 North and South and the major surface streets."

"Thanks, Mike."

Mike nodded and walked away to join the group of officers who had formed behind the crime scene tape. Buck turned and headed towards the two shot-up patrol cars. CBI Agent Ashley Baxter was standing to the side of one of the cars talking with Dr. Sima Kalishe, the forensic pathologist for Grand Junction. Dr. Kalishe was tall and dark-skinned with black hair that she had tied up in a bun. Originally from Kansas City, she had gotten her medical degree at the University of Colorado and stayed in Boulder after graduation.

They stopped talking as Buck walked up, and he shook hands with each of them in turn. He then stepped away from them and walked towards the cars. Both women had dealt with Buck for a long time, and neither was offended by his behavior. One thing Buck always did when he first approached a crime scene was to stand for a minute and look it over. He liked to get a feel for the scene before listening to any of the details. This approach had served him well for a lot of years, and you could almost feel the intensity as he slipped into what he called "investigation mode."

Having gotten the overall picture of the scene, he walked back over to Bax and Dr. Kalishe.

"Ladies. It's good to see you both. Doctor, can you give me a quick rundown on what you see."

Buck and Bax followed the doctor to the first body, where she knelt and pulled back the sheet that covered the body. She held the sheet in such a way as to prevent the police officers behind the tape from seeing the body. Using her pen as a pointer, she started in the area around the ballistic vest.

"Sergeant Smalley didn't die instantly. He was hit with six rounds altogether. Three of the rounds are lodged in his vest, one round hit him in the throat, one in the upper left shoulder."

"What about the head wound, Doc?"

She hesitated for a moment, anger welling up in her eyes. "The head wound was a coup de grâce.

The shot came while he was lying on the ground. I hope he didn't see it coming."

She recovered the body, and they stepped over to the second body. Repeating the same procedure.

"Officer Trujillo died instantly. She was hit twice in the head, twice in her left arm and once in her leg. Buck, this is so tragic. These officers never knew what hit them. How can somebody be this cruel?"

Buck nodded. "Thanks, Doc. As soon as my forensics guys have all their pictures, you can take the bodies."

Buck and Bax stood up and walked towards the forensics team, who had set up a table under a white tent where they were cataloging evidence bags.

"What do you think, Bax?"

"I don't think they stood a chance."

Bax was about five foot six with blue eyes and blond hair she kept tied in a ponytail, hanging through the hole in the back of her CBI cap. She was what some would describe as husky, or what used to be called having a "mountain girl" figure. She wasn't gorgeous, but she was pretty enough to turn men's heads when she walked into a room, at least until they spotted the badge and gun clipped to her belt. She had been with the Colorado Bureau of Investigation over five years, and she had earned Buck's respect numerous times during their time together.

Buck nodded as they stepped into the tent. He shook hands with Richard Goodnight, the lead forensic tech. Buck and Rick went way back, and he knew that Rick would leave no stone unturned in going over the cars and the bodies for evidence.

"Buck, good to see you."

"Rick, what have you got so far?"

"Both officers died where they lie. This was an ambush, straight up and down. The shots came from behind the dumpster next to the roll-up door. We'll run ballistics, but it looks like a .308. The officers didn't stand a chance. We'll gather their clothes once they get to the morgue. We are getting a lot of prints off the cars, but we'll run elimination prints against the first officers on the scene and the EMTs. When you look at the cars, you will notice a couple things. Both dash rifles are gone, so are the laptops, the officer's weapons and their dash and body cameras. These guys were brazen enough to stick around and take their time going through the cars and the bodies. This is some cold shit."

Buck couldn't agree more. He stepped out of the tent followed by Bax, who handed him a pair of blue nitrile gloves, and they walked over to the cars. Pulling his flashlight from his pocket, he opened the passenger door of the first car, knelt and moved the flashlight from side to side. Seeing nothing his techs had missed, he moved around the car and did the same thing on the driver's side. While he was looking through the car, Bax walked over to the dumpster and examined the area around and in it. By the time Buck was finished with the cars, she had finished looking at the dumpster. She seemed perplexed.

"What's up, Bax?"

"I can't figure this, Buck. Was it a crime of opportunity, were they covering up another crime we haven't discovered yet or was it a couple sick bastards getting their jollies off?"

"All excellent questions, Bax. Let's put some of those cops to use." He pointed towards the group that had assembled behind the tape. "Let's start a door-to-door search of these businesses. Maybe somebody caught something on a security camera. Wake up the owners if you have to. There aren't many homes nearby, but have the cops check everything within a thousand yards of where we are and call the office and have our guys check for cameras along each street leading out of here."

"Are you heading to the autopsy?"

"Yeah. I want to send those bullets to Max as soon as possible."

Buck started to walk away, but he stopped and turned around.

"To answer your question, Bax. Sometimes murder is just murder."

Chapter Three

The next two days went by like a blur and sleep was at a premium. Working together with the Grand Junction police as well as the Mesa County sheriff and the state police, the investigation raced at a fever pitch, but by the end of the second day, they were still nowhere. So far, the canvassing had turned up nothing of any value. No eyewitnesses, no video and the evidence was worthless. Whoever the perpetrators were, they were well organized, and they knew how not to leave any evidence. The more Buck thought about it, the more he was concerned that this was a well planned and executed ambush.

Sleep-deprived, he pushed back from his laptop and leaned his head against the back of the chair at the borrowed desk at the CBI field office in Grand Junction. Buck very seldom worked out of the field office, an agreement he'd made with the former director of CBI Tom Cole, a long time ago. Buck had turned down several of Tom's offers over the years he worked for the Gunnison County Sheriff's Office. He thought he was content until the night Tom showed up at his front door in Gunnison and offered him the chance to work out of a new field office he was opening in Grand Junction. The best part was that he could work from his home. A quick discussion between Buck and his late wife Lucy, and a month later he started the second phase of his law-enforcement career.

Buck had drifted off to sleep when Paul Webber woke him up. Paul was a big guy, over six foot four with a muscular physique. He had joined CBI two years earlier after spending ten years with the Dallas, Texas police department. His last post was as a homicide detective. Paul may have seemed like a giant, but those who knew him knew he was a pussycat. He was one of the most soft-spoken guys Buck had ever met. They had first worked together on an arson fire that had almost cost Buck his life when the case got way bigger than just a fire. He was also instrumental in helping Buck unmask a decades-old serial killer in Aspen a couple months before. It was Paul's diligence that led to the information that revealed that the old serial killer's granddaughter, Alicia Hawkins, had taken up her grandfather's cause. She was now somewhere in Florida, keeping the authorities down there on their toes as she honed her deadly skills.

Buck still followed her case whenever he had the chance. He blamed himself for each death that was attributed to her because he was unable to finish the case and arrest her.

"Buck. Sorry to wake you, but Bax called, and they want you back at the scene. She sounded excited."

Buck stretched and wiped his eyes. "Okay, I'm on my way. Any luck with the camera hunt?"

"Not so far. I have a few more stores to call, but

I need to crash for a while. I'm getting cross-eyed chasing store owners."

"Okay, Paul. Grab some shut-eye, and we'll start again later this afternoon."

Paul walked away, headed for the break room, and Buck loaded up his laptop, grabbed his notes and headed for his car. Since there was little traffic at that time of the day, Buck made it to the industrial park in ten minutes. He pulled around the building and parked his state-issued black Jeep Grand Cherokee next to Bax's Jeep and stepped out. Bax and Detective Larry Cooper were standing in front of one of the shops talking with a big burly-looking biker as Buck walked up. Detective Cooper was shorter than Buck and a little heavier, with a receding hairline. He was Buck's liaison with the GJPD. He was wearing a winter coat over his sport coat.

Surprise was written all over the biker's face. "Well I'll be damned, Buck Taylor. How the hell are you? Thought you'd be retired by now."

"Moose? Geez, it's been a long time. You still look the same." He smiled and said to Bax, "What's going on?"

It was Detective Cooper who spoke first. "You two know each other? Why am I not surprised?"

"Yeah," Buck said. "Moose and I go way back. He helped me with a case, must be what, fifteen years ago. Stolen motorcycles. Moose gave me the lead that cracked the case."

Moose smiled. "Yeah, that was fucking something. First time I ever helped a cop. Almost cost me my club affiliation, but believe it or not, Buck talked to the club, and they all backed off. Told me he would, and he did. Knew right then he was a stand-up guy, even for a cop."

Buck laughed, thinking back on all the interesting characters he had met during his thirty-four years in law enforcement.

Bax waved her hand to cut off the conversations and said, "Moose might have the bad guys on video. He just got back into town. Was delivering a motorcycle to a buyer in Vegas. While he was gone, someone tried to pry open his shop door. When he pulled up the CCTV footage, he spotted the car off to one side. There's also a blurry image of two guys, one white, one black, trying to break into his place."

Moose spoke up. "I got broken into a couple years back. Couple high school kids fucking around, looking for a fast score. So, I put in cameras. Haven't had to use them since. I think the wife watches them to make sure I'm working."

That was good for a laugh all around.

Bax had her laptop open on the hood of Detective Cooper's car, and she pulled up the video from the shop door camera. The picture was not the best quality, and the fact it was dark didn't help, but it showed two individuals trying to use a pry bar on Moose's door. The car was visible off to the side.

"Do we know what kind of car that is?" Buck asked, squinting at the blurry object at the edge of the picture.

"We were discussing that when you pulled up,"

said Cooper. "I can have one of the tech guys try to enhance that so we can see it better."

"No need," said Moose. "I've seen it around here before. 1980 Olds Cutlass, burgundy landau roof over a black body. Saw it cruise through the parking lot a couple times in the last week or so. Car like that, you notice."

Buck, by this point, had put on his reading glasses and was looking closer at the car. He raised his head and said, "This was way before your time, but I think Moose is right. I had that same car after I got out of the army. First new car I ever owned."

Buck asked Detective Cooper if he could run the year, make and model and see if anything turned up locally, and he asked Bax to run the video back to the office and have one of the tech guys try to enhance it. He thanked Moose, shook hands and was turning to walk back to his car when he stopped and turned back to the group.

"Who made the call?" he asked.

Bax and Detective Cooper thought about the question, and they both shrugged their shoulders.

Buck continued. "This started with a 911 call of a burglary in progress. We've been working under the assumption that the call was a fake and was made to set up the ambush. But this video says there was an attempted break-in, so who made the call and why did a simple burglary end up with two dead cops? Are we now looking at a crime of opportunity?"

Buck turned back around and stood staring out across the parking lot. There were very few houses in the area on either side of the river, and none of the other businesses were open at that time of the morning, so where would the 911 call have come from?

"Bax, can you pull up the murder book and access the 911 call?"

Buck was a dinosaur when it came to technology, but one of the things that the CBI did a couple years back that made a huge difference in how Buck did his job was to set up a file sharing system. In the old days, all the documents that pertained to a case were kept in a blue three-ring binder. The problem was that anytime someone needed to look at something in the "murder book," as it came to be known, or add information, they had to take the book with them. The new system allowed Buck or any agent to open a new case file, which automatically assigned it a new case number, and then the agent gave access to the file to anyone involved in the case. Documents, lab reports, evidence, photos and all manner of information were inserted electronically by the sender, so anyone with access to the file had instant access to the latest information.

Bax opened her laptop and pulled up the file containing a digital recording of the 911 call.

"Grand Junction 911, what's your emergency?"

"Someone is trying to break into one of the shops in the industrial park on Riverside, north of 25 Road."

"Ma'am, are you in the area now and are you in any danger?"

"Just send the cops."

Noticeable click on the line.

"Ma'am, can I have your name and where you are calling from?"

"Hello, ma'am, are you still there? Ma'am? Hello."

Late-spring snow started to fall, and Buck pulled his collar up against the breeze. By normal standards, it was late for snow to fly, but Buck could remember years when he was younger, and they had measurable snow as late as the Fourth of July. The forecast was for snow showers for Grand Junction, but the mountains could be buried under as much as a foot of new snow.

Detective Cooper was the first to speak. "Definitely sounds like an older woman."

"I don't hear anything in the background that might help us," said Bax.

Buck thought for a minute. "Are there any homeless encampments along the river? Her voice was shaky, like maybe she was cold."

"She could have just been scared," said Bax.

"Let me make a call and find out what we can about homeless people in the area," said Detective Cooper. He stepped away from the group as he pulled out his cell phone.

Buck and Bax watched the video one more time and listened to the 911 call again. Nothing jumped out at them. Buck was going to play the call one more time when Detective Cooper walked back to them.

"I have one of the patrol officers who works

this area coming by. If anyone can tell us about the homeless in the area, he can."

While they waited, Bax pulled up the forensic reports. She was looking for the ballistics report on the bullets that had been pulled from the bodies of the deceased officers. Halfway down the report, she found what she was looking for. The report indicated that the techs found a partial thumbprint on one of the bullets that had been lodged in the vest. The bullet was severely deformed, so it only amounted to a sixty percent print, but AFIS had kicked out a possible hit.

"Hey, Detective," she said. "What do you know about a guy named Henry Jenkins?"

Detective Cooper was familiar with Henry Jenkins, so he filled them in on the details. Jenkins was a local black kid who was always in trouble. If it wasn't the cops who were looking for him, it was the school or a drug dealer, or just about anyone else who lived in the area. His parents were alive but out of the picture, and he spent most of the time couch surfing amongst his friends. He had never been in any real trouble, just youthful indiscretions.

"Why do you ask?" he said.

"The lab got a possible hit on a print found on one of the bullets, and it led back to Jenkins. It's a less than sixty percent possibility, but a possibility nonetheless," Bax replied.

Just then a GJPD patrol car pulled into the lot and parked next to the group. Officer Todd Kearney stepped out of the car and approached the group, shook hands all around and asked how he could help. Buck explained about the call and asked Officer Kearney if any homeless people were living in the area, who might have witnessed the attempted break-in and shooting. Kearney thought for a minute and asked Bax if she could play back the call so he could listen to it.

Bax played the call twice more, and Kearney said, "That almost sounds like Brenda."

He explained that Brenda had been on the streets for as long as he could remember. She was in her sixties and suffered from Parkinson's disease, which she refused to do anything about and could explain the shaky voice. He told them that she lived along the river.

"Would you mind taking Agent Baxter with you and try to locate this Brenda?" Buck asked.

He called his dispatcher and asked her to relay his location to his desk sergeant and told her that he would be on his rover, his portable radio. Bax locked her laptop in her car and grabbed a pair of gloves and her flashlight, and they headed across the parking lot towards the river.

"Detective, can you get an address for this Jenkins character? Let's go figure out why he might have been playing with ammo."

Chapter Four

Buck followed Detective Cooper south on Highway 50 and onto eastbound North Avenue until he turned left at North Fifteenth Street, crossed Glenwood and halfway down the block pulled to the curb. Buck slid out of his car and stood for a minute looking at the ramshackle house that stood before them. At the very least a coat of paint and a yard would have helped, although the snow that was starting to stick to the grass hid most of the yard damage. Best thing would have been for a strong wind to come up and level the house. Buck felt sorry for a kid that had to grow up in a place like this.

With Detective Cooper in the lead, they walked up the cracked sidewalk and onto what was left of the front porch. Cooper knocked on the door then took a step back and slightly left, giving Buck a full view over his right shoulder. From inside they heard a cough and the slow shuffling of feet as someone approached the door.

The door swung open, and standing in front of them in a stained sweater and ripped jeans was a tall, gray-haired black man. He could have been forty, or he could have been eighty, it was hard to tell between the partial beard and the bloodshot eyes. He held a can of beer in his hand.

"What d'ya want?"

"Mr. Jenkins," said Detective Cooper as he held up his badge. "Is Henry here?"

"What he do now?"

"We would like to talk to him for a minute if he's around, sir," said Detective Cooper.

"Ain't seen him in a couple weeks. Now get off my porch and leave me alone."

Mr. Jenkins tried to push the door closed, but Buck reached out his hand and pushed the door back.

Jenkins glared at Buck through bloodshot eyes and then reached for Buck's hand.

"What da fuck?" he slurred. "You got a warrant?"

"Mr. Jenkins, we need to know where your son is so we can have a friendly chat," said Buck.

"Ain't no such thing as a friendly chat when it comes to the police," Jenkins replied. He pushed the door a little harder, but Buck didn't back down.

"Mr. Jenkins. We don't want to cause you any trouble," Buck said. "But it is important we talk to your son. He might be in a lot of trouble."

"This about those two police that got shot?" asked Mr. Jenkins.

"What do you know about that, sir?" asked Detective Cooper.

"Don't know nuttin' about those two police being kilt and neither does Henry or that no good white trash shithead he been hangin' with lately. Told them boys they was gonna have real trouble someday they keep mouthin' off about the police."

"Mr. Jenkins," said Buck. "If you know anything about this and you don't tell us, you could be arrested as an accomplice. You could go to jail, sir."

"Already been to jail, once. Ain't no big deal. Still got friends in Canon. Ain't no big deal."

"Mr. Jenkins," said Detective Cooper. "Who is the white boy Henry's been hanging with?"

"Don't know who he is. Drives an old car. Now, I'm done talkin'. You want anything else, you come back with a warrant."

This time Mr. Jenkins pushed the door closed.

Buck smiled at Detective Cooper. "Think it could be the same old car?"

Cooper thought about it for a minute. "What are the odds of there being two old cars involved in recent crimes? I'm inclined to believe that this is the same car from Moose's video."

"Good," said Buck. "Let's request a warrant to search the house."

Detective Cooper pulled out his phone and called his office. Buck's phone chimed, and he pulled it off his belt and checked the number. "Hey, Bax. What's up?"

He listened for a minute, told her they did a good job and that they would be there as soon as they could and disconnected the call.

"Bax says they found our homeless person. We need to head back to the industrial park."

They each headed for their cars and followed the same route back to the industrial park. When they pulled in, they spotted Bax and Officer Kearney at the far end of the lot talking with an elderly woman.

She appeared to be wearing two or three coats and was stooped over. She wore a knit cap on her head and had on fingerless gloves. Buck and Detective Cooper approached the group, and Buck introduced himself to Brenda.

Bax gave Buck a look that said the elderly woman might not be all there and explained that Brenda was having trouble sleeping the night of the break-in and had walked up from the river to find a place out of the wind. She saw the two men, one white, one black, doing something to the door with a long bar and called the police because most of the shop owners were kind to her and she didn't want them getting broken into.

"Brenda," Buck asked. "Did you see the car they were driving?"

She stood for a minute and stared into space, trying to recall the moment. "Yes, sir, I did. It was an old black car. Couldn't make it out clearly because I lost my glasses a while back. Also saw them hide when they saw the lights from the cop cars."

"Brenda, where did they hide?" Bax asked.

"Right behind that dumpster. They shot those two cops as soon as they got here, but I didn't hear any shots. Saw the flashes from the guns but no noise."

Buck, Bax and Detective Cooper thought about what Brenda just told them. A picture of the attack was forming, and they understood why there was only the one 911 call. The bad guys had used silenced weapons. "Why did you hang up after you called 911?" asked Buck.

She pulled her old flip phone out of her coat pocket and held it up for Buck. "Battery was low. Just like now. Didn't want to be without it during the night."

"Brenda, where do you sleep at night when it snows? Do you go to the shelter?"

Brenda pointed towards a pile of cardboard boxes covered by a blanket. "Over there. I like being along the river. It's peaceful."

Buck saw her makeshift home and offered to take her to the shelter. Brenda shook her head, no. "Can't leave my stuff. Someone will steal it."

Buck walked back to Bax and Detective Cooper, who were standing together watching Brenda head back to her makeshift shelter.

"What a sad life," he said. "Her story backs up the video, so we need to find out who owns that car and also who Henry Jenkins's friends are."

Detective Cooper was about to say something when his cell phone chimed, and he stepped away to answer it. Buck and Bax took a minute to talk about what Brenda had said about not hearing any noise from the guns. This was something new. Although it was easy to buy a suppressor these days, it was still unusual to see them at a crime scene. Buck was about to comment when Detective Cooper ran back over.

"They got a hit on the car description. SWAT is rolling. Chief wants us there, now. He also sent a detective and a couple uniforms over to the

Jenkins's house to execute the warrant. Got a verbal from the judge."

They each jumped into their respective cars, and Buck and Bax followed Detective Cooper as he pulled out of the parking lot and, with lights flashing, pulled onto Riverside Parkway. He turned onto 25 Road heading north, turned right on Patterson Road and turned left on 28 Road, where they ran into a police roadblock. They pulled their cars into the first available spaces they saw, got out, grabbed their ballistic vests and signed in with the officer that was manning the roadblock.

It was a nice-looking house with a well-kept garden out front, and the only thing out of place was the front door hanging off its top hinge. Several SWAT officers were standing out front talking when the trio walked up, and Detective Cooper stepped up to a captain who was talking with one of his officers. They spoke for a few minutes, and then he called Buck and Bax over. He introduced them to Captain Stan Jackson, the SWAT commander, and explained that their suspect, twenty-eight-year-old Edward Michael Seville, was not at the residence. While Bax and Detective Cooper talked with the captain, Buck stepped through the door, noting the damage caused to the lockset and the doorjamb by the ram. There was a heated conversation coming from the kitchen, and he stepped through the door and spotted Chief Whitaker and several plainclothes detectives talking to a middle-aged woman who was sitting on a kitchen chair with her hands cuffed behind her.

From the language coming from her mouth, Buck could tell she was not happy about the damage the police caused when they smashed in her front door. Buck listened for a minute and figured out that she was the mother of their suspect and she had no idea where her son was.

The chief walked away frustrated and spotted Buck standing in the doorway.

"Definitely her son who owns the car. His old man took good care of it, and when he died a year ago, she gave the car to her son. He's got a juvy record and did six months in county for assault. She doesn't know if he is friends with Henry Jenkins. She swears she doesn't know the name."

A detective walked out of a hallway deeper in the house carrying two boxes in his gloved hands. "Chief found these in the bedroom under a pile of clothes in the closet."

The boxes were long and thin, and everyone in the room knew what they once held. "Suppressors," said Buck.

Buck pulled out his phone and dialed Paul Webber. He answered with a sleepy voice and Buck filled him in on recent developments.

"Paul, would you give the forensics guys a call and get them on their way?" He gave Paul the address for both houses. "Also put out an APB for Seville, Jenkins and the car. Bax will text you the details. Let's cover all the surrounding states. Thanks."

He waved Bax over. "Would you send Paul the details on the car, Jenkins, and Seville and then head back to the office and run a deep background check on Seville and Jenkins. We need to figure out where they might run to. I'm going to stick around here and see what else we can find."

Bax pulled out her phone and started texting. Buck was always amazed at how easily she handled technology, but he was glad she could. He didn't know anyone who could do a deep dive on the internet better than Bax.

Chapter Five

The interview with Mrs. Seville lasted well into the evening and Buck, who was already running on little sleep, was wiped out. Although she was still angry about her front door, Mrs. Seville tried to answer their questions about her son as honestly as possible. She knew he was in contact with several people on the internet who seemed to be somewhat radical, but she had no idea who they were or what they were concerned with. The techs were going through his laptop, and they hoped to have some answers in a couple hours. They had not been able to narrow down where he might have run to or even where he got the guns. They found literature in his room supporting gun rights but nothing they would call unusual or even radical. An outsider looking into Seville would have come away thinking he was just a red-blooded American kid who was interested in guns and old cars. Buck still had no idea what had caused this normal kid to murder two police officers.

Chief Whitaker called Buck into his office. "Buck, I can't figure this kid. He seems perfectly normal. What are you thinking?"

"I was sitting here thinking the same thing. I wish we knew more about him, but his mother was no help. Let's hope we see some results from the APB, or tomorrow is going to be a long day."

"Why don't you go crash for a while, you look dead on your feet. I'll call if anything comes in or if any of my detectives find anything interesting. By the way, the search of the Jenkins house didn't give us anything. I guess the father was telling the truth about not seeing his son in a while."

Buck nodded, grabbed his backpack and headed for his car. Before heading for the hotel, Buck had two stops to make. The snow that started earlier had left about an inch on the ground, and as Buck cleaned off his car, he thought about all the nights he and Lucy sat on the front porch of their home in Gunnison and watched the snow come down.

Buck and Lucy were married the month before he joined the Gunnison County Sheriff's Office. They met while they were both in high school. Buck was a standout football player, and until senior year Lucy had avoided him, thinking he was another stuck-up jock. She gave in to the pressure from her friends and went out on a date, and what she found surprised her. Buck barely talked about himself. He was soft-spoken, a little shy, interested in her and when they were together, he made her feel like she was the only other person in the world. After that first date, there was no keeping them apart. Following his enlistment in the army, he came back to Gunnison, accepted the job with the GCSO and proposed to Lucy that same day.

They were together for thirty-four years until Lucy passed away in his arms after a five-year battle with metastatic breast cancer. Lucy's death hit Buck hard, even though they knew that it was coming, someday. Two and a half years after her death and Buck was still dealing with the memories and the sense of loss. He wiped the tears from his eyes, slid into his car and headed for the closest Walmart.

Buck walked into Walmart and headed for the camping supplies. He picked up an inexpensive pop-up tent and a decent winter sleeping bag, then walked over to the deli and ordered a fried chicken dinner. With his packages in his arms, he headed back to his car, loaded everything in the back and headed back to the industrial park. Parking near where Brenda had showed him her pile of boxes, he grabbed his purchases and walked towards her shelter, calling her name as he approached. Brenda poked her head out of her shelter and was having trouble seeing in the dark. Her face showed the fear she felt until Buck told her who he was, and she seemed to relax. Over the next half hour, Buck set up Brenda's new tent, placed her new sleeping bag inside and helped her load her meager belongings into her new home. When he was finished, he wished her a good night, accepted a grateful hug and headed back to his car. He knew Lucy would be proud of him and that made him smile. He pulled onto Riverside Parkway and headed for his hotel.

It seemed to Buck that he had just put his head on the pillow when he woke up to a ringing in his ears. It took him a minute to realize where he was, and he reached over to the nightstand and grabbed his phone.

"Taylor."

"Buck, it's Jim Gilchrist, sorry to wake you but I didn't think this could wait."

Jim Gilchrist was the Boulder County sheriff and one of Buck's oldest friends, going back to grade school. He had been the quarterback of the Gunnison High School Cowboys football team when Buck and his future brother-in-law, Hardy Braxton, broke every state defensive record and were known as the "wrecking crew" for their explosive plays on the field. Buck and Gilchrist had joined the sheriff's office the same year, went through the police academy together and a few years later went through the FBI's National Academy at Quantico. Gilchrist was Buck's best man when he married Lucy, and they had lived and raised their families next door to each other in Gunnison until Gilchrist's wife grew tired of winters in the valley and they headed for warmer pastures in Boulder. He was elected sheriff in 2012, and like his buddy Buck, he never wanted to do anything else.

Buck squinted through the fog in his brain and checked the time on his phone. "Jim, what's got you up so early?"

"I may have your APB in my backyard, so grab the Coke sitting next to you, take a drink and wake up."

This got Buck's attention, and he was now wide awake as he swung his legs out from under the covers, grabbed the warm bottle of Coke off the nightstand and took a big swallow.

"Okay, Jim. You have my full attention. Fill me in."

"One of the Nederland cops spotted the car yesterday outside a liquor store. He remembered it because he's a car guy and you don't find many pristine Olds Cutlasses on the street anymore. He didn't see the APB until a couple hours ago, so he decided to drive around and try to find the car."

"Fuck, Jim. Tell me he found it?"

"You got that right, brother. It's parked at a cabin about two miles west of Highway 72, on County Road 128 West. He spotted it about an hour ago and called us. He says it's buried up to its axles in the driveway. We got about a foot of new snow yesterday, and that's not the best car for driving on back roads in the snow."

"Is he absolutely certain?"

"Plates different but car matches the description. Have you got a couple pictures of the perps you can send me right away? The officer says he got a good look at three of the guys and . . ."

"Wait, a minute. We have two suspects. He's saying at least three guys were in the car?"

"Yeah, they must have picked up some local help along the way."

Buck grabbed his laptop, opened the murder book and clicked on the tab entitled "Suspect Descriptions." He clicked on each picture, attached them to the email and clicked send.

"Got it," said Gilchrist. "Let me send these over to the officer and see what he says. Call you back."

Gilchrist hung up, and Buck sat down at the desk. He had missed a call, and he checked his voice mail and found a message from Chief Whitaker. The tech guys had accessed Seville's laptop, and they found some hateful stuff, directed at a lot of ethnic and religious groups, but a lot of it calling for killing cops. The tech guys were able to open his contact list, and they were running the list to see if they could match names to people.

Buck jumped in the shower, toweled off and was putting on his boots when his phone rang. He checked the number and answered.

"Well?" he said.

"The officer confirmed your two guys were at the liquor store. He also said they identified the other guy in the car. Antonio Rivera. Did a nickel for aggravated assault. They were notified two weeks ago that Rivera was being released from Canon City because they were the ones who arrested him. The cabin they are in belongs to Rivera's uncle, who spends winters in Mexico. The officer thinks there might be as many as five guys in the cabin."

"Sweet. I'm on my way. Can you surround the cabin without them knowing? These guys are bad news, and the tech guys found a lot of hate speech directed towards cops."

The sheriff told him he had already called out his SWAT team and they were on their way to Nederland. He promised he would hold off as long as possible, but he would not jeopardize his guys by waiting too long past sunrise.

"Buck, meet me at the Nederland Police Department, and I will take you in, and one other thing. These are cop killers, and as much as I respect you, they are on my turf, and my SWAT commander will be in tactical command. Okay?"

"Got it. I will be on my best behavior. I should be there by sunrise, but you guys go when you are ready. It's your call. And Jim, be careful. These guys will not hesitate to shoot first."

Gilchrist hung up, and Buck threw his clothes in his go bag, grabbed his laptop, gun and badge and headed for the car. He threw everything in the back, started up and pulled onto Highway 50. As soon as he turned onto I-70 East, he hit the gas and turned on his flashers. His first call was to Chief Whitaker, and he filled him in on the call with Sheriff Gilchrist. The chief was ready to send his entire department to Boulder if need be, but Buck calmed him down and asked him to hold back. This was a different jurisdiction, and the Grand Junction Police had no authority there. He asked him to call Detective Cooper and have him head to Nederland as soon as he could to be their liaison. The chief agreed reluctantly, and Buck hung up and dialed Bax, who answered on the first ring.

"Hiya, Buck. Get any sleep?"

"Bax, don't you ever sleep?"

She told him she was in the office with Paul Webber and they were uploading the evidence from the Seville house into the murder book. She wanted everything in order to take to the judge in the morning. They had gotten the original arrest warrant based on the promise she would bring the judge the murder book as soon as they had everything compiled, and she never broke a promise to a judge.

Buck told her to let Paul finish the evidence log and asked her to email the arrest warrants to Sheriff Gilchrist in Boulder County. He had forgotten to do that in his haste to get on the road. She told him she would take care of it and that she was here if he needed her.

"Buck, I don't know if you went through all the stuff the tech guys found, but these guys are bad news. I can't figure out where they got radicalized in their hatred for cops, but some of this stuff is vile. Be careful, okay?"

Buck thanked her for her help and her concern and promised to be careful. He hung up, pulled the mic for his statewide radio, called the state police dispatch center and told them he was traveling east on I-70 with lights flashing. He didn't have a lot of time, and the last thing he wanted to do was get stopped by a trooper for speeding.

Chapter Six

Buck arrived in Nederland just as the morning sun was cresting the foothills. It was a beautiful morning in the mountain community as the rising sun covered the snow-capped peaks in a soft pink alpenglow. He pulled into the police department parking lot and parked next to the Boulder County sheriff's SUV. Buck slid out of the car, stretched and walked up to the sheriff, who was standing next to his vehicle drinking coffee from a foam cup. He handed Buck a bottle of Coke he had sitting on the hood of his car. Buck's love of Coke was legendary around CBI, and anyone over the years who'd dealt with Buck knew that the man could consume huge quantities of the product. Buck thanked him and took a big gulp before replacing the cover. The look on the sheriff's face told the whole story.

"How bad?" asked Buck.

"We had no choice, Buck. They spotted two of my SWAT guys coming through the woods at the back of the cabin. Guy stepped out on the back porch while it was still pitch black. My guys said they hit the ground as soon as they saw the back door open. Whether he saw them or heard them I have no way of knowing, but he yelled for his buddies, ran back in the house and came out with an AR and opened up on my guys. Two of them tried to make a run for the car, firing their weapons all the way, and my snipers took them both out. We cut down the guy on the porch when he went to reload. There were two more guys in the house, and they opened up from the front and side windows. We lobbed in some tear gas, threw in a couple flash bangs and smashed in the front door. One guy was lying on the floor with a bullet in his upper chest, the other guy died at the scene."

"Are your guys okay?"

"Yeah. One of my guys at the back of the house took a round through his outer shoulder, it's a through and through, and he is on his way to the hospital as we speak. One of my guys got hit in the chest, but the vest stopped it. He'll be sore for a week, but he is happy to be alive."

"Shit, Jim. I'm sorry about your guys. Where's the bad guy?"

"On his way to Denver. He's in critical condition. Flight for Life just picked him up over at the school."

"Well, I'm sorry you guys got caught up in this, but I'm glad you came out ahead. Doesn't sound like you had any choice. Can we get into the cabin?"

The sheriff nodded and told Buck to follow him. They pulled out of the parking lot, jumped on Highway 72 and in two miles turned left onto County Road 128 West. Buck and the sheriff pulled their cars over onto the side of the road, climbed out and Buck grabbed his coat and his backpack. The first thing Buck noticed as they approached the house was the big pile of snow in front of the driveway. Buck pointed to the pile.

"Didn't want them leaving while we were setting up," said the sheriff, "so I had one of the county snowplow drivers make a run up 128, and he made sure that a lot of snow ended up in front of the driveway."

Buck smiled. The sheriff's crime scene unit was already on the scene, and the sheriff stepped away to talk with the three techs while Buck headed towards the house. The first two bodies were right where the sheriff said they would be, in what Buck would assume to be part of the driveway. One body, a young black male, was propped up against the house and had several bullet holes in his chest and shoulders. The AR-15 was lying on the ground, a foot away. The second body, Buck's second suspect, was lying next to the front passenger door of the Olds Cutlass, which was riddled with bullets. Buck observed what appeared to be two exit wounds in the upper back and a lot of blood on the snow under the body. Buck took out his cell phone and took several pictures of the bodies as they lay.

He walked around the house, shaking hands with several of the SWAT officers as he went, climbed up the stairs to the deck and stopped several feet back from the third body. This body belonged to a powerfully built older Hispanic male. He was lying in the snow with just a pair of boxers and a T-shirt on. He had several bullet holes in his upper torso and Buck could see a lot of prison tats on his arms, neck and the side of his face. Buck took more pictures, including a facial close-up.

He had to be careful where he stepped as he approached the back door since there was glass everywhere from the shattered windows all along the deck. He turned and focused on the tree line at the edge of the backyard. He spotted the two red marker flags about forty yards into the woods where the two deputies had been when they were somehow discovered. Buck thought for a minute. At night in the dark, they would be hard to see. He could only imagine that the perp must have heard something. He would need to find out how much moonlight there was at that time of the morning. Buck turned and walked until he stopped at the threshold and peered through the shattered door. The forensic techs, dressed from head to foot in Tyvek jumpsuits, were busy working the scene, so Buck stayed where he was so as not to contaminate the scene.

Buck was pulling out his phone when two men came around the corner of the house. One was Hispanic, average height with a full head of black wavy hair, and the other was a tall black man sporting a thin mustache. Both were wearing jeans and winter coats with the word police written on the back and across the left chest.

"Agent Taylor?" said the Hispanic man. They stepped up on the deck and he introduced himself as Investigator Juan Sanchez and his partner as Investigator Bernard Williams, both with the Boulder County District Attorney's Office. Sanchez told Buck they would be handling the shooting investigation and asked him if they could speak with him in the crime scene trailer. Buck said he would meet them out front in a minute. He needed to call the Grand Junction police chief and fill him in. They nodded and stepped away so Buck could make his call.

Chief Whitaker answered his call on the first ring.

"Buck, glad you called. How are things going?"

Buck filled the chief in on the events of the morning, and when he finished, the chief was quiet for a minute.

"Any doubt that the dead guys are Jenkins and Seville?"

"I'm comfortable. The coroner will confirm their IDs, but I don't have any doubt that these are our guys."

"Thanks, Buck. I appreciate everything you did for us. Please thank Sheriff Gilchrist for all his help and tell him we will be praying for his wounded deputy."

Buck next dialed his boss. Director Jackson answered on the second ring. Kevin Jackson, when appointed, had been one of the youngest directors in the history of the Colorado Bureau of Investigation. He was appointed by Governor Richard J. Kennedy. Before his appointment to the director's position, he had worked for over a decade with the Colorado Springs Police Department where he rose through the ranks with what seemed like light speed. Most of his career in the Springs was on the administrative side, but Buck had learned over their years of working together that Kevin Jackson was also an excellent and intuitive investigator in his own right.

"Buck, what's going on?"

Buck filled the director in on what had transpired so far. The director listened without interrupting until Buck completed his update.

"Honest opinion, Buck. Is it a good shoot or did these guys go cowboy and take out a couple cop killers?"

Buck thought for a minute before answering. He couldn't figure out how the SWAT officers were spotted in the dark, but that would all come out in the DA's investigation.

"From everything I've seen so far, sir, it appears to be a good shoot. I know Jim Gilchrist well, and I know how well trained his deputies are. Anything is possible, but I think this was righteous."

"Good," said the director. "Excellent work on this. I will call and thank Bax and the team in Grand Junction. You finish up there and get some sleep."

Buck hung up and walked around the house to the crime scene van and stepped inside. Sanchez, who was sitting on the edge of the desk reading a report, asked him to have a seat. He moved aside a couple of file folders and asked Buck if he was okay being recorded. Buck said he was okay with that and sat down opposite the two investigators.

Sanchez asked Buck to fill them in on how the investigation in Grand Junction led to the two suspects and how he found out they were here in

Nederland, which Buck was happy to do. He walked through the entire investigation to date, and then he offered to share the murder book file with them. He pulled out his phone, pulled up the mobile file-sharing app and sent a link for the file to the two investigators' emails. The investigator thanked him for his help, and Buck left the van. Detective Cooper was standing next to the van talking to Sheriff Gilchrist when Buck exited the van.

"I see you two already met?" Buck said. He shook Detective Cooper's hand.

"I guess I missed all the excitement," Cooper said. He held on to Buck's hand and said, "I don't know how to thank you, Buck. Our officers will go to their final resting place knowing that justice has been served. Under the circumstances, it doesn't get much better than that."

"You guys need anything from me, give me a call. I gave the DA's investigator access to the murder book, but anything at all, you call. I'm going to swing by the police department and crash on one of their bunks for a while before heading back to Grand Junction. I'm about done."

They all shook hands, and Buck walked back to his Jeep, stashed his backpack in the back and headed for the Nederland Police Department. He didn't feel comfortable driving back to Grand Junction with having slept about four hours in the last five days. He figured he could grab a few hours and a late lunch and head back later that afternoon. He felt good about the work they had done. The two Grand Junction officers deserved the best work his team had to offer, and he was proud of his team. He agreed with Detective Cooper: he wished they could have taken the bad guys alive to stand trial for what they did, but in the end, justice was served.

Chapter Seven

Buck sat for a minute on the edge of the rack in one of the holding cells in the Nederland Police Department's office and stretched out the kinks in his back and shoulders. He'd found over the years he could sleep just about anywhere, but the older he got, the less that seemed to be the case. The day shift officer was kind enough to find him a thin blanket and a small pillow, which made the hardwood rack in the cell a little softer, but not much, but Buck didn't care. He was exhausted, and once his head hit the pillow, he was gone.

The alarm on his phone and his growling stomach told him it was time to wake up. He folded the blanket and left it and the pillow on the desk in the office and wrote a note thanking the officer for his hospitality. He had asked about a place to eat in town, and the officer told him to swing by the Nederland Deli. They served the best sandwiches and soups in town, and he wasn't kidding. Buck finished his huge pastrami sandwich and his glass of Coke and headed for his car. He checked his phone one last time, slid into the seat and pulled out onto Highway 72. He figured he would be back in Grand Junction by early evening and he would stop at the office first to check on progress.

He was about to turn onto I-70 when his phone

rang. Checking the number on the dashboard information system, he hit the green phone button on his steering wheel and answered.

"Yes, sir?"

"Did you get any sleep, Buck?" asked Director Jackson.

"Yes, sir. Couple hours and had an awesome sandwich. I feel alive again. What's up, sir?"

"I hate to do this to you, but the governor called. We have a possible missing person case unfolding in Summit County, and the governor wants us on it. Have you passed the Dillon exit yet?"

"No, sir. Just passing through Idaho Springs. What's the governor's interest?"

"The missing woman is Barb McBride."

The director mentioned the name like it was a name that should be familiar to anyone, and luckily Buck was aware of who she was. Barb McBride was a journalist of the utmost repute. She'd started her career as a television news reporter, spent several years as a national investigative reporter for one of the big networks and eventually went off on her own and was doing investigative documentaries. Over her career, she had won several Pulitzers and several Emmys for her hard-hitting documentaries. By all accounts, Barb McBride was at the top of her game, so her disappearance was going to be a national news story. He understood why the governor would want this handled as fast and as discreetly as possible.

"Sir, can you text me the address and let the sheriff know I'm on my way?"

"Done and done," said the director. "I appreciate you doing this, Buck. You let me know if you need anything and I'll make it happen."

Buck hung up the phone and let out a long sigh. "Fuck. Just what I need, a missing celebrity. This should be fun," he said out loud since there was no one around to hear him.

Governor Richard J. Kennedy was one of those Kennedys, but he never flaunted that fact. It almost seemed to Buck that he tried to avoid the connection at all costs. He was a multimillionaire businessman in his own right and had created and sold several different businesses. He was in his early seventies and had spent twenty years in the state legislature before becoming governor. Somehow over the years, Buck became the governor's go-to guy when he needed an investigation handled with discretion. So far, Buck hadn't disappointed him.

The huge drug bust that Buck had been involved with in Durango, the year before, was one example of their relationship. Buck solved the case and avoided any notoriety, and the governor won praise in the local and national press for his leadership. This was just the way Buck liked it. He avoided the media like the plague, and he always made sure the governor thanked all the people involved. It was not a one-man show, and so far, the governor had not taken advantage of their relationship. He knew Buck was not political at all and that he would not tolerate any political motivation or intrusion in his investigations.

Buck hit the phone button on his steering wheel and said, "Call Bax cell phone."

Bax answered on the second ring. "Hey, Buck, what's up?"

Buck filled her in on the phone call with the director. "Are you in the middle of anything with the Grand Junction package that can wait a little bit?"

"Right now, I'm waiting on the evidence from Boulder, but I don't expect anything to come in for a couple hours. What do you need?"

"Can you do a deep dive on Barb McBride and let's see if there's anything in her past that might have caused her to run? I'd like to eliminate that possibility as soon as possible. Also, call the Summit County sheriff and see if they have her cell phone number and let's get a warrant for her phone records and ask the provider to give us a current phone location."

"You got it, Buck. By the way, the service for the two officers is scheduled for Saturday. I will fill you in on the details as I find out more."

Buck thanked her and hung up. He pulled into the far-right lane, took the Silverthorne exit and headed north on Highway 9. He followed the Blue River through Silverthorne and thought about all the times he'd fished along the Blue River. This was one of his favorite rivers to fly-fish, but it was quite a drive from Gunnison, so he seldom got up this way unless he was on a case. Buck always carried his fly-fishing gear in the back of his Jeep and no matter what the weather, he was always ready to slip into a nearby river for an hour or two of fishing. He was convinced that fly-fishing had kept him sane after Lucy died. As time grew short, Lucy loved to sit on the bank of whatever river Buck happened to be fishing on. She would read or crochet, or sometimes just sit and look at the birds. Even though he was standing in the middle of the river, as long as she was with him, she was content.

Buck had gathered the family together one Sunday morning after Lucy passed away to scatter her ashes at one of her favorite places to sit, a small handicap fishing dock along the Gunnison River at a little park in the middle of town. It was supposed to be a private affair, and everyone got a chance to sprinkle some ashes in the river and say a few words about her. Somehow word had gotten out in the small town, and when they turned to leave, there must have been three hundred people standing behind them in silence, many with their heads bowed in prayer. Their friends and neighbors brought food and drinks, and what started out as a simple family gathering turned into a huge spontaneous party, honoring Lucy. Although she didn't want any kind of service, Lucy would have loved it, because it was so genuine.

Buck wiped the tears out of his eyes and continued twenty miles north of Silverthorne to the address the director had given him. Buck didn't need his GPS to tell him when he got there. The road leading from Highway 9 to the house was full of cars, trucks, county and state vehicles. He counted several Summit County Sheriff's Office

SUVs as well as two state police cars and the van belonging to the Summit County Search and Rescue. He pulled up to the deputy who was manning a makeshift gate, presented his ID and was waved through. He parked alongside the house, slid out of his car and grabbed his coat and backpack.

Buck stood for a minute and admired the house and the property. The back of the property sat right along the Blue River and backed up to what he knew to be national forest on the other side of the river. The house was built to look like an old-style two-story farmhouse, but he could see that it was anything but. The exterior was clean, freshly painted and seemed to have all the latest energy-saving features. A covered porch that ran the length of the house anchored the front of the house, and there was a beautiful, what appeared to be hand-carved front entry door depicting the river, the mountains and a bull elk with huge antlers. Buck was impressed and wondered if he might know who the wood-carver was. People always laughed about it, but the truth was that Buck knew a lot of people all over the state, and it seemed like he remembered and befriended everyone he met.

He stepped up on the front porch and was about to push open the front door when the door opened, and Summit County Detective Carl Chandler stepped out onto the porch.

"Buck Taylor, how the hell are you?" He stuck out his hand, and Buck shook it.

Carl and Buck had worked a murder together when Carl was first promoted to detective after attending the FBI's National Academy in Quantico. It was Carl's first major crime, and he was grateful for all the credit Buck gave him in solving the crime, even though he felt out of his league during the investigation. Buck never saw it that way. He was a rookie investigator once too, just like Carl, and he never had a problem passing along the knowledge he had gained over the years to someone interested in learning and becoming a better investigator.

"It's nice to see you, Carl. How have you been? You look the same as the last time I saw you."

Truth is, Carl was a little heavier and had a little less hair than the last time Buck saw him. He was average height and wore a navy blue SCSO logoed ranch coat over a white shirt and blue-and-red-striped tie that was pulled down at the neck. He also wore glasses, which was something new since the last time, and he had a thick mustache that showed a lot of gray.

"I'm glad you're here, Buck. When the sheriff told me you were coming at the request of the governor, I was thrilled. I haven't handled near as many missing persons calls as you have, so welcome."

"Seems like you got a hell of a crowd inside. Have you started the search yet?"

"Yeah," said Carl. "Took us a while to notify everyone and have them meet out here. The head of search and rescue is inside passing out assignments. We've already been in touch with Grand County and Routt County, and they will start searching along Highway 9 and Highway 40 in their jurisdictions to see if maybe she went off the road. You want to go inside?"

"In a minute. Why don't you fill me in on what you've got so far?"

Chapter Eight

Carl signaled Buck to follow him to the end of the porch. He leaned against the rail, pulled a pack of cigarettes out of his coat pocket, dug out a brass lighter and lit up. He took a long drag, held the smoke for a minute and then exhaled. He offered the pack to Buck, who refused, and he set down his backpack.

"We got the call about an hour ago from Barb McBride's sister, Elizabeth Grainger. Mrs. Grainger lives in Steamboat, and she has been calling her sister for the past two days since she hadn't heard from her. Mrs. Grainger called Jim McBride a couple hours ago to see if he knew where his wife was. The sisters talked every day unless Barb was doing the final editing on one of her documentaries, but she always told her sister when that was happening."

Buck pulled a small notebook and pen out of his jacket pocket and made a couple quick notes. He signaled Carl to continue.

"According to Mr. McBride, he and his wife had an argument three nights ago, and Mrs. McBride left in a huff—his words, not mine. Said she was going to spend a couple days with her sister, got in her car and tore out of the driveway. Until his sister-in-law called today, he assumed his wife was in Steamboat and would come home as soon as she cooled off."

"Okay," said Buck, squinting to read his own handwriting. "So, Barb McBride left home three nights ago and hasn't been seen since?"

Carl nodded. He told Buck that as soon as they got the frantic call from Mrs. Grainger, he was dispatched to meet up with search and rescue and start a road search for Mrs. McBride's car, a 2017 white Range Rover, Colorado plate Victor Bravo Charlie one seven four.

"What time did she leave the house?"

Carl pulled out his phone, opened a notebook app and scanned down the page until he found the entry he was looking for.

"Mr. McBride is unsure of the time. It seems he spent most of the day drinking and was well out of it when the argument occurred. He was having trouble recalling the argument."

The odd look on his face caught Buck's attention. "What?"

Carl hesitated. "From the conversation I had with him, he must have spent most of today drinking as well. Mrs. Grainger, who is very angry right now, says this is a normal state for him to be in. I don't think there is any love lost between those two."

Buck understood the hesitation on Carl's part. Missing celebrity, drunk husband, argument: this was the kind of story that was like a wet dream for the editors of the daily rags. They would pay huge money to anyone willing to talk, and as soon as this became national news, the paparazzi and the national reporters would be all over this. Buck gazed out over the property. One good thing was that with the long driveway they would see the news vans coming and they could stop them from getting near the house. The bigger problem was that behind the house on the other side of the river were thousands of acres of mountains and forests. This was going to be fun.

Buck turned back towards Carl. "Let's go talk to Mr. McBride and the sister."

Carl pushed open the front door, and they both walked into a warm, cozy foyer. The house was as tastefully done inside as it was well cared for outside. Carl pointed towards a double glass panel door at the end of the hall, and they headed that way. They passed what appeared to be the living room or family room just inside the front door. The head of the search and rescue team was pointing to a map laid out on a table and was passing out search assignments to two-man teams. He nodded to Buck and Carl as they passed and went back to his debrief.

They continued down the hall, and the first thing Buck heard was the yelling coming from the office. To his ears, it sounded like a one-sided argument since the only voice he could make out was female. As they stepped into the office, the yelling stopped, and a tall, slender blond-haired woman turned and glared at Buck. Buck figured she was somewhere in her fifties, but she might have been older and in good shape, and she was dressed in jeans and a flannel shirt. He assumed this was the sister.

Sitting in the desk chair behind her was the person Buck assumed was the husband, Jim McBride. He was younger than Buck expected, possibly in his forties. His brown hair was combed back, and he wore jeans and an old University of Colorado sweatshirt that appeared to have seen better days. His eyes were bloodshot, and he held a glass tumbler in his hand, filled with a light tan liquid. He had a couple days' growth of beard and probably hadn't slept in a while.

The sister fixed her gaze on Buck and then on Carl and with fire in her eyes said, "Who the fuck is this and why aren't you out searching for my sister?"

Buck spent his life dealing with people, including the irate relatives of people who were involved in a crime, and he had developed an amazing level of patience over the years. One thing that always worked well for him was to slow down the level of discourse. If the person he was dealing with yelled, Buck would lower his voice, and if they continued to raise their volume, he would lower his. At some point, the person would have to stop yelling because they could no longer hear what Buck was saying.

Buck entered the room and noticed the three broken glass panes that used to be part of the office door and were now shattered in a hundred pieces on the floor, along with the hole in the wall where the doorknob had hit it with enough force to break the drywall. The office was a typical male-inspired office, with dark wood paneling on two of the walls, a large stone fireplace and dark wooden beams at the ceiling. A leather couch sat opposite a beautiful burled wood desk, and there were Western prints on the walls.

Buck could sense the sister getting more and more aggravated, but he also could see her breathing slowing down as she followed him with her eyes as he toured the room. He reached a large picture window that had a great view of the river about fifty yards away, stood there for a minute admiring the view and then turned to face McBride and the sister. The two deputies that were standing against one wall glanced at Buck, and he could tell they were expecting the explosion to begin again. Instead, Buck addressed the conversation to the sister.

"Evening, Mrs. Grainger, I'm Agent Buck Taylor with the Colorado Bureau of Investigation, and I'm here to help with the search for your sister. Is there someplace you and I can go to have a conversation? I promise I won't take much of your time, but we don't want to miss a minute in this search."

The sister, whose mouth was already starting to form the first salvo of the argument she was going to have with this guy, kind of evaporated, and she turned and walked towards the door. Buck and Carl followed her down another hallway to a huge farmhouse gourmet kitchen, where she pulled out one of the stools at an eight-foot-long island counter, sat down and put her head in her hands. Buck let her compose herself for a minute and then he walked over to the sink, took a glass from the drainboard, filled it with water and placed it on the counter next to the sister. She wiped the tears from her eyes, picked up the glass and took a long sip and then set the glass on the counter.

"I'm sorry about that little outburst, Agent Taylor, is it? I'm worried sick about my sister, and nothing seems to be moving faster than a snail's pace."

"No need to apologize, ma'am. This is a terrible situation you are in the middle of, and we will make sure we do everything we can to find your sister. Towards that end, I would like to ask you a few questions if I may?"

Mrs. Grainger nodded and took another sip of water.

"I'm guessing you are not happy with the way your brother-in-law is handling himself, with regards to finding your sister? Can you fill me in on a little of the family dynamics, the relationship between your sister and her husband, your relationship with them, anything at all that might help me understand her state of mind when she left?"

The sister thought for a minute, wiped the tears from her eyes and then opened up in a way she never thought she would, especially to a stranger.

"You're aware who my sister is, Agent Taylor, or I'm guessing you wouldn't be here? She's been in the limelight her entire adult life, first as a reporter, then an as a national news anchor and then creating highly acclaimed investigative documentaries. All that popularity was hard for her to deal with, and it was hard on the family, which is why she quit the TV news business and started doing her own investigations. She married Jim almost forty years ago when they were right out of college and at first everything was great. They were a celebrity couple and went to all the best parties, and they knew everyone."

"They had children early, and they were very happy. Something changed, Agent Taylor, after the kids moved out and Barb started working on her own. By that time Jim's drinking had gotten in the way and was putting a strain on their marriage. Jim was an award-winning cameraman, whose work suffered from the booze, and he found himself out of work and living in isolation out here. He never adjusted to the change, and he blamed Barb because she was the one who bought this property and built the new house and she was the one who kept him in money, but his life sucked just the same. Over the last couple of years, he's grown bitter and angry."

The sister stopped talking and took another drink of water and set the glass down, her eyes filling up with tears, again.

Buck said, "Mrs. Grainger, I understand that your sister was on her way to your house the night she disappeared. Were you aware she was coming? Had you spoken on that day?"

The sister thought back on that day. "No. We hadn't spoken that day, which was not unusual.

Barb was closing in on completing her most recent project, and she would often disappear into her studio for what seemed like days on end to finish editing the documentary. I had no idea she was on her way to my house until I called Jim at around four o'clock today because I was getting concerned that I hadn't heard from her. We might miss a couple days but never more than two or three."

"What happened when you called Mr. McBride this afternoon?"

"Jim told me they had an argument and Barb stormed out of the house. He said she was going to spend a couple days with me to cool down. It was obvious to me that he was drinking and had been for a while."

"Does your sister often visit you on the spur of the moment, like that?"

"Sometimes. We live in Steamboat, and it's a convenient place for Barb to sneak away to if she needs a break. To be honest, Agent Taylor, it was happening more and more frequently over the last couple years, but I was surprised she would leave this close to finishing her project and during a snowstorm. Barb hated to drive in the snow."

"Mrs. Grainger, I don't want this to sound insensitive, but is there anyplace else your sister might go to if she wanted to be away from her husband for a while? A friend, colleague, lover or some secret place she might have only told her sister about?"

"I don't think so, Agent Taylor. Her life was all about work, so I doubt she had time for a lover or anyone else in her life. She hardly ever sees the kids anymore, and they mean everything to her. Oh, my god, I need to call the kids and tell them what's going on. I doubt Jim has done that yet."

"One more question, Mrs. Grainger. Have you ever seen Mr. McBride become angry or violent? I'm sorry, but I have to ask."

"The truth, Agent Taylor, I don't think Jim cares enough about anything to get angry or violent."

The sister pulled out her cell phone as Buck slid off the stool and signaled for Carl to follow him. They had gotten a lot of information about the McBrides but very little that might help them find Barb. Buck walked down the hallway towards the office. Time to talk to the husband.

Chapter Nine

Jim McBride was still sitting behind his desk with the glass in his hand as he stared out the window at the river. For a guy whose wife was missing and lost somewhere in the mountains, he didn't seem at all concerned. He stared out the window and sipped his drink.

"In my own way, I love my wife, Agent Taylor. I can't stand being around her, but I still love her. Is that weird?"

"I guess that depends on a lot of things, Mr. McBride. I'd like to ask you a couple questions if that's okay?"

Jim McBride turned and faced Buck, his bloodshot eyes showing a kind of sadness. Buck couldn't decide if he was sad because his wife was missing or if he was just a sad man to begin with. Right now though, he needed to focus on finding the wife.

Jim McBride set his glass on the desk and picked up a pile of pictures. He leafed through them, studying each one as it passed his eyes. He let out a sigh and slid them across the desk towards Buck. Buck picked up the stack and leafed through them, his eyes showing the surprise. He handed them to Carl and waited as Carl worked his way through the stack, his eyes registering the disgust he felt. He handed back the photos and Buck set them down on the desk.

"Was that what the argument was about the other night, sir?" asked Buck.

"The argument the other night was a continuation of a long line of arguments that's lasted for years. I drink too much, I'm too lazy to find a real job, I've lost my enthusiasm for life, I drink too much. It's been one long argument since the kids all moved out, and no matter what I do, I'm wrong."

"Mr. McBride, where did the pictures come from?"

"Honestly, Agent Taylor, I have no idea. Someone sent them to Barb the other night, why I can't tell you, but she went nuts. Those pictures are disgusting, and it's not something I would do, but I can't explain how there is a picture of a naked teenage girl in our bed." He lowered his head and rubbed his temples.

"And you have no idea who would have sent them to her or try to hurt you in some way?"

He stared at Buck. "I wish I knew. All I can tell you is that it's not me."

"Mr. McBride, has your wife run off before?"

Jim McBride thought for a minute, a furrow forming across his forehead. "This is not the first time she's done this, but she always comes home in a day or two, never this long without any word. She told me she was going to her sister's, but for some reason that didn't happen."

"Sir, is there someplace else she would go if she

were pissed at you, a friend, a lover or maybe a hotel someplace?"

Jim McBride was quiet for the longest time as if he was trying to wrap his alcohol-soaked brain around the possibilities that lurked with that question. He shook his head no.

"Mr. McBride, do you have any idea what your wife was investigating?"

"You don't think she went off on her own, do you? You're thinking foul play?"

"Not necessarily, sir, but we need to cover all our bases. Does she have a laptop here in the house?"

"She probably took it with her, she was almost finished with this latest project, and she would be in the middle of editing. She would have taken it with her."

"Mr. McBride, why didn't you call your sister-in-law to make sure she got there safely? I understand she left just as the snow was beginning. Were you not concerned?"

"I'm sorry now I didn't call, but at the time she left I had been drinking, and I was unaware it was snowing. Hadn't listened to the weather report, and after she left, I must have passed out in my chair."

Buck considered the sad specimen of a man in front of him and shook his head. "Thanks, Mr. McBride. We will do everything we can to find your wife and bring her home. Appreciate your help."

He turned and walked out into the hallway, followed by Carl. When they were out of earshot of the office, Carl said, "What do you make of those pictures?"

"I'm not sure yet. I can see why something like that would piss off the Mrs. enough to leave home, but that seems like an odd response. I would think she would throw his ass out first. I wonder why she left and not him?"

"You got me," said Carl. "But if my wife headed out into a winter storm, I would make damn sure I checked on her. The guy is a real fucking piece of work."

Buck nodded his agreement. He told Carl he needed to check with Bax and see if she'd had any luck with tracking Barb McBride's phone, and he asked him to call his office and have someone type up a search warrant application for any electronics in the house. The pictures bothered Buck, and he wanted to see if they might be on Jim McBride's computer as well since they had to come from someplace. This also meant starting another investigation since possession of child porn was against the law. He was reaching for his phone to call Bax when one of the deputies from outside opened the front door and stepped into the foyer, followed by a younger man, who could have been Jim McBride's brother and in fact was.

"Detective, this gentleman says he lives here." He pointed his thumb over his shoulder. The younger version of Jim McBride was about the same height and weight but appeared to be about ten years younger. He was wearing suede boots, jeans and a ranch jacket over a flannel shirt. His hair was the same color but had more wave to it and hung over his collar. He removed his gloves and stepped up to Carl, reached out to shake hands and said, "Robert McBride, Jim's brother. Can someone tell me what's going on with all these people around?"

Carl studied the new arrival as Buck stepped forward and shook Robert McBride's hand. "Agent Buck Taylor, CBI, Mr. McBride. Your sister-in-law is missing, and we are in the process of organizing a search for her car."

Robert McBride appeared stunned and confused. "That can't be, Jim told me she went to her sister's in Steamboat for a couple days. Have you checked with Elizabeth? Let me call her." He pulled his phone out of his back pocket just as Elizabeth Grainger walked into the foyer from the kitchen.

"She never got to my house, Bob, and that idiot brother of yours didn't even have the decency to check on her."

Robert McBride grew more confused, and there was a hint of anger in the corner of his eye. "What do you mean she never got there? And Jim is no idiot. He's going through a rough patch right now, that's all. He . . ."

Buck waved his hand and cut them both off before this turned into another argument. "Bob, may I call you Bob? When was the last time you saw Mrs. McBride?"

Bob McBride thought for a moment. "That would have been Sunday morning. I left for Denver about two o'clock or thereabouts. Was staying with some friends; we went to a Colorado Mammoths lacrosse game on Monday night, and I didn't want to get caught in the storm."

"How did you find out your sister-in-law went to her sister's house?"

"Jim called me Monday morning before lunch and told me they had another argument, and she stormed out. Said she headed for Steamboat. Are you certain she didn't just go off on her own for a couple days? She's been working hard on her latest project. Maybe she just needed a break."

"Any idea what your sister-in-law is working on? Anything that might have gotten her in trouble with someone?"

Bob appeared confused. "I thought she left on her own. Do you think someone abducted her?"

"No, sir. We just need to cover all our bases. You said you live here sometimes. Do you have a room here in the house?"

"No," said Bob, "I have an apartment over the barn. Would you like to see it?"

Carl explained that the first thing they did when they arrived was go through the house and the outbuildings to make sure Barb McBride hadn't been hiding somewhere on the grounds, so it was not necessary to see his apartment at this time.

Buck smiled at Bob. "Thank you, sir. We will be in touch if we need anything further."

Bob headed for the office to talk with his brother, and Mrs. Grainger returned to the kitchen. Buck could hear a teakettle whistling in the distance. For the moment there was peace in the McBride house. He hoped it would last.

Buck and Carl stepped out onto the front porch. The sun was starting to set, and the clouds had a dark red glow to them. The temperature had dropped a few degrees, making it clear to everyone that the calendar in this part of the country was not always an indicator of the time of year. Winter was hanging on a little longer this year, and Buck pulled up his collar against the cool breeze.

"So, what do you think, Buck?"

"I think we need to see what search and rescue comes up with before we come to any conclusions. This seems to be a pretty dysfunctional family, but right now, I don't feel like anyone is lying to us, at least not outright."

"But you have a feeling like something's not quite right?"

"Maybe it pisses me off that a husband would care so little about his wife as to let her head out in a snowstorm and then not even bother to check to see if she made it to her sister's house. I'm having trouble buying the lack of concern."

Buck said, "Why don't you follow up with search and rescue and Grand and Routt counties and see if anyone has anything we can work with. I want to look in her office and see if there is anything that might give us a clue, if she ran off, maybe chasing a story or something. I will also ask Mr. McBride if I can bring in a tech team to put a trap on his phone."

"You are thinking foul play, aren't you?"

"Not really, but we are already three days behind on this thing, and I don't want to lose any time if we need to move on something. I want to be ready."

Carl gave him a suspicious look and headed inside to the makeshift command center in the living room. Buck walked down the hallway and stepped into the office. The conversation between the two brothers ceased when they spotted Buck.

"Mr. McBride, I would like to bring in a team of tech guys to put a trap on your house and cell phones. Would that be all right?"

"You think something happened to Barb, don't you," said Bob. "You're thinking ransom?"

"No sir, but I like to cover all the bases, and since we are so far behind on this one, I want to be cautious."

Jim McBride seemed hesitant, like he didn't believe him, but he told him to do what he needed to do. Buck thanked him and walked down the hallway and past the kitchen door. Mrs. Grainger was sitting in quiet contemplation, a half-empty cup of tea sitting in front of her. Buck nodded as he passed and walked down the back hall to Barb McBride's office. He wanted to see if he could figure out what she was working on. The little bug that sometimes sneaks into the back of his brain when things don't make sense had started to nag at him, and he wasn't sure why.

At this time, there was no reason to believe anything other than the Mrs. left the house in a huff because of the kiddie porn that was emailed to her. That is the only fact they had to work with, and Buck always worked with the facts. He never speculated on anything until the evidence took him to wherever it was going to take him, which was one of the reasons he was so successful as an investigator. He stepped into Barb McBride's office, turned on the lights and closed the door.

Chapter Ten

Barb McBride's office was not at all what Buck expected; of course, he didn't have any idea what he expected. He thought it would be like his late wife Lucy's office, a mix of creams and pastels with a little desk for writing or bill paying and soft lighting. What he discovered when he turned on the lights was a room stacked floor to ceiling with books and papers. There were file folders all over the place, and the desk was an old solid core door on two sawhorses. This was a working office for someone who did a tremendous amount of research. He sat down in the leather chair behind the desk, the only bit of opulence in the room, and pulled out his phone.

Paul Webber answered on the second ring. "Hey, Buck. How's it going?"

"I'm glad I caught you, Paul. Were you able to wrap up the evidence for the Grand Junction shootings?"

Paul explained that they were still waiting on ballistics from the Boulder shoot-out, but everything else was logged and put in evidence boxes. He also told Buck that the fifth shooting suspect from the cabin died at the hospital.

"Great job, Paul. Do you have anything going right now?"

"No, sir. What do you need me to do?"

"Can you grab the tech guys and head out here? I want to set up a trap on a couple of phones."

"Do you think this is an abduction?" said Paul.

"Not sure yet, but I want to be ready."

Buck scanned the office and considered all the camera gear and the file cabinets. "I could also use a hand going through Barb McBride's files. Her office looks like a bomb went off. I'm not even sure where to start."

Next to Bax, Paul was one of the best computer guys Buck knew, and even though they didn't have Barb McBride's laptop or phone, the rest of the equipment in her office was as foreign to Buck as anything he had ever seen.

"No problem, Buck. We'll be there in a couple hours." Buck gave him directions, hung up and dialed Bax.

"Hiya, Buck."

"Hey, Bax. Anything back on Barb McBride's phone?"

"I should have the call list in a couple hours. The location tracker could take till morning. I told them this was urgent, but you know how these cell phone companies can be. They all take their sweet time."

"Anything in her background material that might give us a clue where she went?"

"Nothing that jumps out at me. I opened an investigation file, and I uploaded what I found so far. Take a look when you can and let me know if you need anything else. I have a call into her executive producer to see if she can shed some light on where she might go. Background on the husband is in the file. Not much on him either, he's kind of a deadbeat."

"Great, Bax. I will read it later tonight. Can you run another background check for me? Mr. McBride's brother's name is Robert. He also lives here on the ranch, and we might as well be thorough, and run Barb McBride's sister as well. Elizabeth Grainger, currently residing in Steamboat."

"You got it, Buck. Do you think this might be more than a simple disappearance? Sounds like you're thinking foul play."

"Nothing specific, just a lot of unanswered questions. Listen, give me a call when you hear back on the phone location, no matter the time."

Buck hung up and scanned the office. He didn't have any thoughts about where to begin or what he was even hoping to find, but he was hoping something in all this chaos might lead him to where Barb McBride might have gone. He knew one thing for sure: wherever she was, it was a good spot. She was a well-known celebrity, and that would make it hard to hide for long.

Buck started with the piles of documents on the work surface, but he soon realized there was not just one cohesive storyline amongst all the folders and newspaper clippings and books. There was information on cattle mutilations in Colorado, there was information about the thousands of Native American women who had gone missing over the last decade, there were piles of information on fracking and mining and there were several files on sexually exploited children and kiddie porn.

It would have been awesome if she had a folder marked latest project, but that was not to be, so Buck started looking through the six four-drawer file cabinets that were against the wall behind the desk. What he found was more of the same and a ton of other items. It seemed to him that every time Barb McBride saw an interesting story in a magazine or newspaper, she pulled it out and filed it away for future use.

One file cabinet was full of folders on unsolved murders around the country. He found a couple files that contained information about killings in England and Europe.

Buck sat back down at the worktable after about an hour of digging through countless files and books and leaned back in the chair. He ran his fingers through his hair and rubbed his temples. This was getting him nowhere. Without having some idea of what she was working on, anything useful he might find was buried in a mass of information. He could have been looking right at it and not have any idea. He was about to give up when a thought occurred to him. Looking around the room, he found what he was looking for sitting next to the file cabinets.

The trash can was full to the top, so he cleared a space on the worktable and dumped the trash out in a pile. It appeared Barb McBride was a crinkler, since the can was full of balls of crushed papers. She also devoured a tremendous amount of energy drinks, evidenced by all the cans he found in the trash can. He set the cans aside and began unfolding the balls of paper and set the now-flattened pages on the corner of the desk. A half hour later and he had a large stack of papers to go through, so he sat back down and started reading.

One paper contained a list of names and phone numbers, several of which were familiar to Buck as they were prominent businessmen and politicians, both from Colorado and from outside the state. He set the list aside. He found several pages that appeared to have been torn from a spiral notebook. Each page was written in something that resembled hieroglyphics. He assumed this must be her personal code. He was aware that many journalists developed their own secret code, kind of shorthand so they could make notes while interviewing a subject, but also to keep other people from reading their notes. He made a mental note to ask Jim McBride if he was able to read his wife's code. When he was finished going through the papers, he had three stacks in front of him. One stack was trash, and those he put back into the trash can. The second stack was the coded notes, which he set aside. The third stack was scraps of paper containing phone numbers, names or email addresses. He would have Bax and Paul start researching those.

Buck, frustrated by his lack of anything significant, leaned the chair back and closed his eyes. He'd gotten about seven hours of sleep in the past week, so he decided to give his brain a rest and call it quits. He checked his phone and was stunned to see that it was almost midnight. He placed the two stacks of papers into a couple of manila file folders he found and left the office.

Carl was standing in the hall talking to the head of the search and rescue teams when Buck walked up. He'd glanced into the office as he passed, but it appeared Jim McBride had gone to bed, as the office was empty. He could tell from the frustrated looks on their faces that the search had failed to yield any sign of Barb McBride.

Carl's tone of voice said it all. "Not a fucking thing. We sent all the searchers home an hour ago and just finished looking over the map, trying to figure out where to look in the morning."

Buck nodded. "Okay, then let's call it a night and try to get some sleep. Please tell the deputy on duty out front that my tech guys should be here in a couple hours. They know what to do, so he just needs to let them in. Did McBride head up to his room?"

"Yeah, about two hours ago. He was totally wasted, so his brother helped him to bed, and then he headed over to his apartment above the barn. Mrs. Grainger is asleep in one of the guest bedrooms. She refused to leave until we have some answers."

"Did you have any luck in the office?" asked Carl.

"No. I have a couple things to follow up on, but nothing concrete. I will follow up in the morning. I'm heading back to Silverthorne to see if I can sleep for a few hours. Let's reconvene in the morning."

They each headed for their cars after leaving instructions with the deputy on duty. Buck stashed his backpack in the back, slid in and headed towards Silverthorne. He pulled out onto the highway and made a beeline for his hotel room twenty miles away. He needed a few hours of sleep to clear his mind. He hated to admit that he wasn't as young as he used to be and that it took longer for him to recover from these long nights, and in the past week he had put in a lot of long nights. He turned up the radio and rolled down the window to keep himself from falling asleep. Tomorrow was going to be another long day.

Chapter Eleven

Bax had spent the past couple hours researching the phone numbers she received from Barb McBride's cell phone provider. She couldn't believe the number of calls this woman made in one day. She must have had the phone glued to her ear. It was still early in the month, and she was sitting at her desk looking at fourteen pages of phone calls just since the first of the month. She knew Buck would want a list of as many names as she could match to the numbers, so she started running the list through the various data banks she had access to.

She started with the most recent calls, the ones Barb McBride made just before she disappeared, and by the time she could no longer keep her eyes open, there were twenty or so names on her list. Some came from watching various news programs, others were foreign to her, but she logged them all into the investigation file so Buck would have them first thing in the morning.

She decided going home was a waste of time, so she crashed on one of the two bunks the staff at the CBI field office set up in the storage closet. She was so tired, all she needed was a pillow and blanket and she would have slept on the floor.

Paul stopped by before she crashed and told her he was on his way to Summit County along with two of the tech guys to set up the phone traps Buck had requested. They took a minute to compare notes, but so far neither one of them had been successful at pulling anything that might help them find the missing woman. Paul headed out, and Bax turned out the light and crashed.

The ringing of her cell phone woke her up, and it took her a minute to remember where she was. She grabbed her phone off the edge of the table next to her bunk, checked the phone number and answered the call.

"Ashley Baxter, Colorado Bureau of Investigation."

"Agent Baxter, Reynalda Swanson, from Enterprise Cellular, I hope I didn't wake you?"

Bax shook the sleep out of her brain. "No, Ms. Swanson, what can I do for you?"

"I have the location information you wanted on the cell phone number you gave us earlier."

Bax was now wide awake, and she grabbed her notebook and pen off the table. "Go ahead, Ms. Swanson."

"The phone is in Bozeman, Montana. I took the liberty of overlaying our cell tower coverage on a city map and the best I can do for you is an area of downtown Bozeman bordered by East Mendenhall Street, East Olive Street, South Grand Avenue, and South Church Street."

"Ms. Swanson, can you tell how long the phone has been at that location?"

"Our records indicate it's been there about two days."

"The list of phone numbers you sent me earlier would include the last two days, so since no calls were listed, that means the phone has not been used at all during the last two days, correct?"

"That's correct, Agent Baxter. I wish I could get you closer to the phone, but that's the best we can do. I hope it helps?"

Bax thanked her for the information and hung up her phone. "Bozeman, Montana?" she said out loud. "What the hell is she doing in Bozeman?"

She stood up and headed out the door to her cubicle and pulled up a Google Earth view of downtown Bozeman. The area Ms. Swanson gave her was just about the entire downtown area. She was going to need help.

Bax pulled up the nonemergency number for the Bozeman Police Department, dialed and waited.

"Bozeman Police Department, how may I direct your call?"

Bax explained who she was and what she needed, and the operator asked her to hold while she connected her to the night supervisor.

"Sergeant Alvarez, how can I help you, Agent Baxter?"

Bax explained about the missing woman, that her cell phone was pinged to Bozeman and she was hoping she could get a little help from the police department in trying to track down the missing woman. After a few back-and-forth questions, Sergeant Alvarez asked her if it would be all right if she called her back in a few minutes. Bax had expected this to happen. You couldn't be too careful anymore these days, and she assumed the sergeant would call her back on her office phone as a means of checking out her identity. Sure enough, two minutes after she hung up the phone, her desk phone lit up with an incoming call.

"Agent Ashley Baxter, how may I help you?"

"Agent Baxter, Sergeant Alvarez, Bozeman PD. I hope you don't mind, but I needed to make sure you were who you said you were."

Bax told the sergeant she understood and then set about putting together a plan. Bax sent the sergeant an email containing information about Barb McBride's car and the woman's vital statistics along with a photo. Sergeant Alvarez told her that she would have her patrol officers start visiting some of the shops in the area to see if any of the shopkeepers might have seen the woman, and they would also be alert for her car.

"May I ask, Agent Baxter, if the missing woman is the journalist who does all those investigative reports on TV?"

Bax responded that she was.

Alvarez continued. "She did a report several years ago about missing Native American women, and it was an excellent report. We've had several women disappear in the last couple years, and it was awesome that she shined a spotlight on the problem. It got a lot of people's attention. I hope we can help you find her."

Bax thanked her and hung up the phone. She needed to call Buck, but first, she called the director. She hated waking him up, but that came with the job.

The director answered with a sleepy voice on the fourth ring. "A little early, Bax."

"Yes, sir, but I didn't want to wait. Barb McBride's phone is in Bozeman, Montana. I spoke to Bozeman PD, and they are going to start a search for her car or herself. I would like to head up there and help with the search, but I wanted your okay to charter a flight."

"No worries, Bax. The governor wants this handled as fast as possible, so I will authorize a charter flight. Do you have someone you can call, or do you need me to find a charter pilot for you?"

"I was going to call Mack Price; we have used him before, and he is based out of here. I'll call him right now, and thank you, sir."

Bax hung up and dialed Mack Price. She knew Mack was an early riser, so she figured she wouldn't wake him, and as it turned out, he was sitting at his kitchen table drinking coffee when he answered the phone. Bax explained what she needed, and Mack was happy to help. They agreed to meet at the Grand Junction airport in an hour, and Bax hung up and grabbed her go bag out of her locker. She called Sergeant Alvarez and told her when she was arriving and asked if she could have an officer pick her up at the airport, and then she called Buck.

The ringing of his phone woke Buck out of a sound sleep. He grabbed the phone off the nightstand, checked the number and answered.

"Bax, do you ever sleep?" he asked in a groggy voice.

"Maybe someday," she said with a laugh.

She explained about the phone location and told him she had already called the director, and he had approved a charter flight to Bozeman. She also took a minute to fill him in on the phone numbers she was able to check, so far, and that all the information was in the investigation file.

"Bax, did anything show up in her background search that would tell us why she would go to Bozeman? Family, friends, anything?"

"Not a thing, Buck. It seems like an odd place to run to, but I guess if you're trying to hide, Bozeman is as good a place as any."

"All right, keep me posted, and if you need anything, call. The sheriff for Gallatin County and I have known each other for a long time, and if you need help, he might be able to spare a couple deputies."

Bax hung up her phone, not at all surprised that Buck and a sheriff in Montana would be friends. It was amazing the number of people in law enforcement, around the country, that Buck knew. What was more surprising was how many of them Buck could reach out to at a moment's notice and how willing they always were to help. It said a lot about Buck, she thought. Bax grabbed her bag and her laptop and headed out the door.

Buck figured sleep was impossible now, so he jumped in the shower, dressed in the cleanest clothes he had, clipped his badge and gun to his belt and headed out the door.

Chapter Twelve

Buck had to slow down a mile or so before he got to the ranch drive because both shoulders along the highway were full of news vans and satellite trucks. The word was out, and the world was waiting for news of Barb McBride's disappearance. He turned onto the ranch road, stopped at the deputy who was trying to keep the reporters and photographers at bay, showed his credentials and proceeded to the house.

He parked out front, slid out of the Jeep, grabbed his backpack out of the back and walked up onto the front porch. He stopped and watched all the media trucks jockeying for the best spots and thought, "This is going to turn into some circus."

Inside the living room, the search and rescue leader was passing out new assignments to his teams. Some of the teams would go back over the routes that were covered the night before, and other teams would start searching along some of the county roads they hadn't covered yet. There were at least a dozen more teams than they had earlier, and they were eager to start searching.

Buck walked past the living room door and down the hall towards the office. He could hear conversation coming from the kitchen, so he continued down the hall and found both McBride brothers, Mrs. Grainger and Carl Chandler all talking with Paul Webber and the two CBI techs, Melanie Hart and George Peterman. Everyone stopped talking as Buck walked in. The smell of bacon frying was overwhelming, and Buck remembered he hadn't eaten a thing since around four p.m. the day before. He was starving. Mrs. Grainger, who was standing next to the stove, filled a plate with bacon and scrambled eggs, handed it to Buck and told him to grab a seat. She picked up the coffeepot, but Buck signaled no thanks. He brought in a warm Coke from his car and with breakfast in hand had everything he needed. He sat down at the table and listened as Melanie Hart explained the process.

Melanie, who was about five foot two, with shoulder-length black hair, wore jeans and a dark gray hoodie and had several piercings. Anyone meeting her for the first time would think she was a high school kid, but she had received her doctorate in computer science from MIT about a dozen years before. She'd joined CBI right out of college. George Peterman, on the other hand, could have passed for her father. George was about the same height as Buck, a shade under six foot, but where Buck still weighed what he'd weighed when he played football in high school, George had added a few pounds over the years. He was bald, by choice, and wore khakis, with a button-down shirt and sweater. He joined CBI after retiring from the navy, where he'd spent his entire career working in cybersecurity.

"So, we have loaded all your cell phone information into the system," said Melanie. "If a call comes in for you it will ring on this console." She pointed towards the laptop sitting in front of her. "All you need to do is keep the caller on the line for twenty seconds, and if you can do that, then we should be able to track a location based on the cell towers that are being used by the call."

Buck finished his breakfast and thanked Mrs. Grainger for her hospitality, then he addressed the group.

"Is there any reason Mrs. McBride would travel to Bozeman, Montana? Does she have friends or relatives up there, or perhaps a business partner?"

The McBride brothers and Mrs. Grainger were bewildered.

Jim McBride, who seemed sober, but with his hair uncombed and wearing the same clothes he'd worn since Buck arrived, said, "Why would you think that? Did something happen?" Everyone leaned into the table and listened to Buck.

"We're not quite sure. We received the location data for her cell phone, and it pinged off several cell towers near the center of town in Bozeman."

Bob McBride stood up from the table. "Well, what are we waiting for? Shouldn't we be heading up there?"

"Please take your seat, Bob. At this point, we have no idea what it means. One of my associates is on her way up there as we speak, to meet with the Bozeman Police Department and see if they can track down either your sister-in-law's car or her phone. We should have more information later today."

"This is ridiculous, Agent Taylor," said Mrs. Grainger. "Why would my sister go to Bozeman? This doesn't make any sense. Are you positive it's her phone?"

Buck told them about the call from the cellular provider and explained that until they were sure, it was best if everyone stayed focused on getting through the day and helping look for Barb. He stood up, put his plate on the counter and signaled for Paul and Carl to follow him.

Buck led them to Barb McBride's office, walked in and closed the door. He pulled the manila folders out of his backpack and handed them to Paul.

"Paul, can you run these names and numbers through the internet and see if we can identify any of these folks on these scraps of paper? I'm going to call Mrs. McBride's producer and see if she can give me any insight into what she was working on before she disappeared. Thanks, Paul."

Paul pulled out his laptop and opened several different databases. He opened the folder and started entering the first name. Buck asked Carl if he would mind going back through some of the files and books in the office to see if there might be something he missed the night before.

Buck stepped out of the office, found a quiet place in the living room, now that all the searchers were out on the road, and pulled up the number Bax sent him for the producer. Bax had called her the afternoon before, but she hadn't returned her call, and Buck needed answers. He dialed the number and waited, got voice mail and left a message. He hung up, frustrated, and opened the investigation file. The background information Bax was able to pull for Bob and Jim McBride and Mrs. Grainger was in the file, and he began to read.

Elizabeth Grainger was squeaky clean, not even a parking ticket in the last twenty years. She was married to Harold Grainger, a retired attorney, and they had lived in Steamboat for the past ten years. They had excellent credit ratings, their house was paid for and they had almost no debt. Their three children were grown and had their own careers and families outside the state of Colorado. She was a member of the Junior League and chaired several charitable organizations in the city. By all accounts, she was a well-respected part of the Steamboat community.

Buck closed her folder and opened the folder marked Jim McBride. Jim and Barb McBride were married almost forty years, and they also had three grown children who lived out of state. There were several newspaper and magazine articles from several years back about Jim, concerning some award he'd won, of which several were mentioned. He was his wife's chief cameraman, and then, suddenly, nothing. Starting about eight years back, he was no longer getting awards and didn't seem to be working at all. He kind of fell off the grid. Bax included a copy of a discharge paper from a substance abuse clinic—how she got that he would never ask—from five years ago showing he had entered an inpatient abuse program at a facility in San Diego. There was nothing since then, and it was apparent to Buck, from the night before, that Jim was no longer on the wagon when it came to booze.

Buck clicked on his credit report, and things got interesting. Numerous settled accounts indicated someone, probably Mrs. McBride, had paid off his debts. What was interesting was the loan he had taken out, using the house as collateral. Buck wrote down the name of the bank so he could follow up. It seemed odd that with so much settled debt anyone would lend him money. He wondered what the money was for and, more importantly, was his wife aware of the loan? He made a note on his pad to find out if Mrs. McBride had a life insurance policy.

He was about to open the file on Bob McBride when his phone rang. He didn't recognize the number, so he answered the call.

"Buck Taylor."

"Uh, hello, Mr. Taylor. This is Regina Cavanaugh. I believe you left me a message a little bit ago. Something about Barb. Is everything all right?"

"No, Mrs. Cavanaugh. I'm afraid Mrs. McBride is missing, and we were hoping you might be able to help."

"What do you mean Barb is missing? She probably just ran off to finish up her latest project."

"I'm sorry, ma'am. She's been gone for four

days with no word to anyone. Does that sound normal to you?"

"I'm sorry, Mr. Taylor. Who are you with?"

"I'm with the Colorado Bureau of Investigation, and we are trying to locate Mrs. McBride."

"You're serious about this? I had no idea. I just got back from a couple days in Cancun, and I tried to call her this morning, and it went to voice mail. She is really missing?"

"Yes, ma'am. I was hoping you could tell me what she was working on?"

"Do you think it's related to her disappearance?"

"Can't say for sure until we can find out what it is."

"Well I have to tell you, Mr. Taylor, this is going to sound a little embarrassing, but I have no idea what she was working on. Barb becomes very secretive when she thinks she's onto something huge. All she would tell me was it involved child pornography, and she was going to bring down some very powerful people."

Buck asked her if there might be someone in Bozeman, Montana, who might be helping her with the story, but Mrs. Cavanaugh was just as confused. She couldn't think of any contacts Barb might have in Bozeman.

"Ma'am, are you able to read her private code?"

"I'm afraid not. More of Barb's secrets. She never wanted anyone to see her notes."

Mrs. Cavanaugh gave Buck a little more insight into her relationship with Mrs. McBride and cleared up some of Buck's questions about Jim McBride.

It seemed Jim wanted back into the TV game, but no one was taking him seriously. His drinking had gotten worse in the past six months, and no one would take a chance on him. Rumor was, he was trying to start his own production company, but Barb refused to let him use the house as collateral for a startup loan. When Buck mentioned the loan he found on his credit report, Mrs. Cavanaugh gave a whistle.

"If Barb ever found out he took a loan against the house without her knowledge, she would kill him. Sorry, Mr. Taylor, that was just a metaphor. Barb is the most easygoing person in the world, but she would be royally pissed."

Buck thanked her for her help and hung up his phone. That was an interesting conversation, and it added a new piece of information into the investigation: motive.

Chapter Thirteen

Mack Price landed his Beechcraft King Air 250 on the end of the runway at Bozeman Yellowstone International Airport, like he was landing on a cloud. He throttled back the power and rolled onto the taxiway, coming to a stop outside the local fixed base operator (FBO). Bax always liked flying with Mack. He was personable and funny, and his white hair gave her a sense of security. Mack was five foot ten and rail thin. He wore his World War II leather bomber jacket with pride, having spent twenty years of his life flying jet fighters, first in Korea and then in the early years of the Vietnam War. After his hitch in the air force, Mack started his own charter operation and, with almost fifty thousand hours of flying, was one of the most experienced pilots Bax knew.

Mack told her he would camp out at the FBO until she was ready to head home, and if she needed to stay overnight, he was okay with that. His next charter wasn't for another seventy-two hours, so he had time to wait for her. She thanked him with a big hug and headed out the front door to the waiting Bozeman PD cruiser sitting at the curb.

Bax was surprised to see an older Latina with sergeant stripes step out of the patrol car. Sergeant Alvarez was about the same height as Bax, several years older, with her black hair tied back in a French braid. She walked up to Bax and extended her hand.

"Theresa Alvarez, Agent Baxter."

Bax shook her hand; her grip was solid and self-assured. "It's a pleasure to meet you, Sergeant, please call me Bax."

"Then call me Terry. How was your flight?"

"It was great. The pilot reminds me of my grandfather. I'm a little surprised to see you here. I figured I'd be going with one of your day shift guys?"

Terry explained that the chief suggested that since she was aware of the situation, if she were willing, he would like her to accompany Bax. She was willing and spent the morning following up with the two patrol officers who were canvassing the downtown area talking to merchants, and if Bax was ready, they would head out and meet with the officers.

Bax thanked her and slid into the patrol car. Since she never worked as a uniformed police officer, Bax always marveled at the amount of electronics that filled the front of a patrol car. Her state-issued Jeep Grand Cherokee had one statewide radio and a GPS built into the entertainment console. She was able to squeeze in next to the laptop and drop her go bag on the floor in front of her, and Terry pulled away from the curb and headed for Bozeman, which was eight miles southeast of the airport.

Bax filled Terry in on what they knew about

Barb McBride's disappearance, and they discussed the approach Terry and the two patrol officers were taking. She divided the downtown area into three zones, and each of them parked their cars and walked from store to store with the picture of Barb McBride Bax had provided to her. While that was going on, two other officers in their patrol cars cruised through the area looking for the car. So far, they had covered about half the area with no luck.

Bax contacted the cell provider while they were heading into town and asked them to confirm the location of the phone and whether it was still in the same area that was first reported. Bax and Terry both thought this was odd. Why would you bring a phone all the way to Bozeman and leave it sitting in one location and never move it? In the back of her head, Bax wondered if Barb McBride was ever in Bozeman or if just the phone was there. Was it possible someone else had Barb's phone?

Terry turned onto West Main Street and pulled to the curb next to a patrol officer who was talking with a middle-aged woman sweeping the sidewalk in front of a small bookstore. They stepped out of the patrol car as the officer thanked the woman for her time and walked towards them. Officer Troy Applegate was young and stood proudly in his police uniform. He filled them in on the area he had been able to cover thus far and reported that no one had seen the woman or the car. Bax thanked him, and she and Terry started off in the opposite direction. They stopped and spoke with a dozen other shopkeepers before catching up with Officer

Tanisha Clark, a tall, older black woman. She told Bax she was originally from Detroit but needed to move her family away from the crime and the poverty, so she'd headed west five years before and fallen in love with her new home. She too reported no luck with the woman or the car.

The rest of the afternoon went by just as the morning had, and they all reconvened at the end of the day shift at police headquarters to see if there were any new results. Other than sore feet, the results of the search were fruitless. No one in the downtown area saw either the woman or the car. Bax thanked the officers for their help and sat back in the chair in the interview room. She could see the frustration in Terry's eyes.

"What are we missing?" she said out loud.

Terry, who was now well into her second full shift, sounded beat. "We hit every store and apartment building in the area. If her phone is here, it must be hidden really well."

Bax stood up to stretch and noticed the large map of downtown hanging on the wall. She knew she was overtired, but her mind cleared, and she walked over to the map. Terry stood up and followed behind her.

"You got an idea?"

Bax pointed to a spot on the map and smiled. She wondered why she hadn't thought about this before. Terry shifted her eyes to where she was pointing. "Shit, the post office." She checked her watch. "We still have time before they close. Do you think it could be that simple?"

Bax laughed. "Let's go find out."

Bax grabbed her backpack, Terry grabbed her coffee cup, and they headed for the patrol car. They arrived at the post office with ten minutes to spare and were lucky enough to catch the postmaster just locking up his office. Harold Bronson was friendly and quiet as Bax told him what she was looking for.

"Have you received any small packages in the past couple days addressed to someone 'in care of' the general post office, that were mailed from anywhere in Colorado?"

Harold picked up his phone and called someone in the sorting area, explained what he was looking for and hung up.

"This might take a little while. It's hard to believe so many people still use the general post office as their mailing address. If we do find something, you will need a search warrant before we can turn it over to you. I hope you understand."

Terry stood up and stepped out of the office. Harold asked Bax to tell him what she could about the case, and he sat and listened with interest as she explained what had transpired so far. He was a big fan of Barb McBride's work, and he hoped everything would turn out okay. Just then his phone rang, and he picked it up, spoke with the person on the other end, hung up and stood up. He asked them to follow him to the sorting area. He explained as they walked that there were six packages in the GPO that had been shipped from Colorado. The sorting area was huge and stacked floor to ceiling with packages. One of the sorters stood next to a long table containing the six packages in question.

Bax stepped up to the table, picked up each package, and read the shipping labels. The first two had postmarks that put them well before the disappearance—she slid those to the side—and one of the four remaining packages had been shipped from Alamosa, so she slid that one aside too. She pulled out her phone, pulled up Barb McBride's phone number and dialed. The noise in the sorting area was loud, so Harold asked his crew to stop what they were doing and turn off the equipment. Bax redialed, hoping the phone hadn't died. They each stood near a box and listened, and there it was, almost too quiet to hear. They slid the package in question closer, and they all listened as she dialed again. They all glanced at each other. Bax smiled.

"Son of a bitch."

Terry pulled out her phone and dialed a number. When she was done talking, she hung up and put her phone away.

"The chief already spoke to the judge about the warrant. He will call us back in a minute."

The chief called her back a few minutes later. He told her one of the patrol officers was swinging by the courthouse to pick up the warrant and would be there momentarily. Bax pulled out her phone and took pictures of the box from all sides and a close-up of the shipping label. It had been shipped at a pack and ship place in Breckenridge the day after Barb McBride was reported missing. She opened her backpack and pulled out a couple of evidence bags and a pair of nitrile gloves. The wait for the patrol officer was the hardest part and felt like it took forever.

The patrol officer came through the post office and handed the warrant to the postmaster, who read it and then folded it in half and put it in his pocket.

"Agent Baxter," he said. "It's all yours."

Bax pulled a knife out of her pocket and flipped it open with one hand. She slit the tape on the top of the box while Terry used Bax's phone to record the process. Bax opened the top flaps and pulled out a massive amount of cotton wadding and paper. It explained why they had barely heard the phone ringing in the box. Someone had gone to a lot of trouble to make the box as soundproof as possible.

Bax placed each new piece of batting or paper into an evidence bag and then slit the bubble wrap that encompassed the phone, putting all the wrap in a bag as well. She held the phone so Terry could complete the video and then took several still photos of the now-empty box and the phone before placing it in an evidence bag. She slit the tape on the bottom of the box and folded the box flat before placing it in a bag. She let out a sigh, almost like she had been holding her breath through the entire process.

The last thing she did before placing everything into her backpack was to dial Barb McBride's phone number. The screen lit up with her number. She had everything she needed. She packed up her backpack, thanked the postmaster for his help, called Mack Price and told him she was finished and heading back to the airport. Terry led the way as they exited the post office and walked down the street to her patrol car.

The drive to the airport took less than ten minutes, and Terry pulled up in front of the FBO. Bax reached across the laptop and shook Terry's hand.

"Thanks for all your help, and please tell the chief we appreciate all the cooperation. You guys were awesome."

Terry thanked Bax, wished her luck with the case and asked her to let them know how it all turned out. Bax nodded, slid out of the car, walked into the FBO and found Mack waiting for her at the counter. She presented her ID to the front desk clerk and was buzzed through the security gate.

"It appears you had a good day?" said Mack, noticing the big smile on her face.

"You bet. But I'm ready to head home."

Mack led the way out onto the tarmac, stowed her backpack and climbed the stairs into the plane. While Mack started the engines and went through his checklist, Bax called Buck and filled him in. They had their first break in the case, but it also came with more questions than answers. Bax hung up her phone, fastened her seat belt and was asleep before they took off.

Chapter Fourteen

Buck and Carl were sitting at the back table in a small family-owned Mexican restaurant in downtown Frisco. It had been a long, frustrating day with nothing to show for everyone's tireless efforts. The waitress came by with a plate containing a huge beef burrito for Buck and a taco platter for Carl. They both dug in like they hadn't eaten all day, which was true, since they hadn't. They talked about the investigation thus far and what the next steps would be. They knew they had to solve this soon, before things got any crazier out on the highway.

Earlier in the day, a couple of deputies had to break up a fight between two cameramen because their drones collided over the field in front of the house. One of the deputies told the assembled crowd watching the argument that he was going to shoot down the next drone that flew towards the house. Of course, in today's world, it was only a matter of minutes before the deputy's words were all over social media, which did not make the sheriff very happy.

Buck was able to calm the sheriff down, but the crowds were getting unruly, and they were getting complaints from some of the neighbors about noise and traffic and farm animals being harassed.

Buck was reaching into his pocket for the cash to pay for dinner when his phone rang.

"Hey, Bax. You got any good news for me?"

"We found the phone."

"Damn, Bax. Great news. Where did you find it, and was Mrs. McBride with it?"

Bax explained about the search of the downtown area and about her hunch about the post office. She told him she would upload the pictures to the investigation file as soon as they landed in Grand Junction and then she would overnight the evidence to the State Crime Lab. The phone she would drop off with the tech guys so they could charge it and try to access it.

"Listen, Buck. I need to hang up now. Mack got permission to take off, and I'm wiped out. I will call you in the morning."

Buck hung up, and Carl could see a wave of excitement wash over Buck's face. He filled him in on the short conversation, which pleased Carl, but just like that, the conversation took a bad turn.

"What the fuck is going on?" said Buck. "Finding the phone is going to push this investigation in a different direction."

"You've kind of been thinking foul play all along, but this makes it pretty obvious. No wonder we haven't had any luck finding the car. Fuck, Buck, her car could be anywhere."

Buck sat for a minute and let his head clear. It was apparent now that Barb McBride either had help disappearing or someone made her disappear. The question was which one? It was quite possible she'd driven down to a pack and ship place and mailed the phone herself to throw off anyone her husband might send to find her, or she might have been abducted, and the perp mailed the phone to throw off the investigation. Buck ran his fingers through his salt-and-pepper hair, which had a lot more salt than pepper, and he was reaching for his phone when he received a text notification. He opened his phone and smiled. Bax sent him a picture of the pack and ship label, which he was glad she did. He would have hated to wait a couple hours before he had that information. He showed the text to Carl.

"You know the owner of this place?"

Carl read the label. "Yeah, let me call the office and get a number for him, and we can run over there and see if he has CCTV or can remember who shipped the box."

Carl stepped away from the table and walked out the front door. Buck could see him through the window as he answered his phone, hung up and dialed a number. He hung up from his call and walked back into the restaurant.

"The owner will meet us at the store in twenty minutes."

Buck paid the waitress and left a decent tip on the table, and they headed for their cars. Heading south on Highway 9, they passed Jefferson Avenue and pulled into a parking lot for a small strip center on the left.

The parking lot was empty except for a white Land Rover that was parked in front of the

Breckenridge Pack and Ship store. Carl parked on one side of the Rover and Buck parked on the other. The owner met them at the door.

Carl introduced Buck to the owner, Andy Skidmore, a tall, gray-haired transplanted New Yorker. He was dressed more like a cowboy, with his cowboy hat and shearling coat, than anyone Buck had ever met from New York. He had a warm, easygoing manner and he was happy to look at the picture on Buck's phone. He asked them to follow him into the back of the store to the office, and he opened a window on his computer and pulled up the camera.

He explained that they might be in luck because the system only kept the last seven days, and he began flipping through the digital tape until he came to the time that was stamped on the delivery label. On the screen was an average-height man of undetermined age wearing jeans and a black hoodie pulled up over his head. Buck could make out sunglasses covering his eyes, but that was about it. The man had no distinguishing features, and neither did his clothes. The only thing that stood out was that he was wearing gloves. He was plain and average in every way, and it frustrated the hell out of Buck.

The owner could sense Buck's frustration. "I wish this was more helpful, I'm really sorry."

Carl, who was as frustrated as Buck, said, "No worries, Andy. We appreciate you taking the time to meet with us. If you think of anything else, please, give me a call." He handed him one of his business cards.

Buck thanked him, and they stepped out into the cool night air.

"Well, that was unfortunate," said Buck. "The one good thing we now know is that unless she had someone working with her, Barb McBride did not mail her phone herself. I'm going to run out and fill Jim McBride in on what we found and then see if I can get some sleep. Why don't you head home to the family and let's meet back there in the morning?"

Carl nodded, slid into his car and pulled out of the lot. Buck stood for a minute and took a deep breath to clear his head. The little bug in his head was growing louder, and he was starting to believe they would not find Barb McBride alive. He slid into his Jeep, pulled out of the lot and headed up Highway 9. He wished he had better news to give Jim McBride.

As he drove through Silverthorne, he called the director to fill him in. He was aware the director was under a lot of pressure from the governor to find Barb McBride, and he felt like he was letting the director down. He knew this was just tired thinking, but he couldn't shake it. He figured Lucy would not be happy with him right now. She would tell him to snap out of it and get his shit together, or she was going to kick him in the ass. The thought made him laugh and brought tears to his eyes.

It was two and a half years since Lucy had passed away and it seemed like he missed her more each day. She had been his sounding board when an investigation seemed like it had no place left to go, and she would walk him through the evidence until something clicked. He wished she was here now.

The director listened as Buck filled him in on the investigation so far, and they knocked around a couple of ideas. When Buck hung up the phone, he felt a little better. He also realized that what he needed was a good night's sleep.

Buck drove past all the media trucks and vans parked along the highway and pulled into the driveway. There seemed to be a lot of activity going on as Buck pulled past the throngs of reporters and checked in with the deputy working the barricade.

"What's going on?" he asked the deputy.

"Someone in the crowd got word a ransom note was delivered to the husband's computer, then all hell broke loose."

The deputy moved the barricade, and a surprised Buck pulled through and parked in front of the house. He jumped out of his car, grabbed his backpack from the back, almost ran up the steps and pushed open the front door. Paul was walking down the hall towards the office, and Buck called to him.

"Paul, what the fuck?"

Paul jumped like he was surprised to find someone behind him. "Geez, Buck. Scared me half to death. I was just about to call you."

"Jim McBride got a ransom note? When did this happen?"

"We found out not two minutes ago. The deputy

at the gate called me, and I was heading back to the office to see what the hell was going on. The note arrived here at the same time it hit all the news outlets."

Buck followed Paul down the hall to the office and stepped behind the desk to look over George Peterman's shoulder as he clicked keys on Jim McBride's laptop. Jim McBride sat in the easy chair next to the desk and watched with a stunned look in his eyes and a drink in his hand.

George stopped clicking keys and pulled up the email containing the ransom note. He slid out of the seat and let Buck sit down. The email note was your typical cut-and-paste-letter ransom note you see on television cop shows. The letters, even though they were digital, gave the appearance they were clipped from different magazines and newspapers and pieced together haphazardly. Buck clicked on the forward button and sent the email to his email address, and then he printed off a copy to the printer behind the desk.

"Mr. McBride, when did you first see this note?"

Jim McBride took a sip of his drink. "I was watching a news website when Agent Peterman rushed in and asked me to move out of the way. He opened my email, which I always keep open, and clicked on an email that landed in my junk folder. This is what came up when he clicked on the attachment."

Buck took the printed copy out of the tray and read the ransom note.

WE HAVE YOUR WIFE. WE WANT $ONE

MILLION DOLLARS BY MIDNIGHT TOMORROW. WE WILL BE IN TOUCH. NO COPS.

Buck handed the printed copy to Paul. George tapped Buck on his shoulder and signaled for Buck to follow him into the hall. As he entered the hall, Mrs. Grainger came out of the kitchen.

"Is it true?" she asked. "It's coming up on every news site I follow on my phone. Oh, my god."

Buck asked Mrs. Grainger to go sit with her brother-in-law, and he would be right in. He followed George and Paul down the hall to the kitchen where Melanie was monitoring multiple news channels on her laptop. She stopped watching as they entered.

"The ransom note hit every news outlet I can find, at the same time. Whoever sent it to McBride's email sent a blast email to every TV, radio and internet news channel."

Buck turned to George. "George, what's on your mind?"

"We're gonna need a search warrant."

That caught Buck and Paul off guard.

"Okay, fill us in," said Buck.

George lowered his voice. "I backtracked the email through about fifty different servers all over the place, but the email originated on McBride's laptop. He made a hell of an effort to hide it, but he's not as clever as he thinks he is."

Buck and Paul stared at him. "Are you sure?" asked Paul.

"Not only that but as I was going through his

computer, there is a bunch of kiddie porn on it he also tried to hide. We are going to need to tear into his computer life."

Buck sat down on one of the stools at the long counter and struggled with his next thought. "Do we think the drunk down the hall kidnapped his own wife?"

Paul said, "It would make sense, but I don't see it. He seems as surprised as we are that the ransom note hit his email."

Buck thought for a minute. "There is a lot about this that doesn't make sense. The first thing is the timing. We just uncovered her phone in Montana, and within hours we are getting a ransom note, then he lets you go through his computer and doesn't seem the least bit concerned that there might be porn on it. Either he is a lot cleverer than we have given him credit for, or he is as much in the dark as we are."

None of them were sure of the answer. George spoke first. "Buck, I agree the timing is odd, and he didn't do a very good job of covering his tracks with the porn. It's possible for someone to hack into his computer and put all that stuff in there, but to what end?"

"That's what we need to find out. Paul, let's write up a warrant request and see what else is lurking in his laptop. In the meantime, I'm going to have a heart-to-heart conversation with Mr. McBride." That conversation didn't happen.

Chapter Fifteen

Archie Whitefeather and Charlie Gomez had been friends for almost all their seventy-some years on this earth. They grew up next door to each other in Kremmling, Colorado, and met while they were both attending first grade. Archie was part Arapaho and part Mountain Ute, and he wore his gray hair in a long braid down the middle of his back. As a kid, he was picked on repeatedly in school since he was the only Native American in the small elementary school. Charlie Gomez, who was bigger than most of the kids in first grade and the only Hispanic in the school, came to Archie's defense, and they became fast friends. Charlie still towered over everyone he met and was the most soft-spoken, imposing figure you would ever meet.

Life was hard for the two boys, but they persevered, and after graduation from high school, they both headed to the Colorado School of Mines and graduated as mining engineers. After school, they never lost touch, and even though they both traveled all over the United States and several places around the world, they stayed friends.

When their wives passed away, and they retired from mining, they decided to head back to Kremmling, and they were now residents of a small senior citizen apartment building on the corner of

Highways 9 and 40. Retirement was good for these guys. Blessed with good health and still wanting to be active, they pursued their passion, fishing, and traveled all over the state. Not a day went by, no matter the weather, that they were not on a lake or river somewhere in the state casting their flies and lures. They never kept anything they caught because it was more about keeping each other company and enjoying a sport they loved than about eating their catch.

It was fishing that morning that led them to turn into the Cow Creek South campground on the east side of Green Mountain Reservoir. Due to the snow the week before and the cold temperatures, the campgrounds were still closed, and they were able to pull into a space right alongside the lake.

Green Mountain Reservoir sat between Highway 9 on the east and the town of Heeney on the west and straddled the Blue River. It was the first project built by the Bureau of Reclamation as part of the Colorado-Big Thompson Project, which over the course of the project would include five other impoundments. Completed in 1942, it was now a popular destination with campers and fishermen and women.

The ten-year drought in Colorado had taken its toll on water storage in the state, and the reservoir was at its lowest level since it was first filled. This meant the fish would be gathered in the deepest pools, and Archie and Charlie had their eyes on one location they were confident would hold a lot of Northern pike. Colorado Parks and Wildlife had placed a twenty-dollar-per-head bounty on this invasive predatory fish earlier in the year, and these two fishermen were hoping to clean up today.

The ice was starting to thin near the edges of the lake but Charlie, tied to a long rope, walked out about fifty feet and drilled a test hole using his electric drill with a long ice blade. The ice on the lake was still over twelve inches thick, so they decided to proceed. Pulling the little plastic flat-bottomed Jon boat out of the bed of Archie's pickup, they loaded all their gear into it and stepped out onto the ice, pulling the boat behind them.

The Jon boat, as well as the life preservers they wore, were a compromise they'd made with Archie's son and daughter. If they were going to go ice fishing, which the kids were not happy about due to their age, the kids wanted to make sure they had something to jump into if the ice gave way. Archie didn't mind the boat or the compromise. It made it easier to haul their gear to the fishing spot.

Their destination was a side channel on the other side of the spit of land from the campground, a walk of about a quarter of a mile. It was a beautiful morning, and the sun was coming up over the mountains to the east; the temperature was still brisk, but the day would be clear and bright.

They had been told by a friend of theirs that the side channel was typically around a hundred feet deep, but since the water level was down almost sixty feet, the deepest pools would be easily accessible. Of course, that didn't take into account the foot of new spring snow that was sitting on top of the ice from the recent storm. The trek to the spot they intended to fish took almost an hour, but they finally got there, pulled out their twelve-inch augers and drilled a couple holes.

Archie was sitting in the Jon boat rigging up his rod, so Charlie decided to have some fun first. His son had given him an underwater camera for Christmas that attached to his smartphone, so he unspooled the ten-foot cable that came with it and dropped it into the first hole. The view was incredible, and he saw several large trout swim by the lens. He panned the camera around and with a shout fell back into the Jon boat, almost landing on Archie.

"What the hell, Charlie? You almost crushed me."

He glared at Charlie, and all he saw was fear in his eyes. Charlie sat there, not saying a word.

"Looook," was all he could say, and he held up the phone, so Archie could see the screen. When he fell back, he'd pulled most of the camera cable out of the water, so all Archie could see was a black screen.

"What am I looking at?"

Charlie glanced at the screen and was able to catch his breath. "There was a woman's face in a car."

Charlie slid out of the boat and moved the camera around until he spotted the hood of the car. He called Archie to take a look. Archie climbed out of the boat and stood next to Charlie as he moved the camera around. There on the screen was the cold white face of a woman. Archie let out a gasp.

"Holy shit."

"Yeah," said Charlie. "We better call somebody; this can't be good."

"I don't think we're gonna get any fishing done today," said Archie as he pulled out his phone and dialed 911.

****

Trooper Will Hutchison was the first officer to arrive at the scene. He had been driving his patrol route and was between Green Mountain Reservoir and Kremmling when the Summit County dispatcher called their closest unit. He swung his patrol car around and headed for the campground. He pulled in next to the pickup truck, saw the footprints in the snow heading around the land spit and decided to head back onto the highway and stop where Highway 9 passed over the side channel. He pulled his car over, turned on his flashers, stepped out and walked to the guardrail. Some eighty feet below him and about twenty-five yards from the nearest shore, he spotted the two old-timers and their Jon boat. They waved to him, and he waved back. The first Summit County deputy pulled to the side of the road, put on his flashers and stepped out of his SUV.

The two officers shook hands and studied the scene below.

"Damn, that's a long way down," said the deputy. He keyed his mic, called his dispatcher and requested they roll the search and rescue team. With almost vertical cliffs on both sides of the inlet, the shortest way down was by rope. He also knew his only other option was to follow the trail the two old-timers left. He asked the trooper to keep an eye on the two fishermen from the guardrail, and he climbed back into his SUV and headed for the campground.

He parked next to the pickup truck, pulled on a pair of heavy-duty snow boots, his winter coat and hat and followed the trail across the ice. By the time he reached the two old-timers, there were several more emergency vehicles parked along the guardrail. He walked over to the two fishermen. They talked for a few minutes, and then Charlie held up his phone and dropped the camera back into the hole.

Even in death, the face was recognizable, and the deputy knew precisely who the face belonged to. Rather than use his radio, he pulled his cell phone out of his pocket and called dispatch.

"This is three-one-seven," he told the dispatcher. "You'd better call Detective Chandler and the CBI folks. I think we found that missing woman, McBride."

Chapter Sixteen

Buck stood next to the guardrail alongside Carl Chandler as they observed the activity below. Buck and Carl had interviewed the two fishermen earlier and watched the camera image Charlie Gomez saved to his camera. The woman was definitely Barb McBride, which filled him with mixed emotions. He was glad she had been found, and the family could now deal with the healing and hope for some kind of closure, but he was also perplexed. The ransom note earlier that morning left a vast number of questions, the biggest of which was why? Why did the ransom note come in within hours of Bax finding the phone in Bozeman, and what did it mean now that they found the body? Was the ransom note a scam, or was it a misdirection? Nothing about this case made sense.

Earlier that morning he'd met with Jim McBride and Mrs. Grainger and filled them in on the search for the missing phone that led them to Bozeman, Montana. They were both shocked and confused, and neither one could understand how her phone ended up in Montana. Buck did not want to speculate in front of them, so he kept the conversation simple, but since they each agreed Barb McBride didn't know anyone in Montana, he decided to let the question linger. He could see the anger building in Mrs. Grainger's eyes as she stared at Jim McBride. He was lucky she kept her cool and didn't explode, and Buck waited a beat to see if that might change.

Mrs. Grainger couldn't contain her anger any longer, and in another fit of anger directed at Jim McBride, she blamed him for her sister's disappearance and told him she didn't have any problem believing that either he or his brother, Bob, might be involved in the disappearance. Jim McBride took it all in stride, poured himself another drink and ignored her comments, but Buck could see that the woman was starting to get under Jim McBride's skin.

Buck had ushered Mrs. Grainger out of the room and was about to walk back in so he could have a deeper conversation with Jim McBride when his phone rang. He checked the number and answered.

"Hey, Carl. What's up?"

"Morning, Buck, hope I didn't wake you. A couple ice fishermen found a car in Green Mountain Reservoir. Our deputy on the scene is calling for search and rescue. There's a woman in the car, and it appears to be Barb McBride."

"Shit, Carl. You on the way?"

"Yeah, just leaving home. I'm going to close the highway at Heeney Road at both ends of the reservoir and try to keep the press away until we figure out what's up."

Buck filled him in on the ransom note, and Carl was a bit miffed that Buck hadn't called him right away, but he understood that Buck was trying to let him have a little sleep, which he appreciated. Buck hung up, found Paul in the kitchen, told him what was going on and headed for the front door. He threw his backpack in the back of his Jeep and headed down the ranch road, turning north onto Highway 9, and drove the five or so miles to the scene now unfolding at the reservoir.

He could hear the press yelling his name and yelling questions as he drove by, but he ignored them all. He saw a couple of the smaller media vans pull out and follow him, and he was glad Carl had thought to close the highway, forcing anyone on the road to drive along the opposite side of the reservoir and over the dam. He pulled up to the barricade, presented his ID to the state trooper and proceeded up the highway. He spotted the emergency vehicles, pulled off onto the shoulder and walked to the guardrail, where a couple of deputies and a trooper were standing by talking. Buck knew most of the deputies, and he introduced himself to the trooper.

The first deputy on the scene, named Ortega, filled him in on what he found when he and the trooper first arrived. Buck, who was familiar with the reservoir and the surrounding area, wondered how they were ever going to retrieve the car from under all that ice. Deputy Ortega told him that the two fishermen were sitting in their pickup truck at the campground getting warm, and another deputy was keeping an eye on them until Buck could speak with them.

They stopped talking as Reed Cunningham, one of the heavy search and rescue team leaders, stepped up to the guardrail. Reed appeared to be in his fifties but was still in excellent shape. He had curly brown hair and stood about six feet tall. Reed hadn't been involved in the earlier search for Barb McBride, but he volunteered to run this recovery so the other members of his team could grab some rest. He was also one of four certified cold-weather divers on the team. He stared down at the ice below.

"Whereabouts is the car?"

Deputy Ortega pointed towards the ice. "See those two small holes about twenty-five yards offshore? The car is right below the closest one to us, in about fifteen feet of water."

Reed studied the surrounding cliffs.

"This is not going to be easy. I'm going to stage in the campground. I'm also going to call for a twenty-ton crane. We will have to lift the car straight up once we have her uncovered; otherwise, she is going to get caught on the slope. I need to call Dillon and the county and ask them to roll the fire departments and the heavy rescue equipment. We are going to need a lot of manpower."

Reed stepped away from the group, pulled out his phone and started making calls. A search and rescue truck pulled to a stop alongside him, and he spoke to the driver through the window and pointed towards the campground. The truck pulled forward and headed down the hill to the campground.

Buck stepped away from the group, pulled out his phone and dialed the director.

"Hey, Buck. The news about the ransom note is all over the news and the internet. I hope that information didn't come from someone involved in the search?"

"No, sir. We received the note the same time the press received it. It was like a coordinated attack. I think someone didn't want us to sit on the ransom note."

"Any idea why?"

"To be honest, sir, I can't decide if it was someone trying to play the family and make a buck or if it was a misdirection."

Buck gave the director a quick briefing on what had transpired during the past couple of hours. The director was quiet for a minute.

"Fuck, Buck. The governor is not going to be happy about this. Any idea if what she was working on could have led to this?"

"At this point, we have no idea what she was working on, so that's a question we can't answer yet. Maybe the search of the husband's laptop and phone will yield something useful. I'm going to need a forensics team out here as fast as possible. It might be faster to pull a team out of Denver instead of Grand Junction."

"Okay, Buck. I will call Max and have her roll a team. Anything else you need right now?"

"Until we lift the car, which is going to take several more hours, I think we are okay. I will keep you posted."

Buck hung up and walked back to the guardrail. For the next couple of hours, he watched as the various fire departments from around the county lugged their equipment out to the site. He could hear the sounds of the first big gas-powered circular saws being fired up as the firefighters started to cut big chunks of ice out of the reservoir and pull them ashore, clearing an ever-increasing hole in the ice.

The dive team was assembled near the hole, and they were in the process of checking each other's equipment and getting ready to enter the water. Several rolled-up lifting straps were piled up next to the hole waiting on the divers. The crane Reed had called for was parked across both lanes of the highway, and the boom was extended out as far as it could go. Everything was ready for the lift, and concern was running high. This was a dangerous operation, and Buck appreciated the professionalism of everyone involved.

They all watched as the divers entered the water and descended to the car. The divers wore full face masks and were miked up so they could talk to each other and the firefighters. The divers must have called for the first lifting strap, and Buck felt the engine of the crane rev up as the hook began to descend.

The plan, according to Reed, was to raise the car out of the water and then drag it along the ice before the lift could begin. The crane could not extend out closer to the hole, so they would use the weight of the car to break the ice as it moved towards the side wall that was under the guardrail. The firefighter had lowered two rescue boats, and they were now positioned on the ice along either side of the path they intended the car to follow, so they could keep it moving in the right direction and ensure their own safety as the ice broke under them.

The divers all climbed out of the hole, and everyone grabbed the gear and moved towards the shore. The crane revved up again, and Buck could see the strain on the boom as the car started to rise. The back end of the car appeared above the ice, and then ice broke under it as the car was dragged forward. The firefighters in the rescue boats used hooks to keep the car on course, and there was a loud crack as one of the rescue boats crashed into the water as the cracked ice broke up underneath it.

The car reached the final lift point, and slowly it rose out of the water, leaving a trail of broken ice under it. The crane operator brought the car up above the height of the guardrail and then lowered it onto the ground near where Buck and Carl stood. Their crime scene had arrived. Several firefighters and search and rescue guys moved in to remove the lifting straps, and as they worked, one of them walked over to Buck and handed him the radio. The searchers decided to use a unique law enforcement frequency to keep the radio transmission from being picked up by the press.

"This is Buck, over."

"Buck, it's Reed, there's another car under here, much older than the first one. Appears to have been here a long time, over."

"You have got to be shitting me. Can you reach it and hook it up, over?" asked Buck.

"Yeah, have my guys send the straps back down with the hook. We'll bring it up. Over and out."

Buck turned to Carl. "What the hell do you think that's about?"

"You got me, Buck."

The firefighter standing by took back the radio and ran back to his partners, who unhooked the straps from the car and lowered them back down to the firefighters in the rescue boats. Buck watched as the divers reentered the water and swam to the second car. They accepted the lift straps and dove under the ice.

The divers followed the same procedure as before, and the car, a much older, faded sedan, was lifted to the highway and set down next to the first car.

Buck and Carl cleared everyone from around the cars and asked the forensic pathologist to come have a look. Carl had called him earlier in the day and asked him to be present once the car was lifted to take charge of the body.

Dr. Stanley Worth stepped up to the car and tried to open the driver's side door, which was jammed from the collision with the ice below. He called the firefighters over, and they used the Jaws of Life to spring open the door.

Colorado is one of about a dozen states that use the coroner system instead of the medical examiner system. The coroner is an elected position and does not require any kind of medical background. The state legislature passed a bill requiring all elected coroners to complete a death investigation class so they would be aware of the process and procedures involved in dealing with such cases. In the event an autopsy was required, the coroner would hire a licensed forensic pathologist to perform the needed autopsy and tests. To keep the costs down, a pathologist might work for multiple counties on an "as needed" basis.

That was the case with Dr. Worth. He was a retired medical examiner from Ohio who wanted to keep his hand in the game, so he hired on as one of several forensic pathologists for Jefferson County. Due to a lack of facilities, all autopsies in Summit County were handled by Jefferson County. He got to live in Colorado, work part time at something he loved and golf and fish the rest of the time.

While Dr. Worth examined the body seated in the car, Buck stepped over to the other car. The faded tan 1970 Dodge Dart showed considerable wear, but he couldn't be sure how much of the wear came from the time in the lake or from a hard life on the road. There was no visible evidence as to why this car was in the lake. He stepped to the back of the car and asked the firefighters to pop open the trunk. A crowbar in the hands of a burly firefighter made short work of the trunk, and Buck lifted it.

"Fuck. What is this?"

Carl stepped up alongside him and peered into the trunk. "Shit," was all he said.

Inside the trunk was something wrapped in plastic that appeared to be the size of a small child. Buck and Carl stepped back and waved over Dr. Worth. He stepped over, gave the package a cursory examination and called his assistant to bring over the gurney.

"I don't want to speculate. We'll open it up back at the morgue and see what's inside."

Buck didn't need speculation. He had a sick feeling in his gut, which was not a good thing in his line of work. They stepped back away from the car as Dr. Worth and his assistant removed Barb McBride from the driver's seat and put her in a black poly body bag. They loaded her into the waiting ambulance and then came over and lifted the wrapped bundle out of the back of the older car. The plastic was crisp, and Buck was afraid it might break open before they could move it into the body bag, but they worked quickly and soon had the bundle sitting on the floor in the ambulance.

Dr. Worth signed the transport order, and his assistant climbed into the back of the ambulance with the body and the bundle. Until the body reached the morgue in Golden, Colorado, it would not be alone. This was not only out of respect for the dead, but it was also part of the chain of evidence.

Dr. Worth told Buck and Carl he would give them a call when he was ready to start, and he headed for his car, stripping off his gloves and Tyvek suit as he went.

Buck and Carl could not believe how quickly things had changed. They moved out of the way as the forensics team from Denver gloved up and went to work on the cars. Buck could see the cracked steering wheel in Barb McBride's car, but any closer examination would have to wait until the forensics team gave him the okay. He knew it would take a while, so they headed for their cars. It was time to make the death notification.

Chapter Seventeen

The voice on the other end of the phone was not happy. "The news media is reporting a body has been found. You assured us no one would find the body for years. What the fuck happened?"

"We did everything we could to make sure it wouldn't be found. It was just dumb luck a couple old fisherman had an underwater camera and they spotted the car."

"Whose bright idea was it to put the car in the lake in the first place? We told you when you first approached us with this that we thought it was a stupid idea. You were supposed to make the body disappear forever, not four days."

"Look, we all agreed I would handle this as I saw fit. Well, it didn't quite work out like we planned, sometimes shit happens."

"Let me stop you right there. Maybe in your world shit happens, but in our world, we plan things out until we are certain nothing can go wrong. The members are getting nervous, and you have put us in a bad position. Are you certain everything she was working on is on the laptop?"

"Yes. Once we crack her password, we can destroy everything, and then we will be in the clear. Nothing to worry about."

"You better make sure that's the case, because

we will decide what we worry about and the last thing you want is for us to worry about you."

The evenness in the tone of voice on the other end of the phone was more frightening than if he was being screamed at, and it unnerved him.

"What do you want me to do to fix the problem with the body?"

"We don't want you to do anything. You have done quite enough already. We will take care of this ourselves to make sure it's done right. You focus on getting into her computer. We need to find out what she was able to discover, and then we need to make sure we destroy everything. Do you understand?"

"Yes, sir," he said, but he realized the phone was already dead.

He sat back in his chair and brushed the sweat from his forehead. This was not what he'd expected. What a clusterfuck.

He felt like he was no longer in control. His hands were shaking. He tried to calm himself by slowing his breathing, but it didn't work. These were not people you screwed around with. These were powerful people who had a lot more to lose than he did, and they took this shit seriously.

He leaned back in the chair and closed his eyes. He wondered what it meant that they would take care of this themselves? To him it sounded like a threat, but what could he do? How could it be his fault that those two fishermen found the body? The members had to understand that once in a while things didn't work out as planned. Or did they?

He reached into his backpack, which was sitting

next to his chair, and pulled out her laptop. He fired it up and then sat there looking at the password screen. He'd promised them he would have no trouble cracking the password, but now as he sat there looking at the screen, he wondered if that was a lie too. He was good with computers, very good, but this might just be out of his league.

Over the past couple days, he'd tried every combination of every word he could think of that she might use as her password, to no avail. If he couldn't crack her laptop, he was afraid of what the membership might do. He entered a few more random combinations of letters and numbers but got the same result as before.

He picked up his cell phone and dialed a number. He knew someone not connected with the membership who might be able to help. The phone was answered by an electronic voice, and he left his number and nothing else.

Five minutes later, his phone rang. The voice on the other end had a metallic scratchiness to it. Encrypted.

"Thanks. I need help cracking a password. I've tried everything I can think of."

The metallic voice on the other end said, "Five thousand, same place as before and I will send you a link."

The metallic voice hung up, no discussion, no negotiation, nothing, just hung up. He opened his laptop, entered an exclusive website not available to the general public, entered his security information and pressed enter. Seconds later a payment page appeared, and he entered the number from a foreign bank account that was in a fictitious name and clicked enter. The screen went blank, and he closed his laptop. Now he just had to wait.

He sat back and thought about how they had gotten involved with these people. He remembered it was a fraternity party his sophomore year. He thought it was cool to have rich and powerful friends. He also thought it was funny how people with the same proclivity tended to find each other in a crowd.

At the time he was a good photographer, and he was discreet, so the membership had no problem sending him to foreign places for special photography assignments. He loved the work and the travel, and it made him feel like he was part of the greater good. Over the years, he soon realized he had a limited picture of what was going on and how big this thing was. He felt left out when he realized he was more of an employee than a part of the membership, but he also knew there was no way he could ever cover the initiation fee or the monthly cost. So, he kept his mouth shut and did his job.

His phone chimed, and he checked his messages. There was one message, and all it had were five numbers: 47531. He opened his laptop to another nonpublic website and entered the five numbers. He clicked download on the screen and then sat back. When the download completed, he was taken to a new page. He plugged his laptop into Barb McBride's laptop, clicked start and then sat back and waited while the NSA code-cracking program went to work on the password. Now all he had to do was wait.

Chapter Eighteen

Buck watched the faces of the family members as he explained what they found at the reservoir. He was watching them even though there was zero evidence any of them were involved in Barb McBride's disappearance; the little bug was still banging around in his brain.

"The car was found a few miles from here in the reservoir. At this moment it appears she could have driven off the road in the snowstorm, but with the situation around her phone and the ransom note, we are not going to rule out foul play."

Mrs. Grainger fell apart and sat at the kitchen table, crying into a kitchen towel. Bob McBride was more questioning. "How is this possible? Why would someone hurt Barb? All she ever did was try to help people who needed someone to care. This is a nightmare."

Jim McBride, with his ever-present drink in his hand, stood up from the table, walked out the kitchen door, stood on the back deck and stared at the mountain. Two of his three children who had arrived earlier in the day were now sitting there in shock.

Kenny, the oldest, a tall, good-looking young reporter, had flown in from a national assignment in Georgia covering an odd, off-season tornado that devasted a small town. His sister, April, thin, blond and beautiful had been in New York City on a modeling assignment when she received the call that her mom's phone was found in Montana. She caught the next flight and had arrived the night before.

The youngest daughter, Tina, a fall-term graduate of the University of California at Berkeley, was working with Doctors Without Borders somewhere in the Democratic Republic of the Congo and was out of touch. The U.S. Embassy was working on getting word to her.

Kenny followed his father out onto the deck, while April, with tears in her eyes, tried to comfort her aunt. Buck watched the interaction between father and son and could see that the gestures were getting more and more heated. He debated intervening when Kenny grabbed the glass from his father's hand and threw it across the lawn. He turned, walked off the deck and headed for the river, while Jim McBride stood there fuming.

Buck wanted to have that heart-to-heart conversation with Jim McBride, but he decided to wait and let Jim cool down. He turned and walked down the hallway to Barb McBride's office. His team had vacated the kitchen when Buck called about the body, and they set up all the electronics gear in there where they would have a little more peace and quiet.

Before stepping through the door, he pulled out his phone and called Bax.

"Hey, Buck. Heard you found a second body in the reservoir. That's crazy."

"Yeah, this entire case is getting crazy. Are you all wrapped up with Grand Junction?"

"Yes, sir. All the evidence has been filed, and I've closed out the investigation file."

"Great work, Bax. Have you started anything else?"

"Nope. Was waiting to see what you had."

"Great. Grab your gear and head this way. Let's meet at Giovanni's Italian Restaurant in Frisco so we can figure out a game plan."

"On my way."

Buck hung up and stepped into Barb McBride's office. Paul Webber was sitting at Barb's desk sorting through a stack of file folders, while George and Melanie were busy typing away on their laptops. Paul set the folders down.

"We got a call from the judge. We have the warrant for the electronics. The judge gave us wide latitude, but he told me this was not a fishing expedition and he would squash anything we found that he deemed improperly seized. I didn't want to serve the warrant on a guy who just lost his wife."

"No worries. I'll serve the warrant. Can we grab his brother's laptop too?"

"Judge didn't say we couldn't; as long as it's on the property, because I went for the whole property, not just the house."

"Good move, Paul."

The conversation was interrupted when Carl stepped into the office. "Hate to interrupt. Dr.

Worth called. He is scheduling Barb McBride's autopsy for tomorrow at nine a.m. He will open the other package once he's finished with McBride."

"Thanks, Carl. Let's plan on getting out of here around seven thirty. We can grab breakfast at my hotel before we head down."

He turned back to Paul. "Why don't you and Carl pay a visit to Bob McBride and pick up his laptop and phone. Melanie, when they bring you the phone, can you call the cell provider and have them send his call log?"

George and Melanie nodded and went back to their typing. Paul set his file folders aside and was getting up from the desk when Buck said, "Anything in the folders you've been through so far?"

"No. There are files here covering every subject imaginable, from child porn to alien abductions. Whatever she was working on is someplace else, cause it sure isn't here."

"Okay. Paul, once you and Carl are finished, meet me at Giovanni's in Frisco. Bax is on her way so we can come up with some kind of plan. George, why don't you and Melanie wrap up after you secure Bob McBride's phone and laptop and we can pick it up in the morning. Thanks, all."

Buck left the office and walked down the hall towards Jim McBride's office. As he passed, he noted that the kitchen was empty. He wondered where everyone had gone. Jim McBride sat alone in his office, staring into space. He turned, gazed up at Buck with bloodshot eyes and pointed towards the empty chair in front of the desk. Buck sat down and pulled a small notebook out of his pocket.

"Mr. McBride, I realize this is a hard time right now, but I need to ask you a few questions. The faster we do this, the faster we can find out what happened to your wife."

Jim McBride nodded and took a sip from the glass on his desk. He set the glass down.

"Why would someone hurt Barb? Everyone loved her." Tears formed in his eyes.

"Mr. McBride, are you certain you have no idea what your wife was working on?"

Jim McBride nodded. "I wish I did, but she was always very secretive about her work."

"We've been through most of her files. Is there any place else she might have kept her work, either in the house or someplace else, maybe some secret place she liked to work?"

Jim McBride thought for a minute and then shook his head no.

"Okay. Do you know if she received any threats, either on her laptop or her phone, or was she scared of anything or anyone? No hang-up calls or suspicious people lurking about?"

Buck could see this conversation was going nowhere fast, so he decided to take a different approach.

"Mr. McBride, what about you? Anything going on in your life that might cause someone to want to hurt your wife?"

Jim McBride took a long time to answer. "Do you think someone killed her because of me? Other than the porn Barb found on her computer that morning, there is nothing going on in my life."

"Speaking of the porn on her computer, I would like to have my computer people go through your laptop and your phone to make sure someone didn't hack into your computer as well. I can request a warrant if you would like, but it should only take a couple hours, and we can have it right back to you."

Jim McBride picked up his phone off the desk and handed it to Buck and pointed towards his laptop. Buck accepted both and walked out of the office. That worked out better than he'd planned, since he was hoping Jim McBride would give him the electronics without having to use the search warrant just yet. If they found anything on there that might incriminate him, then they would expand their search and use the warrant. Right now, he wanted to keep McBride talking.

Buck took the phone and laptop back to the office and placed them in an evidence bag, signed and dated the tab and sealed the bag. He handed the bag to Melanie, and she countersigned the seal. She placed the bag in her backpack since they had no secure storage on-site. The evidence bag would stay with her all night.

She was shutting down her laptop when Paul and Carl walked into the office.

"Any problem with Bob McBride?" asked Buck.

"No," said Paul. "He couldn't be more accommodating. Never asked to see the warrant, never asked for an attorney, just told us that if it helped with the case and helped to find out who put the stuff on his sister-in-law's computer, then he was all in."

Carl said, "This whole family seems a little too good to be true."

Buck nodded, and Paul grabbed an evidence bag and followed the same procedure Melanie used on Jim's electronics. With both evidence bags secure in Melanie's backpack, she and George grabbed their backpacks and headed out, followed by Buck, Paul and Carl.

Buck thought about what Carl had just said. He was thinking the same thing. Either this was the most accommodating family ever, or he was missing something. He intended to find out which was true.

Chapter Nineteen

Buck, Paul and Carl stepped through the front door of Giovanni's Italian Restaurant in downtown Frisco, and it was like stepping back in time to a country inn in Tuscany. The smells were almost overwhelming, and they found it hard to figure out the various aromas. It was heaven, or at least what heaven should be if you believed in heaven. The dark wood walls and massive stone pizza oven in the open kitchen created an air of sophistication in this little mountain town.

Buck was talking with the hostess at the podium near the door when a voice he hadn't heard in years yelled, "Buck Taylor, geez, what's it been, about a hundred years?" Tony Giovanni Jr. walked through the door and gave Buck a huge hug, which was no easy feat. Tony Giovanni was about five foot ten and weighed close to three hundred pounds, with a bald head and grayish goatee. He had a dynamic personality, and Buck couldn't ever remember seeing Tony without his trademark smile.

"Tony, it's great to see you. How ya been?"

"Can't complain, besides, nobody would listen anyway. Am I right?"

"Hey, how's your dad doing? Last time we talked he had some kind of heart thing going on. He okay?"

"Hey, Dad is Dad. Nothing stops him. Yeah, he's doing great. Cleaned out a couple arteries and he feels like a new man. He and mom are in Denver visiting friends from Italy. He ain't gonna be happy he missed you."

"Well, you give him my best. How about a quiet table in the back? And we're waiting on one more."

"Pretty blond girl with a gun and a badge? She's already here. Got her set up back by the bar. Follow me."

Tony led Buck and the others to a table for four, just outside the double doors leading to the bar. Bax was already seated, looking at the menu and biting down on a piece of Italian bread covered in olive oil and herbs. With her mouth full, she just smiled as they each grabbed a seat.

Tony handed out menus and then said, "Whatever you want tonight is on the house."

Buck responded with a crooked smile. "You know that's not gonna happen."

Tony laughed a deep belly laugh. "I've been trying for years to buy this guy dinner, and he always turns me down. Okay, Buck, but if a bottle of Chianti should appear at the table, I had nothing to do with it." And almost miraculously, one did.

Tony called over the waiter, told him to take good care of his friends and headed for the kitchen. Bax had finished the piece of bread she was eating and was reaching for another piece.

"This bread is amazing. You need to try this."

Carl, who knew about Giovanni's but never wanted to fight the crowds, picked up a piece of bread. "Is there anyone in Colorado you don't know?"

Bax and Paul laughed. Buck smiled. He'd met Tony while in boot camp, and they became fast friends. When Tony's dad, Tony Sr., opened this place, he and Lucy would stop by if they were in the area. It became an annual pilgrimage. He hadn't been in since Lucy got too sick to travel. He choked back a tear and picked up the glass of Coke the waiter set down in front of him. For a few minutes they discussed the food, and Buck offered suggestions for dinner and then everyone ordered, and the waiter thanked them and headed off towards the kitchen.

Buck knew not to start discussing the case before dinner arrived, because once the food hit the table, there would be no talking at all, just eating, so they made small talk until the first course arrived. Dinner went on for what seemed like hours, and once the dessert course was finished, everyone sat back in their chairs.

"That was amazing," said Paul. Everyone nodded in agreement. Tony stopped by the table a couple times, and now he showed up with the waiter, and they removed all the empty plates. He told them to take their time, and he told the waiter not to bother them unless they asked for something. Buck felt bad taking up one of the waiter's tables, but he knew Tony would take care of him.

"Okay, now that everyone is well fed, let's get back to reality. There are a lot of things about this case that are bugging me and I think you all feel the same, but I want to walk through what we have so far and try to weed out the crap."

Bax pulled her laptop out and fired it up. She pulled up the investigation file, opened to the timeline and entered a note about who was at the table. She turned the laptop so everyone could see.

Buck started. "We have the time Barb McBride left the house, and we have the location where she died. Those are about the only facts not in dispute."

Buck walked them through the timeline, stopping now and then to discuss the evidence or lack thereof that led them to that place on the line. They all agreed that the phone and the ransom note were red herrings designed to throw them off track, so for now, they agreed to set those aside. The phone and the box were now with forensics, and Bax was waiting to hear back from the techs to see if there were any fingerprints or DNA from someone other than Barb McBride.

Now that they had Bob and Jim McBride's laptops and phones, they could do a more thorough search to see if, like George believed, the child porn that had been sent to Barb's email came from Jim's computer, and if so, how it got there. The big question around the table evolved around Jim and/or Bob McBride's involvement in the disappearance. Paul spoke with the friends he was visiting in Denver, and they all agreed Bob was there the entire time or at least the entire time they were with him, but Jim didn't have a real alibi. According to him, he was drinking and fell asleep, with no one to verify that.

"But that leads us to the bigger question," said Bax. "Why would someone want Barb McBride dead?"

Carl was the first to respond. "Revenge for something she wrote, to stop her from writing something, money, jealousy from a rival. Or a homicidal maniac. Do we have any active serial killers working in the state?"

Buck made a note on his pad. "I can check with the Feds and see, but I haven't heard of any. Of course, that doesn't mean there aren't any."

He checked his notes. "Paul, was there anything in her files that might have gotten her killed?"

"The last documentary she produced was almost a year ago. Why would someone wait this long?"

"Excellent point. Take a look at her last couple documentaries and see if anything jumps out. So, what are we left with, jealousy, money and to stop her from writing something? Bax, check with her producer and see if she has any rivals. I doubt someone would kill to take her place as a TV giant, but anything's possible. Also, ask the producer if Barb McBride received any hate mail or death threats recently. We have no idea if someone is trying to stop her from writing something because we have no idea what she is working on. We need to find something. Paul, can you keep working that angle? Talk to her husband and find out who her friends or coworkers in the industry are and see if they can give us a lead."

"What about the money?" asked Carl. "You kind of stepped over that one."

"Yeah," said Buck. "The money has been bugging me since we found the phone. Do we know how much life insurance Barb McBride had?"

Bax spun the laptop around, clicked through a couple of files and found what she was looking for.

"According to her production company documents, she has ten million dollars of life insurance. It doesn't look like she draws a salary, and most of the income comes from sponsors and TV advertising. There are some big names here."

"That's great. See if you can find out who benefits from her life insurance and see what happens if she goes missing. There's no way her husband, if he's the beneficiary, could collect on a missing person for several years, so I don't see this as a motive, but let's see it through and let's see if she has an accountant and run an asset search. Bax, call the office and see who's available to take this project on."

"Buck, what about the stranger angle? Maybe not a serial killer, but what about a Good Samaritan thing gone bad?"

"Good thought, Paul, why don't you and Bax hook up with the forensics guys, find out where they have the cars and let's see if they can find something that might lead us in that direction."

"Buck, did you look through the deep dives I did on Bob and Jim McBride?" asked Bax.

"I read the one on Jim, but Bob kind of got stepped on by the body. I'll go through it tonight. Anything jump out?"

"Look at his work history. A little sketchy for a guy his age," said Bax.

"Let's request a search warrant to pull up his bank records as well as those of Jim McBride. Might be something there. Carl and I will be at the autopsy in the morning, and we'll find out what's in the bundle from the second car. By midafternoon we will most likely have two active cases running, so let's work fast. Everyone get some rest. Tomorrow's going to be busy."

Buck called over the waiter and handed him his state-issued American Express card, while the others gathered up their backpacks. He paid the check and left the waiter a nice tip. He thanked Tony on the way out and promised to stop by to see his dad, and they headed to the hotel in Silverthorne.

Chapter Twenty

Bax pulled into the hotel parking lot behind Buck and parked next to him. She grabbed her backpack and go bag out of the back and called to Buck, who stopped and turned around.

"Buck, something's got you bugged, what's going on?"

Buck stood for a minute thinking about what she'd just asked him. He knew she could read him like a book. They'd spent a lot of time working together since Lucy died, but he didn't know if he could communicate what he was thinking since it was all a jumble. They started walking towards the hotel.

"I think we're missing something. I can't put my finger on it, but I'm starting to wonder if we have multiple scenarios at play here, and until we find that one piece that makes it all come together, we are going to keep grasping at straws."

"You think the family is involved, don't you?"

"I think there's a strong possibility either Bob or Jim McBride, or both, are involved in some way. Not sure how, so we need to look at everything. We can either eliminate them or go after them once we have something solid. Like I said earlier, the money makes some sense, but why put the body where no one will find it if you are trying to collect the inheritance? Her inheritance would be tied up in court for years. We are missing something."

Bax thought for a minute. "That makes sense, I'm beginning to see why you think there might be a couple different pieces to this. Let me think about it tonight, and we'll see what the science tells us tomorrow."

The elevator opened, and Bax stepped off on the second floor and wished Buck a good night. Buck continued onto the fourth floor, opened the door to his room and dropped his backpack next to the desk. He pulled a cold bottle of Coke out of the room refrigerator, pulled his laptop out of his backpack and opened it. While he waited for the computer to start up, he pulled out his phone and dialed Hank Clancy.

Hank Clancy was the special agent in charge of the FBI's Denver Field Office, and he and Buck had worked together on several cases over the years, most recently the serial killer case in Aspen, Colorado. Hank answered on the third ring.

"Buck Taylor, how the hell are you?"

"Fine, Hank, you doing okay?"

"Can't complain. So, I hear from your director that you caught the Barb McBride missing person case. You making any headway, or do you need the Feds to come in and help you out?" Hank laughed.

"As a matter of fact, we have."

Buck filled Hank in on recent developments in the case, and he listened intently.

"Drowned in her car or dead beforehand?"

"Not sure, Hank. We'll have more tomorrow,

but listen, that's kind of why I called. You guys working any new serial killer cases in the area I'm not aware of?"

"You got something in mind?"

"No, we just want to cover all our bases, since this is such a strange case."

Hank and Buck had spoken often since they were unable to capture their last serial killer, Alicia Hawkins, and Buck took every one of her killings as his failure because he didn't catch her before she left Colorado and headed for Florida. Truth is, no one would ever blame Buck for her getting away, but the case still haunted him, and several times he'd woken up in a cold sweat after dreaming that Alicia Hawkins killed his wife, Lucy.

Buck never let his cases get under his skin, but there was something different about her case that was making him lose sleep. He employed several news-clipping services to alert him to any cases, from around the country, that had victims who died under similar circumstances, but so far everything he had came from Florida. If the tally was correct, she had already killed six people in Florida and was no closer to being caught.

"As of right now," said Hank, "we don't have anyone active in Colorado, Utah or Wyoming, so unless this is another startup, you can probably discount serial killers. By the way, we may have another victim in Florida. The task force is in Clearwater right now looking at a sliced-up body found in a storage unit. Local ME figures the victim's been dead three, maybe four weeks."

"She's getting more and more active. That's not good."

"Yeah. We'll have more information in the next couple days. I'll keep you posted."

Buck thanked Hank and hung up the phone. He didn't like the idea that Alicia Hawkins was moving about almost without fear. This was one criminal he wanted, no, needed to stop.

He'd just turned back to his laptop when his phone rang. He checked the number, smiled and answered.

"Hey, kiddo, how you doing?"

"Hey, Dad. David said you were working on the missing reporter case and I wanted to see how you were doing."

Cassie was Buck's middle child, and she was every bit a middle child. In high school, she played soccer, ran track and played volleyball. She lettered in all three sports. She was also the one who got in trouble for violating curfew, drinking and whatever other mischief she could find. Buck was surprised when she was accepted to the University of Arizona with a full scholarship for volleyball. He was even more surprised when she was accepted into law school. Cassie was never much for regimented education.

Two and a half years ago, she dropped out of law school, and her career path took a different track. She joined the Forest Service and was now working as a wildland firefighter with the Helena Hotshots. The Helena Hotshots were one of the elite firefighting teams based out of Helena,

Montana. Buck was not surprised. He never saw her sitting behind a desk as a lawyer. She loved the outdoors, and she was as tough as they come. Lucy hadn't been pleased she quit school without any discussion, and she worried whenever Cassie was called out on a fire, but she also knew her daughter and if this was where she was happy, then so was her mom.

David was Buck's oldest son. He looked just like his dad at that age, was a little taller at six foot two and a little heavier, but the resemblance was almost scary. David was a patrol sergeant with the Gunnison Police Department. He also played guitar in a local bluegrass/country band. David's wife, Judy, had taken over Lucy's little ice cream shop in Gunnison and, with Buck's three grandchildren, was making a real go of it. For Lucy, it had been more of a social gathering place and almost a hobby. He was glad Judy was taking it seriously.

Buck filled Cassie in on the case, and she tried to help him figure out the bug in his brain. That used to be Lucy's job, but since her death, Cassie tried to fill the void. They talked for a while about Cassie's job and the fact her team was between fires, which had not often been the case during the past year, due to the drought conditions. She was hoping to take some time off in a month or so and was planning to come home for a couple days. That made Buck smile. He missed her a lot. They finished their conversation, Cassie wished him luck with the case and they hung up.

He decided to finish up the night with a call

to his youngest son. Jason was an architect, and he lived in Boulder with his wife, Kate, and their three children. Of all of Buck's kids, Jason was the one who had continued to follow Catholicism, just like his mom, and he became more involved in his church after Lucy died.

Jason answered the phone and proceeded to tell Buck about getting final planning approval for the Lucy Taylor Memorial Riverwalk. The walk along the Gunnison River, on the shore opposite where the family had scattered Lucy's ashes, was a gift to the city from Buck's brother-in-law, Hardy Braxton, and his family.

Hardy was married to Lucy's younger sister, and after Lucy died, they'd decided to buy a one-mile stretch of riverfront and build a family-oriented trail along the river in honor of Lucy. Jason, along with a landscape architect from his architecture firm, developed the plan, and Jason was overseeing the construction. The trail was planned to open in a little over a month, and he was thrilled to report that the pedestrian footbridge across the river had been installed that morning. The bridge was the key to the entire project and had taken months to build off-site and then truck to the river.

The river improvements were already complete, and the fishing along that one-mile stretch of river was something Buck thoroughly enjoyed. They spoke for a few minutes about plans for the ribbon cutting, and then Buck hung up. It was time to focus back on the case.

Chapter Twenty-One

Buck was having trouble sleeping, and at three a.m. he found himself standing along the Blue River where it flowed behind his hotel. The air was still crisp, but the trees along the river were starting to leaf out, and the flowers in the beds around the hotel were starting to bloom. The river was running about half of what it would be running in a few weeks as the snow began to melt, but it was already high and fast. Buck decided he would make sure to drop a couple of flies before he was finished with this case.

The river, any river, was where Buck found solace. The sound of the water flowing over the rocks was enough to clear his head. Fishing was a part of Buck's life, and he carried his fishing gear with him no matter where he traveled. Since Lucy died, this was where he went for answers. It was what he loved about fly-fishing: once you set that little fly down on the water, you had to focus one hundred percent on catching the fish. There was no room for random thoughts. During many investigations, it was those moments when his mind would clear that he could see whatever he was missing. So far it wasn't working.

He walked along the riverbank for a mile or so and then headed back to his room. His mind was clearing, but there were still too many questions floating around to find any clarity. He closed the door behind him, sat down at his desk and fired up his laptop. He pulled up the material Bax was able to find on Bob McBride and started reading. Forty-five minutes later, he scanned his notes and was amazed at how many questions he had.

Bob McBride was Jim's younger brother. He was a TV producer by trade and had worked closely with his brother on several of Barb McBride's earlier projects when she was still with the networks. Something changed a few years back, and his involvement with his sister-in-law stopped.

Buck read back over his notes about Jim McBride and noticed that his involvement with Barb had stopped at about the same time. He wondered what might have changed in their relationships that might have caused the split to occur. Since that time, Bob had been involved in several TV projects on his own, but he hadn't been involved in a successful project in the last year and a half or so.

Buck made a note to look into his finances to see where his income was coming from. He also wanted a better handle on his debt situation. Bax couldn't confirm an address for him, and Buck wondered if the room over the barn was a bit of charity on Barb McBride's part.

One interesting item he found was his arrest record. Bax noted that Bob McBride had spent three years in jail, early in his career, for fraud and writing bad checks. There was no other criminal activity listed, but Buck wanted more information, so he clicked on the link and pulled up the arrest report.

Bob McBride had been involved in a scheme to defraud several investors. He was able to attract some big-name investors to put up a considerable amount of money for a science fiction thriller he was going to produce, but in the end, there was no script, no actors and no movie, just an elaborate scheme to get money for his own personal use. It always fascinated Buck that rich people could be taken in by these kinds of schemes. In the end, the district attorney in Los Angeles decided to press charges, and Bob was convicted and sentenced to three to five years. He served three years.

It was almost ten years before Bob McBride showed up as a TV producer on Barb McBride's nightly news program. Buck wondered if it was a little more charity; he also wondered where Bob McBride had been for the last ten years. He needed more information.

Buck closed his laptop, put it in his backpack, showered, dressed and got ready to meet Carl for breakfast. He clipped his badge and gun to his belt, grabbed his backpack and left his room.

Carl was already sitting in the small restaurant attached to the hotel when Buck walked in. He sat down and ordered a couple eggs over hard with bacon and French toast and a large Coke in a to-go cup.

"You look like you didn't sleep much," said Carl.

Buck took a sip of his Coke and started filling Carl in on the deep dive material he'd reviewed overnight. Carl's eyes brightened when Buck told him about the arrest for fraud.

"You think he could be back to his old ways and maybe Barb found out?"

Buck sat back as the waitress brought over his breakfast. When she left, he leaned forward. Several of the reporters he had seen on the street in front of the McBride house were having breakfast, and he didn't want to be overheard.

"I think it's worth taking a deeper look at his financials. Something happened a couple years back that caused Barb McBride to cut off financial ties to both her husband and her brother-in-law. We need to find out what that was. It might mean nothing regarding her death, but I think it's a factor."

Carl nodded and finished his breakfast. Buck picked up the check, left cash and the tip on the table and they stood up and headed for the door. Several of the reporters tried to ask them questions as they passed, but they continued straight ahead and headed towards Buck's car.

The drive to Golden took a little over an hour, and they turned off I-70 onto C-470, followed it around as it merged with Highway 6, turned right onto Jefferson County Parkway and pulled into the parking lot of the Jefferson County Coroner's Office. They checked in at the front desk and were escorted to the morgue in the basement, where they found Dr. Worth about to start on Barb McBride.

Dr. Worth acknowledged them with a nod, adjusted the microphone and the overhead camera and pulled back the sheet covering Barb McBride. The first thing Dr. Worth commented on was the bruising on her forehead. He signaled for Buck and Carl to take a closer look.

"This is where she hit the steering wheel, but if you look closely, gentlemen, you can see three distinct bruises, here, here and here."

He asked his assistant to pull up the X-ray of her forehead, and the fractures were easy to spot.

"First appearances would indicate that her head hit three times as the car bounced down the side of the reservoir, but the X-ray, coupled with the bruises, indicates to me her head was violently slammed into the steering wheel. We noted the fractured steering wheel on our report when we removed the body."

Buck examined the bruises.

"So, there's no possibility this was an accident?"

Dr. Worth turned the head and pulled back her hair. There were several purple spots on the back of her neck. "Not when you include these."

"Are those fingerprints?" asked Carl.

"Yes." Dr. Worth stepped back. "The bruises on her forehead are spaced too close together—almost overlapping—to be accidental. I would say someone grabbed her by the back of the head and slammed her into the steering wheel until she was unconscious. This took a hell of a lot of force, enough to fracture her skull and crack the steering wheel. This was a savage attack. You can also see that there is no bruising on her shoulder or chest to indicate the seat belt was restraining her. She was not wearing her seat belt when she hit the wheel."

Three hours later, Dr. Worth stood back, turned off the microphone and the camera and removed his gloves. He took a big gulp from his water bottle while his assistant finished sewing up the *Y* incision.

"We'll send out samples for a tox screen, but I saw nothing that would indicate she was drugged before her death. The water in her lungs indicates the cause of death as drowning, but based on the skull fracture and the fracture on her spinal cord at the base of the skull, I will rule this as a homicide; the aforementioned damage will be listed as contributing factors."

Carl was making notes in his notebook as Buck stepped closer to the body. Dr. Worth stretched and pulled off his gown. He needed a break before they opened the other bundle.

Chapter Twenty-Two

Buck and Carl walked over to the café counter at the Jefferson County Justice Center and grabbed a quick lunch, while Dr. Worth took a break. Carl sat at the table in the lobby and read his notes.

"Fuck, Buck. It would take a huge amount of force to cause that much damage. We're talking about being able to move her head maybe two feet, from upright to the steering wheel."

"Yeah, but it hadn't been enough force to kill her, so she was alive when she hit the water. One thing we will never know is if she regained consciousness after she hit the water and realized what was happening to her. What a shitty way to die."

Buck checked his phone, swallowed the last of his Coke and they headed back to the morgue for round two. As they entered the coroner's office, he stopped. The revelation in his eyes spoke volumes.

"She knew her killer?"

"Why do you think that?" asked Carl.

"She unhooked her seat belt. It makes sense. She wrote about some bad people. She was careful. She would not have gotten out of the car unless she knew the person who stopped to help her, especially being a woman alone on a dark highway. The question is, why did she stop on that stretch of highway in the first place? Did something happen, or did someone force her off the road?"

Carl could almost see the wheels turning in Buck's head. He stood there and let Buck continue.

"Why would a woman alone stop her car on a deserted stretch of highway, in the dark, in a snowstorm? Her car was only a year or two old, so if it wasn't mechanical, then what happened, and why that specific spot? If I remember correctly, that is the highest point on the drive around the reservoir, the one place where the water comes up almost to the edge of the road, the only place where the guardrail is open on either side of the drop-off. It's like the perfect storm, and now that we've determined she didn't drive off the road accidentally, we need to figure out why she stopped there."

Buck pulled out his phone. George answered on the second ring.

"Hey, Buck. What's up?"

"George. Barb McBride drove a Range Rover. Does that car have something like OnStar, where someone could shut her car down remotely?"

George thought for a minute. "Her car doesn't have OnStar, specifically. Range Rover has its own system called InControl. It's got some of the same features. We couldn't use it to locate her car because the system fried when it hit the water. Why do you ask?"

"I'm wondering what would make a woman stop on the side of the road, in a secluded spot, in a snowstorm. Could someone have hacked into her system and shut her car down at that exact spot, or was there a mechanical reason it stopped there?"

"I can't answer that, Buck. It's possible. People don't realize how easy it is to hack into a car's information system. If they did, they might not want the system in their cars. The forensic guys commandeered a garage bay over at the CDOT shop just as you enter Kremmling. They are going over both cars as we speak, and I think Bax and Paul are there as well. Let me head over there and see if we can find something that might answer that question. Maybe it wasn't in the water long enough to corrupt all the data."

Buck thanked George and hung up. Carl nodded and said, "Now all we need to do is figure out who she would stop for. You might be onto something, Buck. I always tell my wife that when she is alone in the car, not to open the window or unlock the door, even for a cop, until she calls 911 and checks to make sure the cop is real. Barb McBride didn't call 911 or anyone else, at least according to her phone logs. Who would she open the door for in the middle of nowhere: cops, tow truck, neighbor?"

"Family," was all Buck said, and he pushed the down button for the elevator.

Dr. Worth's assistant was rolling the gurney containing the plastic-wrapped bundle from the second car to the autopsy table when Buck and Carl entered the morgue. The doctor handed Buck and Carl each a pair of nitrile gloves, and the four men lifted the bundle onto the table. He then handed them a small jar of Vaseline, and they each put a small amount under their noses. They put on Tyvek jumpsuits, surgical masks, and plastic safety goggles. Until they opened the bundle, Dr. Worth was not taking any chances.

Buck and Carl stepped back from the table, and Dr. Worth started the camera and the recording system. He adjusted the microphone. He gave his name, the names of those present, the date and a brief summary of where the bundle was found.

Taking a pair of scissors, he began cutting what was left of the tape that was holding the bundle together. A lot of it started to disintegrate as he cut it, but he was able to expose the edge of the plastic, which was also very brittle. He peeled back the black plastic, and the first thing they noticed was the smell of human decomposition.

He nodded. "It's human."

Dr. Worth continued removing the plastic, which kept breaking off in small strips. As he removed the second layer of plastic, they saw what appeared to be a pair of jeans and a faded red T-shirt. With the help of his assistant, they were able to spread the plastic apart. A foul-smelling fluid sloshed out onto the table. Dr. Worth asked his assistant to fill an evidence jar with the liquid so they could send it to the state lab.

The body, appearing to be a young boy, was in remarkable shape considering it had been underwater for such a long period. Dr. Worth suggested that the cold water of the reservoir had probably stopped the decomp and preserved the body. He rolled the body so his assistant could pull the remaining plastic out from under it. The plastic was placed in a large evidence bag and set on the counter. Under the body, he found what appeared to be flower stems, like someone had put a flower bouquet in the bag before it was sealed. He put those in a separate evidence bag.

Dr. Worth cut away the jeans, T-shirt and white underpants, which he sealed in additional evidence bags. The boy was barefoot. He took scrapings from under the toenails and fingernails and pulled a couple pieces of the shoulder-length blond hair. Hair was a great place to find chemical or drug residue.

He commented that the body appeared to be somewhat malnourished. Buck observed that the legs and arms seemed odd, almost like they were twisted. Dr. Worth asked his assistant to bring over the portable X-ray machine. The county had invested in a digital X-ray machine, which gave the doctor instant access to the X-rays, and he pulled up the pictures on his laptop. After a few minutes of looking at the pictures, Dr. Worth told Buck that he believed the boy probably had either muscular dystrophy or some other neuromuscular disease.

After a thorough examination of the body, noting a couple unusual bruises and lacerations, he pulled down the spray nozzle and washed the body, collecting the additional fluids from the table in several five-gallon buckets.

At one point he stopped and pulled down a lighted magnifying glass to study something on the boy's left thigh. He asked Buck and Carl to have a look at where he was pointing.

"Needle mark?" asked Buck.

"Yeah. Could be nothing, but we'll take a piece for testing."

He took a scalpel and cut out the skin around the needle mark, which he placed in an evidence jar. The rest of the autopsy was uneventful, and while his assistant closed the incision, he countersigned all the evidence bags and jars and set them in a box to be shipped to the lab. He removed his gloves, stepped up to the light box and examined the X-rays his assistant had taken after the body was cleaned.

Looking perplexed, he turned to Buck and Carl.

"Cause of death is inconclusive. We will need to wait on the lab results, but other than one needle stick, there is no evidence of foul play. We'll have the lab run all the usual tox screens and DNA, but right now I don't have any idea what killed this child. The one thing I can say for sure is the child was dead before he went into the water. I guess that's a blessing."

Buck thanked the doctor, and he and Carl walked out of the morgue and headed outside for some fresh air.

"Buck, what do you think about the flowers we found in with the body? A sign of respect, maybe?"

"That's what I'm thinking. Somebody cared for this kid and was sad when he died, yet he was also malnourished."

He pulled his phone out and speed-dialed a number. The director answered immediately. Buck filled him in on the autopsy findings for both bodies. The director asked a couple of questions, and they discussed how he wanted to proceed. The director agreed and told Buck to call if he needed anything or any more help. Buck hung up and speed-dialed another number and waited as the phone rang. Max Clinton answered her phone as she always did.

"Hey, Buck. How's my favorite cop?"

Dr. Maxine Clinton was the director of the State Crime Lab in Pueblo. She was a matronly woman in her late sixties, about five feet five with short gray hair. She probably thought she carried around an extra fifteen pounds she didn't need, but she was still a handsome woman. Married for forty years, Max had four children, eleven grandchildren, and six great-grandchildren. She lived in a one-hundred-fifty-year-old farmhouse in Pueblo, where she liked to tend her garden and sit on her porch and drink iced tea. She was also a bourbon girl and could drink most people under the table. She was loud and outspoken, but she knew her job.

Max had received her PhD in biology from the University of Colorado and worked as a biology professor for twenty years before taking over the crime lab, a job she enjoyed. She was a tough taskmaster, but she had a belief system that didn't allow for defeat. Her goal was to give the crime investigator, no matter which department or municipality they worked for, all the information they would need to solve any crime. She held that as a sacred obligation to the victims. She was a dedicated professional, and her team at the lab practically worshipped her.

Buck would have been included in that group. Many times, during a rough investigation, it was Max and her team that lit the spark that led to a breakthrough. Max was one of Buck's favorite people, and she felt the same way about him.

Buck told her about the results of the autopsies and asked her if she could put a rush on the results. She promised to put his samples at the top of the list as soon as she received them. She also told him she would call the director and see if they could do an overnight DNA test on the little boy. This was an expensive test and was not a common procedure. Buck had received permission to use this test on several occasions, but he'd never put Max in a position that would cause her trouble. Max ended the call like always.

"You're a good man, Buck Taylor, God will watch over you." Max hung up.

Buck didn't care much about religion. He hadn't been to church in probably forty years. He had been raised Catholic but left the church right after Confirmation. He always had too many questions about the teachings and too many people telling him he had to have faith. The answers he was seeking had nothing to do with faith. He had a lot of friends, Max among them, who always offered up a prayer, especially when Lucy was dying. He never once rejected any of those offers, often smiling and thanking them for their kind thoughts.

Buck had realized a long time ago that God and

faith weren't the problem, it was organized religion. In his many years in law enforcement, he had seen too many times the aftereffects of someone's religious beliefs. It amazed him that so many people of faith could cause so much hatred and crime. But then, nonbelievers created just as much havoc.

Buck believed there was a higher power out there, but he didn't believe that, whatever that power was, it cared about one individual over another. His football coach had always offered up a prayer before each game asking for help in defeating the other team. He always suspected the other team's coach was doing the same thing. How did God decide which team should win?

He knew a lot of people who'd said a lot of prayers for Lucy over the five years she was sick, but in the end, she still died. She was the last person who should have gotten cancer, but Buck didn't carry any hatred. Who could he possibly be mad at? Who could he blame? He figured you couldn't be mad at something if you didn't believe in it, to begin with.

Buck believed there were spirits or a force all around us, and he always thanked them for allowing him to enjoy the hike, or for allowing him to catch fish, or see the sunrise and the sunset. He didn't think of it as a religion. It was something deeper. Something Buck didn't understand. He just accepted it. But no matter what, he always appreciated it when Max told him God was watching over him. After all. What could it hurt?

Chapter Twenty-Three

Bax and Paul pulled into the gravel parking lot at the Colorado Department of Transportation garage just south of Kremmling and parked next to the CBI forensics van. The forensics guys had been able to commandeer one of the garage bays and move both cars into the space. They were going over Barb McBride's Range Rover when Bax and Paul walked in.

They signed in on the visitor log, put on Tyvek jumpsuits, booties, hats and nitrile gloves and walked up to Jerry Harcourt, the lead forensic tech.

"Hi, Jerry. Any luck so far?" Bax asked.

"Hey, Bax, Paul. Not much so far, but we just started the detail work on this one. I can tell you one thing for sure. The Range Rover was not involved in an accident, at least not one that left any paint or residue. We pulled the hard drive and have it drying out in a bucket of rice. It fried when it hit the water, but we might be able to pull something off it."

Bax stepped over to the driver's side door. She pointed to the cracked steering wheel. She had to lift the airbag remains out of the way with her gloved hand to see the wheel.

"Could this have cracked when the car hit the ice in the lake?"

"It's possible, but I doubt the body would have

hit it hard enough to do the kind of damage we see here, especially with the airbag in the way. I think something else happened."

Paul was looking in through the passenger side door.

"Jerry, was she wearing her seat belt when the pathologist pulled her from the front seat?"

Jerry walked over to his laptop, opened his photos from the crime scene, found a clear picture and spun his laptop so Paul could see it.

"Not from the pictures. The water floated her around a little, but when the car hit the ground after the fire department lifted it, she was slouched across the seat and the center console. No seat belt."

Paul pulled out his notebook and made a note to himself. Bax nodded in agreement. She walked over to the table they had set up in one corner of the garage and started looking through the evidence bags. The table didn't hold much evidence, at least nothing that seemed promising to Bax. She turned back to the car as two of the forensic techs carried in a large plastic tent.

"What's the tent for, Jerry?"

"We are going to try to lift some prints off the car."

"The car was submerged for almost a week; I would assume the fingerprints would have washed off everything."

"That's what most people would think, but a lot of us have had good luck pulling prints off submerged metal using cyanoacrylate fuming. Basically, superglue on steroids. The DNA will be gone from the print, but we may still find a print. Ain't science amazing?"

Jerry removed a packet from his toolbox, broke it open and set it inside the tent. He closed the flap to the tent and told her it would take about an hour. While they waited, they were going to start on the older car. Bax watched the tent fill up with a white cloud. Maybe they would get lucky.

Jerry joined the two other techs at the 1970 Dodge Dart. He made a note of the mileage: over one hundred sixty-two thousand. Someone had driven this car for a long time before it found its way into the reservoir. He checked the corner of the dashboard, but the VIN tag was missing. He checked inside the driver's door, but there wasn't one there either. With no license plates and no VIN, it was going to be difficult to find the owner of the car. Bax noted the frustrated look on his face.

"VIN's gone?" she asked.

Jerry nodded. "We might still be okay. The manufacturer also puts the VIN on the chassis and on some of the main components. Hopefully, whoever removed these didn't find them all."

Bax stepped away, and the techs crawled all over the car. She was walking back to check on the fume tent when George Peterman walked through the door.

"Hey, Bax. Buck wants me to look at the computer system on the Range Rover. He thinks someone might have hacked the system and stopped her car."

"Jerry said it might be fried, but he put the hard drive in rice to dry it out."

She pointed to the five-gallon bucket on the table, and George walked over and tapped Jerry on the shoulder. Jerry made his way out of the car, spoke to George for a minute and they walked over to the bucket. Jerry handed him a clipboard, while he put the lid on the bucket and sealed it with a couple of pieces of red evidence tape. George signed the transfer form on the clipboard, nodded to everyone and walked out the door.

Paul walked up to Bax. "Hacked her car? That would explain why she stopped on the road. Is that even possible?"

Bax thought about the possibilities. "I guess it could be possible. In an emergency, OnStar can do it. Shit, what a scary thought that someone could shut your car down whenever they wanted."

It was late afternoon when Paul headed back to the McBride ranch to check on George and Melanie. He was hoping they were able to gather some of the information Buck was looking for. Bax stayed behind at the garage and watched Jerry and his team tear apart the old Dodge. One of the other techs slid out from under the car and handed him his phone. Jerry was pleased with the image that was on the screen. He waved Bax over as he walked towards the table his laptop was on.

"What have you got?"

"We were able to pull another VIN off the chassis."

Bax took the phone and read off the numbers as he typed them into the DMV database.

While this was going on at the old Dodge, the other tech was going over the Range Rover with a magnifying glass looking for fingerprints. She worked her way around the car and stopped at the driver's door frame. She studied the frame and then took a high-resolution digital photo of the print she found. She also photographed it from a little distance to give it perspective. She found two more prints on the headliner over the door on the inside of the car. She photographed those as well. On the trunk lid, she hit pay dirt. There was an almost perfect palm print with three quality fingerprints next to a large smudge. She photographed the palm print.

Bax walked over, and the tech handed her the phone. The prints were of good quality. Bax positioned herself outside the car door, and with the help of the tech placed her hands where the prints were found. After moving around and changing positions, she was able to match things up, and she saw that there would be no reason for someone's prints to be in those locations unless they were pushing the car with the driver's door open or the window rolled down.

Bax was pleased and amazed they were able to pull fingerprints off a submerged car. She stepped out of the way as the tech moved to the inside of the car, and she saw her take several more prints off the steering wheel and the gearshift knob. When she was finished, she uploaded the prints to the investigation file, and Bax created a digital package and uploaded them to the Automated Fingerprint Identification System, AFIS for short.

Bax knew using AFIS was not like what people saw on those television cop shows. You didn't receive a response back within a few minutes so you could solve the crime within the one-hour-allotted time frame. Sometimes you didn't get a match at all. It was now a waiting game.

Chapter Twenty-Four

Buck pulled off the highway and turned onto the McBride's ranch road. There seemed to be about half as many media trucks and vans parked along the highway. He pulled up to the deputy manning the barricade.

"Where'd all the media folks go?"

"The family headed into Silverthorne to meet with the funeral director at Henderson's Funeral Home. As soon as they left, everyone followed. They told me they got the call saying the body was being released. It was like a parade heading out of here. The sheriff called in extra help to keep them out of the mortuary."

He moved the barricade and Buck pulled through and parked between the house and the barn. He and Carl checked in with the deputy at the door and walked back to Barb McBride's office to check in with the tech team.

Paul and Melanie were hunched over a laptop on one end of the desk, while George worked on his laptop and what appeared to be an external hard drive on the other end. Paul smiled as they entered.

"Good, you're here. We were just going to call you," said Paul.

"Whatcha got?"

"Melanie may have found something. I'll let her explain."

"We were watching a couple of Barb McBride's other documentaries, looking for a reason someone might want to kill her. She sure covered a lot of controversial subjects over the past couple years, but nothing that made sense to us, that someone might want her dead. Her last documentary was over a year ago, and it was about missing Native American women. It was an incredible program but didn't really indict anyone, but we did notice something in the credits. She uses a post-production company called CRT Production Services to handle the final editing and to prepare the documentary for broadcast."

She stopped talking for a minute to let that sink in. Carl was the first one to talk.

"Do we have a name of someone who might be able to tell us what she was working on?"

Melanie smiled. "Better than that. Paul and I have a meeting as soon as we can get to Denver, with the guy who handles all her work. He won't talk about it on the phone, but he will have the entire program loaded and waiting for us to view at his facility. We were getting ready to head out."

"That's awesome. Don't let us keep you," said Buck. "Great job."

Paul and Melanie grabbed their backpacks and headed out the door. Maybe this was the break they needed.

Buck walked over to George. The desk was

covered with the hard drive, the laptop and a bunch of electronics he hadn't ever seen before.

"Is that from the Range Rover?" he asked.

George sat back in his chair. "Yeah. I was on the phone for a couple hours with the Range Rover tech support folks. The system fried once the car hit the water, but we've been working on repairing the fried components. We just about have it, but I'm waiting on a part they found me at an RC store in Leadville. I called the owner, and he was going to have his son drive the part down here. Should be here in about an hour."

George stopped to take a breath. "The other thing the tech guys told me was that their system is cloud-based. They are having one of their computer guys run through the programming to see if the system might have been hacked. If it was hacked, the hacker would have either gone through the hard drive in the car or gone through the cloud-based software. Either way, the tech guys say the hack would have left a fingerprint in the system."

"Shit," said Buck. "Maybe things are finally coming together. Were you able to find anything in the McBride brother's laptops or phones?"

"Not so far. I wanted to work on the car stuff first. I downloaded everything off their phones and laptops onto an air-gapped laptop. I can work on it when I'm done here, and we can give them back their electronics."

Carl noticed the questioning look on Buck's face, but before he could ask, Carl answered.

"An air-gapped laptop is one that hasn't ever

been connected to the internet. That way, the data can't be hacked or corrupted." George nodded his head approvingly and went back to soldering a small resistor in place.

Buck thanked him, pulled out his laptop and opened the investigation file. Buck noted that Dr. Worth had uploaded the autopsy report for Barb McBride. Buck opened the report, and with Carl sitting next to him, they read the report. There was nothing new revealed in the report that they hadn't talked about at the autopsy.

He noted that the blood alcohol test came back showing a blood alcohol level of .05, not drunk by legal standards, but she did have a few drinks that night. The stomach contents showed she had cheese ravioli, a salad and bread for dinner. Buck made a note on his pad to ask Jim McBride what they'd had for dinner the night she disappeared to make sure she hadn't stopped someplace after she left the house.

Buck closed the autopsy report and opened a separate email from Dr. Worth. This one contained the autopsy on the six-year-old boy. Buck hadn't had a chance to open a separate investigation file for the new case, so he took a few minutes to open a new file, enter the information he had and email the link to all concerned.

There were no surprises in this report either. Buck checked his email to see if any of the lab results were back, even though he knew the state lab had only received the box of evidence a few hours earlier.

He closed his email and reopened the McBride file. He clicked on the communication section and found an asset report on the McBrides that the office in Grand Junction had completed. According to the document, Barb McBride had a personal worth of about twelve million dollars. The house and ranch, which were in her name, were valued at around ten million, and she had stocks and personal bank accounts worth another two million.

Jim McBride, by comparison, was a pauper. He had personal bank accounts worth a little over twenty thousand and no property assets. Even his car was in Barb McBride's company's name.

Bob McBride did not have any assets of his own, and he had a small checking account. The auditor had made a note to look at his income. Buck ran his finger down the income statement. Bob received a payment of fifteen hundred dollars every month from something called Skylark Holdings, LLC. There was no indication what this was for, but the odd thing Buck noticed on his expenses page was his credit card balance, which up until a couple months ago was running around forty thousand dollars, but in the last month the balances were wiped clean.

Buck thought back to the conversation he had with Jim McBride about him starting his own production company, and he wondered how he intended to do that with so little money of his own and no assets. He also wondered who paid off Bob's credit cards.

He opened a search engine on his laptop and

entered Skylark Holdings, LLC. He got 457 hits. He clicked on the first one and got a small news blurb about Skylark Holdings, LLC, opening a new office in Hong Kong. He clicked on the next several and found more worthless information. He couldn't locate a website for the company or any information about what type of business entity it was.

He perused his notes, found the number he was looking for and dialed. Regina Cavanaugh, Barb McBride's producer, answered.

"Hi, Ms. Cavanaugh, Buck Taylor with the Colorado Bureau of Investigation. I was wondering if you could answer a question for me. Have you ever heard of a company called Skylark Holdings, LLC, based out of Hong Kong? Could they be someone working in your industry?"

"Not that I'm aware of," she said. "Do they have something to do with Barb's death?"

"Not sure right now, just a name we came across, but I can't find anything about them on the internet."

"I'll tell you what. Let me make a few phone calls. If they are in the industry, someone will have heard of them. I will call you back if I hear something."

Buck thanked her and hung up.

"That's odd," said Carl. "A company with no internet presence. I didn't think that was possible?"

Buck agreed, and he pulled out his phone and speed-dialed a number.

Hank Clancy answered on the third ring. "Hey, Buck, twice in one week, what's up?"

Buck explained about Skylark Holdings, LLC, not having an internet presence and he wondered if the FBI might know who they were or what type of business they were. Hank didn't recognize the name, but he told Buck he would run it up the flagpole and see if anyone else at the bureau did.

Buck thanked him and hung up. He closed his laptop. They had made a lot of progress today, but they still had a lot of irons in the fire. He needed something to break. He closed his laptop, told George not to work too late and he and Carl grabbed their backpacks and headed for Buck's car. Carl had a school recital to get to, and he didn't want to be late.

Chapter Twenty-Five

Paul and Melanie made good time getting to Denver in spite of the rush-hour traffic. They exited off I-70 at Washington Street and followed the directions to a small industrial park north of Fifty-Eighth Avenue. CRT Production Services was on the back side of a nine-unit concrete office warehouse. There was one small sign indicating the office, and Paul stopped in front of the stairs leading to the front door of the unit.

Melanie rang the doorbell, and they waited until a tall, thin, bearded man unlocked the door. He was dressed in jeans and an old Grateful Dead T-shirt. His dark brown ponytail hung down almost to his waist.

"Agents Webber and Hart, Colorado Bureau of Investigation," said Paul, as they held up their credentials.

"Come on in," the tall fellow said. He locked the door behind them. He stuck out his hand. "Tom Cranston," he said. "I'm the *C* part of CRT."

"Not an easy place to find," said Melanie.

"Yeah. We like it that way. We have another office a few miles from here, but this is where we deal with Barb's projects."

"Why would that be?" asked Paul.

Tom Cranston signaled them to follow him.

They passed through a small office space with a couple desks and computer monitors and entered a large studio area. It was like walking onto the deck of a high-tech starship. Green and red lights flickered on dozens of computers, hard drives and monitors, and green screens covered one entire wall.

Tom Cranston led them to a bank of computer monitors at a large control console and invited them to take a seat.

"Let me start," he said, "by asking that you not tell anyone, other than members of your team, what you are about to see. Barb was incredibly security-conscious, and even though she is no longer with us, I'm under an obligation to her to make sure nothing changes. This is going to seem like a strange request, but I would also prefer that you not take any notes. To be honest, our attorneys were not very happy when they found out you were coming here, so this request is a compromise."

Paul and Melanie nodded their approval, and Tom Cranston continued.

"Barb used us to put the final package together before it was sent off to the network. She never told us who did the filming, especially since she dumped her husband as her cameraman a few years back, and we didn't ask. We would take care of the final editing, correct anything that needed correcting and give her a finished product."

"Barb was a real professional, and our work was mostly superficial, but I think she valued our input. The package you are about to watch would have been shown on the network sometime in July. The network told her producer that they still want it, so we will deliver it. All I'm gonna tell you about it is that it's going to embarrass a lot of powerful people."

He asked them to put on the headsets that were lying on the console, and then he clicked a couple keys on the console and all but the two monitors in front of them went black. Paul and Melanie sat back and watched the two-hour video, and when it ended, they sat there staring at the screens. They pulled off the headsets and sat there without saying a word.

"Holy shit," was all Melanie could say as she set the headset on the console.

Paul was almost speechless. "Fuck. What the hell have we gotten in the middle of?"

"Yeah. If the evidence she presented in her report is true, it's no wonder someone killed her to keep it quiet."

"The evidence is all true," said Tom Cranston as he stepped back into the control room. "Barb had more integrity than anyone I have ever known. Nothing she ever said on air was faked or not thoroughly vetted. Now you understand why we kept her projects away from the rest of the company. The people who work in this section have been vetted like they were going to work for the CIA. Barb insisted."

"Are you guys concerned about your own safety, since she was murdered?" asked Paul.

"We weren't until you called today and

mentioned her being murdered. We have a protocol set up to deal with this. It's not the first time one of her reports led to death threats, but it's more volatile than anything she's done before."

"Does anyone outside your company know what's on this tape?"

"No, Agent Webber, it's the five people that work in this building, Barb and her cameraman, whoever he is. Our lawyers have no idea, and neither do the security people we hired to stay with our people until this is released to the network."

"What would we have to do to get a copy of this tape?" asked Melanie.

"Not to sound smug, Agent Hart, but there is nothing you could do. We have the best first amendment lawyers in the country working on Barb's projects, and they would fight you all the way to the United States Supreme Court. And we would win."

The look in his eyes told Paul and Melanie that he was not joking around.

"Let me ask you this," said Paul. "Barb McBride's laptop has not been found. It's possible it's sitting at the bottom of the reservoir, but we think someone took it from her car. How much of a problem will that be?"

Tom Cranston thought for a minute. "Unless whoever took it gets someone from the NSA to break the password, then not much of a problem, but that may not be as far-fetched as it sounds. Barb hired the best cybersecurity people to create her file protection. She was paranoid to the nth degree. It was the only way to protect her family from harm. If anyone knew what was on this tape, her family wouldn't stand a chance. If they have her laptop, then they might believe they have everything she had in the way of evidence. They will be shocked when this comes out. But once it's out, then her family is safe."

Paul thought for a minute. "Anyone that worried about her safety wouldn't keep all her evidence in one place. Do you have any idea if she had a secret place she kept her project notes, or evidence or anything else?"

"Whenever Barb did a report on a criminal matter, her evidence was always placed in the hands of a third party. Once the program aired, the evidence was then sent to the appropriate authorities."

"Any idea who that would be?"

Tom Cranston got a faraway look in his eyes, and he turned away from them and headed towards the door to the office.

"I want to thank you for coming," he said. "I wish we could have been more help, but you know everything we know. Now, I must ask you to leave. I need to secure the tape and head home."

"Look, Mr. Cranston, Barb McBride was murdered by someone who didn't give a shit about her. It was about protecting his ass. You guys have worked with her for years. You owe it to her to help find out who killed her. We need your help. We can stop these people, but we need someplace to start, and right now we're in the dark. You helping us could help you guys in the long run. I can't promise we can keep you all safe, but you stand a much better chance if we put the bad guys away first."

"I'm sorry, Agent Webber, we have done all we can do, and I would not try to get a subpoena to raid our office and seize the tape. By the time you get back here, we will have relocated this entire office to a new place."

He stopped at one of the desks and made a notation in a ledger. He then led Paul and Melanie to the entry door, which he unlocked. He shook Melanie's hand and then reached out to Paul.

"Again, I'm sorry we could not help you more."

He shook Paul's hand, let them out the door and locked the door behind them.

Melanie started to say something, but Paul held a finger to his lips and pointed towards the car. They climbed into the car, and Paul pulled out of the parking space and pulled around the building and back onto Washington Street. He drove north and pulled into the Burger King drive-thru. They placed their order, paid and collected their food. He pulled onto the street and pulled into a King Soopers parking lot and pulled into a space.

Melanie wondered what was going on until he held out his closed fist and opened it. In his hand was a small piece of paper, which he opened.

"Son of a bitch," he said.

He handed the slip of paper to Melanie. She read it and smiled. "Shit, Paul."

Chapter Twenty-Six

The forensics team finished up their work later that evening. They wrapped both vehicles in the same kind of plastic wrap you see boats in marinas wrapped in for the winter. They called the State Crime Lab and arranged to have the cars picked up by a secure hauling company and locked up the shop. Earlier in the afternoon they had dropped off the evidence boxes at a pack and ship store in Kremmling and sent everything overnight to the lab.

Bax wished them a good night, climbed into her car and headed south on Highway 9 towards Silverthorne. She was hungry and tired, and she wanted to put her feet up.

She was approaching the north entrance to Green Mountain Reservoir when the sky behind her lit up like someone had turned on a bunch of stadium lights. She pulled her car over, opened her door and stared back down the road. The sound of the explosion reached her car about two seconds later.

She jumped back into her car, made a quick U-turn and hit her flashers. She stomped on the gas pedal. She was reaching for her radio when the call went out on the Summit/Grand County mutual aid frequency. There was an explosion and fire at the

CDOT garage on Highway 9 in Kremmling. Grand County Sheriff's Office and the Grand County Fire Brigade were responding.

Bax pulled to the side of the road just north of the Colorado River and ran towards the CDOT garage. What she saw when she arrived stunned her. Where she had been standing not ten minutes before was gone. In its place was a smoldering pile of rubble and the twisted wreckage of the two cars and two snowplows that were in the other two bays being serviced.

A Grand County deputy started to tell her she had to move, but she flashed her badge in his face. Her concern was for the three forensic techs she had left the building with. She had no idea if they were okay or not.

The fire department made short work of what was left of the building, and while they put out hot spots, she pulled out her phone and called Buck, who answered right away.

"I'm on my way. I'll be there in twenty minutes. Are our people okay?"

"I can't say for sure. Jerry's not answering his phone, but I don't see their van."

Her phone chirped with an incoming call.

"Let me call you back," she said, and switched to the other line. "Jerry, thank god. Are you guys okay?"

"Yeah, Bax. We were having dinner in Kremmling when the explosion happened. We stayed back out of the way to let the fire guys through. Once they let us through, we'll be there."

"Okay. I will talk to the deputy on the scene and have you cleared through."

She hung up, dialed Buck and told him that the team was okay, hung up and went in search of the on-scene deputy. She found him talking to the Grand County Fire Brigade Chief. She stepped up, flashed her badge and introduced herself.

"I have a forensics team just north of the scene, can you call the deputy at that end and have him clear my guys?"

"That's convenient that you have forensics guys already here. Were they working on the missing woman case?" asked the chief.

"Yeah. Those two lumps of burned shit lying on their sides are my evidence. We wrapped up and had headed out when the explosion happened."

"Fucking lucky," said the deputy, whose name tag said sanchez. He keyed the mic that was attached to his shoulder and asked the deputy in town to clear the forensics van.

"Thanks. Chief, any thoughts on the source of the explosion?"

"Most of the damage seems to have occurred at the back of the building. The GCSO investigators and my arson guys are on the way. Should be here in about a half hour. With the help of your guys, maybe we can figure this out. Did all your evidence go up in smoke?"

"No," she replied. "We shipped most of our stuff to the state lab earlier today."

She was about to go into more detail when Buck badged his way past the deputy guarding the gate to the facility and walked up. Buck reached out his hand.

"Chief, nice to see you again." With an experienced eye, he took in the leveled building. "Everyone accounted for? Anyone hurt?"

"Some minor injuries. Some of the neighbors had their windows blown out by the force of the explosion. Nothing serious, thank god."

"Bax, are our forensics guys on the way back?"

"Yeah, they were still in town having dinner, they should be here in a few minutes."

Buck nodded and stepped away, pulling out his phone. He speed-dialed and waited.

Paul answered on the second ring. "Hey, Buck. We're almost to the ranch. What's up?"

Buck told him about the explosion. "Get to the ranch as soon as possible, grab all the electronics and all the information we have collected so far and take it to the sheriff's office in Breckenridge. The sheriff is sending a few more deputies along with Carl to the ranch to help. Keep your eyes open for anything suspicious."

"You think we're in danger?"

"I'm not taking any chances," said Buck. He hung up and faced Bax with concern in his eyes.

"I'm not sure if we were attacked or not, but the timing makes me suspicious. Grab a roll of crime scene tape and have the deputies give you a hand. Once the firefighters are finished, let's get everyone off the property except for the arson guys and the sheriff's investigators. Use our forensics guys however you need them. Let's see if we can get a preliminary cause as soon as possible. When you're done, meet me back at the ranch. I need to talk to Paul and see how his visit to the production guys went."

"You got it, Buck." She headed to her car for the tape.

Buck thanked the chief for his help and told him he was leaving Bax to work with his guys to find the cause. He turned and headed for his car. He pulled his phone out and dialed the director.

"Fuck, Buck. I just heard. Was anyone hurt?"

"Couple cuts and scrapes from broken glass."

"Do you think this was because our evidence was in the garage?"

"Yes, sir. I do. I'm pulling our people out of the McBride's ranch and moving them to Breckenridge. The sheriff will set up more security on the family until we can figure out their involvement in all this."

The director interrupted. "You still think the family is involved?"

"Yes, sir. I should have more information once I talk to Paul. He had a meeting with Barb McBride's post-production guys and is on his way back to the ranch. He didn't want to talk over the phone."

"Okay, Buck. Keep me posted. I need to talk to the governor."

Buck hung up, slid into his car and headed south on Highway 9, heading back to the ranch. One more mystery, he was thinking. "Why blow up the garage after the evidence was already collected? A warning?"

Buck was pissed. The explosion may have happened after his team left the garage, but it seemed like it was directed at them. That was unacceptable on way too many levels, and some son of a bitch was going to pay.

Chapter Twenty-Seven

Buck turned off Highway 9 and onto the ranch road. He stopped at the deputy at the barricade and checked in.

"Is the family back?"

"No, sir. Mr. McBride and his brother returned about an hour ago; I understand the rest of the family is staying in Frisco. Seems they had a big fight at the funeral parlor. Something about burial versus cremation."

Buck thanked him, waited while the barricade was moved, pulled forward and parked next to Paul's Jeep. Carl was loading a box in the back when Buck walked up.

"We've gotten almost everything out of the house. Do you think we were targeted?"

"I wish I knew, but I'll feel better with my guys working out of your office. It's a bit farther to drive, but this investigation is moving from a kidnapping to a murder, and I'm still not convinced the family is not somehow involved. Where's Paul?"

Carl told him Paul was in the office helping dismantle the phone traps, and Buck headed that way. He passed George in the hallway heading for the front door carrying several laptops.

"Any luck with the McBrides' laptops and phones?"

"I think I'm close. I have a few more things to work through, but I figure another hour or two and we should have something to talk about. Melanie was working on their phones. She should be right behind me."

Buck found Paul and Melanie wrapping up the surveillance equipment. They loaded the last monitor into a box, and then Paul signaled Buck to follow them, and they went out through the sliding door and onto a back deck. They stepped off the deck and walked towards the river. When he felt they were far enough away from the house and out of sight of the media trucks, they stopped along the bank.

"You are not going to believe what she was working on," he said.

Buck listened as Paul and Melanie took turns describing the information that was on the video. Between the two of them, they had tried to remember as much about the program as they could, and as much about the evidence that was presented. Melanie handed Buck a list of names she remembered from the program, which Buck opened and read.

"Are you guys sure about this information? This is hard to believe if it's true."

Buck continued reading down the list. A couple times he let out a low whistle. "No wonder someone tried to destroy the evidence from the car. Some of the names are downright shocking.

"Okay, we have the names of some of the people involved, but who is running this thing? It takes a special kind of sicko to possess child porn, but it takes an even bigger sicko to sell and distribute the stuff."

"The impression I got," said Melanie, "is this is some kind of exclusive club, almost like a membership kind of thing. How sick is that?"

"Yeah. The problem is we have no evidence to support any of the claims she made in the video."

"Can we subpoena the video?"

"No. I mean, we could try," said Paul. "This Cranston guy has the video, but none of her evidence. He told us the evidence was with a third party and will be sent to the authorities after the video airs."

"Do we have any idea who the third party is?" asked Buck.

Paul reached into his pocket and handed Buck the folded piece of paper Tom Cranston had passed to him during their goodbye handshake.

"What's this?"

"Cranston gave me that when he shook my hand as we were leaving. It's a site online, and I think that's where all her evidence is hidden."

"All right, head back to Breckenridge and track this down. If it is what you think it is, let's gather it all up and put it under lock and key until we figure out how to deal with it. We are stepping into some uncharted waters here, and if any of this is actionable, we need to make sure we have done everything we can to protect the integrity of the information."

Paul and Melanie headed back to the deck and

entered the office, closing the sliding door behind them. Buck walked over to a huge rock that sat along the river and sat down. He stared at the river for a few minutes, trying to calm his mind.

Three days ago, they were asked to investigate a missing celebrity, yesterday it became a murder investigation and suddenly it was a huge worldwide conspiracy involving powerful people along with possible threats to his people. Plus, they still needed to deal with a dead six-year-old. How the hell had it come to this?

Buck sat on the rock for about an hour. The more he thought about the names on the list and the information in the video, the more he wondered how deep this investigation could go. Many of the names on the list were friends of the governor, and a lot of them lived in Colorado. Coordinating a multipronged arrest strategy was going to mean getting the Feds involved, which was something Buck didn't want to do.

He wondered how the McBride brothers fit into all this. Neither one of them were rich or famous, at least not like the people on the list. He decided sitting on a rock was getting him nowhere and what he needed was a decent meal, since he hadn't eaten all day. He was walking back to the house when he spotted Bob McBride walking out of the barn. He turned and walked towards Bob McBride, who stopped next to his truck when he saw Buck walking over.

"Evening, Agent Taylor. I heard on the news that there was some excitement in Kremmling this evening. Did it have something to do with Barb's car?"

"Can't say for sure, Mr. McBride. We're looking into it. I would like to ask you a question though."

"Anything I can do to help solve this. Barb was an incredible woman, and she deserved better."

"Have you ever heard of a company called Skylark Holdings, LLC?"

Bob McBride tried to look serious as he contemplated his answer, but Buck saw it in his eyes before he could hide it. Recognition mixed with a little fear. "No, the name doesn't ring any bells. Does this have something to do with Barb's death?"

"No, it was something that came up during the investigation. We're having trouble finding any information about them, so we wondered if maybe they were involved in the television industry."

"Sorry, I wish I could have helped. Now, if you'll excuse me, I'm meeting some people in Frisco for drinks."

Bob McBride climbed into his pickup truck, glanced over his shoulder at Buck and drove down the ranch road. He passed through the police barricade and was swarmed by reporters when he came to a stop before turning onto Highway 9.

Buck watched him go. He hoped he hadn't made a huge mistake, but he needed to try to shake something loose. Bob McBride had secrets, and Buck was going to find out what they were. He walked towards the back door to the house, checked in with the deputy on duty and walked into the kitchen.

He found Jim McBride sitting behind his desk in his normal condition. The drink sitting in his hand was tipped to the side and had dripped on his pants.

Buck walked in and sat down. It looked like Jim McBride had been crying, although his bloodshot eyes could have been the results of too much alcohol.

"I miss her so much, Agent Taylor. How am I supposed to go on without her? She was the one person who seemed to care about me, and I pissed it all away for this." He held up his glass almost like a tribute.

"I have nothing. She didn't trust me with money, which I can't blame her for. The kids want nothing to do with me. They won't even stay here in the house; they hate me so much. They blame me for her death like I had something to do with it."

Buck sat back and let him ramble on. "We were separated, but she never left me alone. I'm a worthless human being." Tears flowed from his eyes, and he wiped his face with his sleeve. He closed his eyes, leaned his head back in the chair and fell asleep.

Buck heard the front door open and close, and Bax walked into the office. She saw Jim McBride passed out in his chair. "Shit, Buck, this guy is a mess. How does anyone constantly drink like that?"

Buck shrugged his shoulders. Buck never took a drink, but he was very familiar with people who drank to excess. Bax set her backpack on the floor next to the desk. "The explosion started with a propane water heater. All outward appearances say the gas line ruptured and filled the garage up with propane and then the heater kicked on and boom, all she wrote."

"So, accident? Just happened to happen right after you left the building, and it filled the space up that fast?"

"That's the part that doesn't make sense. The rupture would have to be huge. None of us are buying it, but it got too dark to see under all the debris. The sheriff assigned two deputies to guard the building, and we are going to meet again in the morning to take another look. Some of the debris was still too hot to move."

Buck took the next half hour to fill her in on the video Paul and Melanie had watched earlier in the day. When he was done, she stood there with her mouth hanging open. She regained her composure and said, "What the hell are we going to do? If the information in the video is correct, we have opened a shitload of trouble. Have you filled in the director?"

"Not yet, I got sidetracked with the brothers."

He told her about his conversation with Bob McBride and his suspicions about Bob's relationship with Skylark Holdings.

"I need to process this all," she said. "I'm gonna head for the hotel and put my head down for a couple hours." She had just reached down to pick up her backpack when the picture window overlooking the river exploded.

Chapter Twenty-Eight

The bullet blew through the double-pane glass, shattered the whiskey glass Jim McBride had resting against his chest and slammed him into the wall behind the desk. Buck dove off the couch and kicked the lamp off the end table, causing the bulb to blow out. He hit the floor and pulled out his Kimber.

Bax dove under the desk and pulled the plug on the desk lamp, sending the room into darkness. She had her Sig in her hand and dragged her backpack under the desk. She opened her backpack and pulled out her night vision goggles.

The two deputies from the front and back doors came running down the hallway with guns drawn.

"Kill the lights!" Buck yelled, and the hallway lights went out.

"Bax, Bluetooth, see what you can see from upstairs and be careful."

Bax clipped her Bluetooth to her ear, and Buck pulled his phone and dialed her number. She answered almost before it rang, crawled out from under the desk and raced up the stairs, turning off lights as she went.

The two deputies crab-walked into the office.

"Guys, watch the front and kitchen doors. Until I give you the all clear, you shoot anyone that walks through either of those doors. Call for backup and medical."

They both scooted back into the hallway and positioned themselves at opposite ends of the hall. Buck heard one of them yell into his microphone, "Shots fired, officers need assistance, also need an ambulance." He gave the dispatcher the McBride's address.

"Bax. You see anything?"

"Wait one." She paused. "Buck, I've got movement on the other side of the river. Maybe a hundred and fifty yards. Hunkered down in a rock outcropping."

Buck knew he couldn't reach his car, which was right out in the open between the house and the barn, and he'd never hit anything at that distance with his pistol. He needed some firepower. Taking a chance, he raised his head above the couch and spotted the gun cabinet on the wall next to the window that had blown. He could get there without being seen.

"Buck, the shooter is up and moving down the slope, heading this way."

"Okay, keep an eye on him. Do not let him cross the river."

Buck slid across the floor to clear the window and approached the gun cabinet from the dark side of the room. He reached it, found it locked and, using the barrel of his pistol, hit the glass, which shattered on impact. He checked the assorted rifles that were on display.

He was looking for something that could shoot

fast, cover the distance. He didn't want to work a complicated sight. He found what he was looking for. A custom-built Salsbury Armory lever action rifle chambered for .500 S&W Magnums. He picked it up, opened the lower drawer, found a box of cartridges and loaded the rifle. It might not be the most accurate gun in the cabinet, having metal sights, but he figured the noise alone might stop somebody in their tracks.

"Bax, give me a landmark."

"Between the two big cottonwoods, about ten degrees up the slope. He's working his way down the slope sighting through the scope."

"Okay, when I tell you, hit a light up there and kick open the French doors and stay down."

Buck worked his way out into the hallway and opened the front door. The two deputies from the barricade were stepping up onto the front porch when he opened the door; both men froze as they saw Buck coming out the door with the rifle.

"Stay here and keep your eyes open. We have one shooter, but there could be more."

Both deputies nodded, and Buck stepped off the porch and headed around the building until he got to the corner that would give him the best view of the shooter's position. He took a quick glance around the corner and spotted the shadow on the other side of the river. He pulled back and took a deep breath.

"Bax, now."

He saw the upstairs deck light come on and heard the French doors slam open and hit the wall.

He stepped around the corner, raised the rifle and fired; he worked the lever and fired five more times before he ducked back behind the corner and reloaded. The noise was deafening, and he had no idea if he'd hit anything or not.

"Bax, anything?"

He saw the deck light go out and for more than a minute nothing happened.

"Buck, I don't see the shooter."

He could hear the sirens coming from both directions on Highway 9, and he could see some of the media vans firing up their high-pressure sodium lights, which were pointed at the house. Under normal circumstances, he might have been pissed with all the lights, but right now they gave him a little comfort as they lit up the house, the barn and part of the area on the other side of the river.

He called for the two deputies that were still on the porch, and they came around the building and stood next to his position.

"We need to find the shooter. Follow me but stay low. Bax, keep watching. Anything moves, yell."

"Be careful," came her reply.

Staying low, Buck made a run for the back wall of the barn, followed by the two deputies. So far, so good. No one shot at them. He worked his way across the yard from tree to tree until he was crouched alongside the river. He made a walking motion with his fingers and pointed to the deputy's guns and then to their eyes. They nodded. He wanted them to cover him as he crossed the river.

The two deputies spread out and got as low as

they could. Buck, with the rifle leading the way, stepped into the frigid river. He didn't know if the shiver was from the cold or the fear. The river was about forty feet across at this point, and he was able to keep his balance by leaning on a tree that was lying across the river. The current made walking difficult, and several times he almost fell due to slippery rocks and debris.

Staying low, he crouched against the opposite bank. Behind him, several more deputies gathered behind the barn, and he saw them and waved. The first two deputies entered the river, and they were soon crouched next to him as several other deputies with rifles gathered along the riverbank.

Slowly, Buck moved up onto the field next to the river. He didn't want to draw his flashlight, and at the moment the media lights were giving him enough light to see by.

"Bax, can you guide me to the last location of the shooter?"

"Straight ahead from your position about fifty yards. I don't see anything moving."

Buck, leading with the rifle, stepped into the field and made his way to the position Bax indicated, swinging the rifle from side to side as he went. The two deputies moved off his back about ten feet to either side.

"Buck, you should be right where the shooter was," said Bax.

Buck knelt and pulled out his flashlight. He reached down and touched a dark spot on the ground. His finger was red and sticky. Blood, and a lot of it. The blood trail led off towards a couple large boulders on the slope, and Buck indicated for the two deputies to spread out and follow. He raised the rifle and followed the blood trail.

Several more deputies crossed the river and were spreading out behind Buck and the first two deputies. Buck approached the boulders and signaled the deputies to stop. There was a lot of blood on the ground, and Buck steeled himself to swing around the boulder.

The shooter was propped up against a small boulder with his hands gripping his stomach, blood dripping from both hands. His rifle lay on the ground next to him.

"Don't move," said Buck. The shooter's reaction surprised him.

"You a sniper?" he said weakly.

"No, just a cop," said Buck.

"Fuck, done in by a local yokel. How fucking embarrassing." He laughed, and blood dripped down the side of his mouth.

Buck set down the rifle. "Try not to move. Help is on the way."

The shooter's hands were covered in blood, and he knew he was dying. "Don't bother, Officer. I'll be dead in a minute or two. I had a good run, but all things must come to an end. You'll find my truck about two miles down the road on a little side road." He coughed, and more blood came from his lips. "In the glove compartment, you'll find a picture of a little girl. There's an address on the back." His body shuddered.

"Just tell her that daddy loves her and I'm sorry."

The shooter closed his eyes and took his final breath.

Chapter Twenty-Nine

He sat in his truck watching the forensics guys come and go from their van. They had the doors to the shop closed, so he couldn't see what was going on inside, but they didn't move like there was a sense of urgency. If he'd had the location of the shop earlier, he would have destroyed the car before they had a chance to work on it. He doubted they would find much in the way of evidence. From what he was told, the car had been submerged in the lake for several days before it was discovered.

He did wonder about the second car they had in the shop. He was only told to deal with the Range Rover. He didn't care where the other car came from, since that wasn't part of his job, even though it was going to be destroyed anyway. He checked his watch. The CDOT mechanics that were working in the other bays of the garage left the shop at six p.m. and locked the door behind them. He didn't have any qualms about killing civilians, but he hated to do it. Those guys were just doing their job and didn't deserve to die.

His cell phone rang, and he noted the unknown number that popped up. He answered the call but didn't speak.

"Are you on-site?"

"Yeah."

"Will you have any problem?"

"No."

"Will you have time to handle phase two today?"

"Yeah. I've got this covered."

"Then phase two is a go."

He clicked off his phone, settled in and watched the building. He hated small towns like this one. People were nosy, and he hated when someone would come up to see if he needed help. Luckily, there was a small parking area so folks could stop and fish the Colorado River. He parked next to two other cars and waited.

It was several hours past full dark when he noted movement at the side door. His timetable was going to hell, and he was going to have to get moving to keep to his schedule. The three forensics people, still dressed in the Tyvek suits and booties, stepped out the door followed by the blond woman. The forensics guys loaded a couple of toolboxes in the back of the van, stripped off their suits, climbed into the van and pulled out of the parking area. The blond woman checked the door, made sure it was locked and climbed into her Jeep and pulled onto the highway.

Out of habit, he slid down in his seat, even though he knew there was no way she would be able to see him as she drove by. As her taillights crested the hill and disappeared, he grabbed his backpack, slid out of the truck and opened the rear toolbox. He pulled out a pair of adjustable pliers and an adjustable wrench, climbed over the low fence surrounding the parking area and ran across the field to the rear of the building.

Using his lockpicks, he made quick work opening the rear service door, stepped into the building and pulled the door closed. The two cars were parked side by side in the first bay, with two big snowplows sitting in the other two bays.

He moved to the rear of the building and found the small restroom. Taking his wrench and pliers, he disconnected the pipe and listened as the propane started to flow into the shop. He pulled a small timer with an electrode out of his backpack and placed it under the water heater. Once the time hit zero, the electrode would heat up until it was hot enough to set off the gas. It worked like a pilotless igniter on a stove or a fireplace. Anyone investigating would find pieces of burned metal that appeared to belong to the heater.

He grabbed his backpack and tools and headed for the door. He'd given himself five minutes, so he locked the back door, closed it and headed for his truck. Once clear of the building and safe in his truck, he pulled out of the lot and headed for the small dirt road he found about two miles from the ranch house.

The explosion lit up the sky behind him, and he continued driving. A few miles ahead, he saw the blond woman's Jeep stopped in the middle of the highway; she made a U-turn and, with her flashers on, drove past him headed back to the shop.

He continued south as more emergency vehicles passed him heading north. A half mile south of

Heeney Road, he found the dirt road he'd scoped out earlier, turned off his lights and turned down the dirt road. He traveled back about half a mile and stopped on the road.

He pulled the rifle case from behind the seat, removed the rifle and installed the suppressor on the end of the barrel. He pocketed three, ten round clips, locked his truck and started walking along a barely discernable trail until he came to the river. Although it was pitch-black, he walked the trail as if he'd done it a thousand times before. He spotted the house as he cleared the trees and made his way to the rock outcropping he'd chosen for his nest.

The house was a buzz of activity with a lot of people moving about inside carrying boxes. His position did not give him a view of the front yard, but as he sighted through his scope, he had a great view of the desk in the office. He checked the wind and the distance one more time and dialed in the scope.

A while later, he spotted movement in the office, picked up his rifle and sighted through the scope. He recognized his target from the photo he'd been given, but he confirmed it by opening his phone. He kept watching his target until he appeared to fall asleep. The glass that was resting on his chest would make an excellent target, so he made his final adjustments, aimed for the glass, let out a half breath and pulled the trigger.

He kept looking through the scope as the window shattered, as did the glass sitting on his victim's chest, and then the victim slammed into the wall behind him. He watched as lights began getting turned off all over the house.

Confident no one was targeting his position, he made his way down the slope from his nest. His orders were to set the house and barn on fire once his victim was dead. With all the news vans he'd seen parked along the highway earlier, he was certain he would see the fire on the late news.

He was about fifty yards from the river where he intended to cross when a light came on. He zeroed in on the light on the upper deck, when the French doors flew open. He froze, adjusted his rifle and aimed for the doors.

The first bullet flew past his left shoulder and he felt it go by. His first thought was, "Ambush," as he turned to see where the shot came from. The second bullet slammed into his stomach and knocked him backwards. Four more shots followed those as he lay on the ground. Ignoring the pain, he tried to stand and run. He managed to half run, half crawl and made it as far as a small rock outcropping and fell amongst the boulders.

The pain was intense as he lay there holding the wound. His hands were covered in blood. "They must have had a sniper watching the victim," he said to no one. "Of all the stupid luck."

He lay still for a while as he listened to people approaching his position. He tried to shift his body so he could use his pistol, but he couldn't pull the gun from his belt holster with all the blood on his hands. Twenty-five years of serving his country as a warrior all around the world, and he was going to die on a hill in Colorado. He thought about his daughter and how he was never going to see her grow up.

He picked his head up as a face holding a huge bore rifle stepped around the boulder. The end of the barrel looked as big as a train tunnel.

"Don't move," said the voice behind the rifle.

"You a sniper?" he said weakly.

"No, just a cop," said Buck.

"Fuck, done in by a local yokel. How fucking embarrassing." He laughed, and blood dripped down the side of his mouth.

Buck set down the rifle. "Try not to move. Help is on the way."

The shooter, looking down at his hands covered in blood, said, "Don't bother, Officer. I'll be dead in a minute or two. I had a good run, but all things must come to an end. You'll find my truck about two miles down the road on a little side road." He coughed, and more blood came from his lips. "In the glove compartment, you'll find a picture of a little girl. There's an address on the back." His body shuddered.

"Just tell her that daddy loves her and I'm sorry."

The shooter closed his eyes and took his final breath.

Chapter Thirty

Bax was standing next to Summit County Sheriff Ryker Morgan when Buck stepped into the office. He handed the rifle he'd used to the shooting team detective and stepped into the office. He shook Ryker's hand. Ryker was tall and stocky with light brown hair. He had first been elected sheriff five years earlier after serving almost twenty years as a deputy.

"Fuck, Buck, explosions, shootings. You sure have a way of keeping things exciting." He smiled.

Buck nodded as he stood there dripping on the hardwood floors. The team from the coroner's office was taking pictures of the body of Jim McBride. They would wait for Dr. Worth before removing the body, a call the sheriff had already made. Two more bodies. Dr. Worth was going to be a busy man.

Ryker signaled for Buck to follow him as he walked down the hall and into the kitchen.

"We'll need a shooting statement, of course, but that can wait till later. Lucky shot?"

"Must have been. I've never been that good with a rifle, especially without a scope and in the dark. This guy was a pro. All I wanted was to keep him from coming to the house. Thought the noise from the big gun might scare him off. Surprised the hell out of me that I hit him."

"Buck, level with me. What's going on? There are a bunch of rumors circulating through the county, and I'm going to have to make a statement after this."

Buck thought for a minute then walked over and closed the kitchen door. "We're still speculating at this point, but here is what we do know so far."

A half hour later, Buck stopped talking, and the sheriff stood there shaking his head. "Jesus, Buck. If only half of this is true, this is going to cause one monumental shit storm. These are the friends in high places most people talk about. Shit."

"Look. Keep a lid on this when you make your statement. Right now, it's an isolated crime, no connection to the explosion at the CDOT shop, more to follow. Assure the citizens that they are not in any danger. I need a little more time to sort this all out."

"Okay, but we need to wrap this up as soon as possible. Keep me in the loop."

The sheriff was about to step out of the kitchen when the door opened, and Hank Clancy walked in. The FBI special agent wore jeans, boots and a flannel shirt instead of his typical business suit. He carried a tan Stetson in his hand. The sheriff glanced at Hank and then at Buck.

"Shit, this can't be good."

Hank shook Buck's hand and then the sheriff's. He spoke to Buck.

"I was never here, if anyone ever asks."

"What's going on, Hank?"

Hank checked behind him to make sure no one was standing outside the door listening.

"Whatever you're into concerning Skylark Holdings sure got a bunch of people up the food chain excited. I've been ordered to discontinue any interest in that company. This didn't come from the director; this came from somewhere way above him."

"Any explanation?" asked Buck.

"No, and I'm not going to ask for one. All I can figure is you stepped in the middle of a huge investigation, and you need to back away for your own good."

"Hank, look around you. I've got three dead bodies, someone trying to destroy evidence and a shitload of unanswered questions. The guy we killed tonight was a professional. Someone hired this guy."

"Buck, you're not listening. Stay away from Skylark Holdings. I didn't mention your name when I sent out the inquiry, so right now it's my ass on the line, but that's gonna change, and soon."

Buck decided to take a chance, so he told Hank the same story he'd told the sheriff. Hank listened without saying a word. When Buck finished, Hank pulled out a kitchen chair and sat down at the table.

"Can you prove any of this?"

"Not yet, but my tech guy is trying to get into Barb McBride's cloud server. If we can get in, we may have everything we need. It should be enough for a couple warrants."

"Can you tell me if Skylark Holdings is involved in this child porn ring?"

Buck thought for a minute. "Not at this time. The name came up as part of our investigation, but we have nothing indicating they are involved in any of this."

"Once you request those warrants, people are going to find out, which means you might have twenty-four hours to move on them before the federal government swoops down on this like nothing you have ever seen before. I can cover your ass for a while, but once my boss asks me about my interest in any of this, I'm going to have to answer him straight."

"Okay. Do you have any idea what Skylark Holdings is or what they do?" asked the sheriff.

Hank hesitated. "One thing I did find out before the lid clamped shut is that they are supposed to be a multinational think tank. I think what that means in Washington speak is they come up with ways to solve problems for the more elite among us. It could also be a cover for something a lot more sinister. If they are tied to your investigation in any way, you better watch your ass. This could get even more ugly. I did find out before the hammer dropped that the Hong Kong address is a front. Word is they operate out of Beaver Creek, Colorado."

Hank stood up. He put on his Stetson and walked to the door. "I will try to cover you but wrap this up quick and maybe someday you can tell me what this was all about over a beer."

Hank walked through the door and left Buck and the sheriff sitting there, wondering what had just happened. Bax walked in and saw the perplexed look on their faces.

"Was that Hank Clancy that just walked out of here?"

Buck nodded. "Yeah, he was never here. He was warned off pursuing any information on Skylark Holdings."

"Shit, that doesn't sound good. Does he have a clue why?"

"No," said Buck. "It came from Washington."

Bax shrugged her shoulders.

"Okay, then. Oh, we have an ID on the shooter. A deputy found the truck parked along a dirt road not far from here. They're running the VIN, his fingerprints and his name." She handed Buck a picture. "Deputy said you asked him to bring this to you. Is that the guy's kid?"

"Yeah. He asked me for a favor before he died."

He put the picture in his shirt pocket.

"I need to change out of these wet clothes. Let's meet at the sheriff's office in two hours so we can talk about our next moves. Bax, have George and Melanie meet us there and call Paul."

Buck got up from the table and headed towards the front door. Bax said to the sheriff, "The FBI trying to stop this investigation is going to have the opposite effect. Buck's gonna be more determined than ever to solve this."

"Yeah. That's what I'm worried about."

Chapter Thirty-One

Buck took a long, hot shower to get the chill from the river out of his bones and found some reasonably clean clothes to put on. He sat down at the desk in the room and opened his laptop, but then sat there and stared at the blank screen.

He was worried about Hank. He had never seen him look nervous about anything in all the years they had known each other. The inquiry into Skylark Holdings and the shutdown from up the food chain had him concerned. The more Buck thought about it, the more pissed he got. He had an obligation to his victims to find the truth, and he didn't care who got crushed by that, so he decided he was not going to back down. He felt they were too close to stop now.

He started his laptop and opened the investigation file he'd created for the little boy. He opened the lab reports folder and spotted a report that had been uploaded a few hours before. He read through the report. The test results showed advanced muscular dystrophy, just as Dr. Worth suspected. The skin from the thigh showed signs of insulin at the injection site. It was severely degraded, but there was enough residue left to identify it.

Buck sat back in his chair. He felt like this little

kid had been thrown away. He wondered why. Someone gave this kid insulin and then buried him with a bouquet of flowers. That had to mean something. He just couldn't figure out what. He checked the DMV report on the VIN search. There was nothing in the Colorado DMV database. He pulled up the request and resent it, but this time he set a nationwide search criteria. He closed the investigation file and was about to open the McBride file when his phone rang. He didn't recognize the number, but he answered it anyway.

"Buck Taylor."

"Agent Taylor, it's Richard Kennedy."

"Good morning, Governor," said a surprised Buck. "What can I do for you, sir?"

"Agent Taylor, I received a call from the U.S. Attorney General. He told me in no uncertain terms that we were running an investigation that was about to interfere with something they had going on, and we were meddling with national security. He demanded we cease and desist. Are you meddling with national security, Agent Taylor?"

"Not that I'm aware of, sir."

"Good. I would hate to think of you as a meddler. Now, two things piss me off. One is phone calls from those idiots in Washington telling me what I can and can't do in my own state. The second is when someone throws around words like national security. Does what you are looking into have anything to do with the Barb McBride murder and now the murder of her husband?"

"We can't say for sure, sir. A company name

came up during the investigation, and at this point, we have no idea if or how it is connected."

"Do whatever you need to do to wrap this up. I don't know what line of questioning you are following, and I don't want to know, but I do not want anything going on in this state that concerns national security. You need anything, you call me. Oh, and by the way. You may want to be quick about it because I think we can expect a visit from the Feds here pretty soon."

The governor clicked off, and Buck sat staring at the phone. The governor never called him directly, choosing instead to go through the director of CBI. The call from the attorney general must have really pissed him off.

Buck clipped his phone back on his belt, clipped his badge and gun on, grabbed his laptop and backpack and headed out the door. It was time to make something happen.

The rest of the team were standing in the sheriff's conference room talking when Buck walked in. He set down his backpack and fired up his laptop, as everyone took a seat.

He walked over to the whiteboard, picked up a marker and wrote a name on the board. Skylark Holdings, LLC. He turned and faced everyone. George was the first one to talk. "Who are they?"

"We can't answer that. Bax found the information when she did a deep background check on Bob McBride. He receives a small payment, each month, from this company, yet when I approached him about it, he said he had never heard of them. The Feds do not want us looking into these guys, but we need to either eliminate them from the investigation or bring them in deeper. George, do you have a discreet way to look into this company without raising any red flags?"

George thought for a minute. "I think I might. Give me a little time. I'm waiting on a call back from Range Rover."

"Okay. Melanie, can you handle the website you and Paul got from the production guy, or do you want to push it to the office?"

"I can handle it with Paul's help."

"Okay, we have a lot of information floating around out there, and we need to break some of it open. Let's wake some people up if we need to, but let's push for some clarity. Carl and I need to go talk to Bob McBride's family and do another death notification. Be careful. I don't want to do any more."

Bax hung up her phone. "We got the print results from the Range Rover." Everyone stopped what they were doing. "The prints inside the car belong to Jim McBride, which would not be unusual if he drove her car occasionally. However, the prints we got off the driver's side window frame and the trunk lid belong to Bob McBride."

"Shit, he killed his own sister-in-law," said Buck. "Bax, write up a warrant and get it to a judge. Sheriff, can you have your guys at the ranch bring Bob McBride in for questioning?"

Sheriff Morgan nodded and walked out the door of the conference room. Bax opened her laptop, pulled up an arrest warrant application and started typing.

Buck and Carl left everyone busily working, and they walked out to the parking lot. Once in Buck's Jeep, they turned north on Highway 9 and turned down Main Street in Frisco.

The hotel where Barb McBride's family were staying was a block down on the right, and Buck pulled into the lot. They walked into the hotel lobby, flashed their badges and asked for the rooms the family was using.

Buck knocked on Kenny McBride's door, and after a minute Kenny's sleepy voice said, "Who's there?"

"Mr. McBride, it's Buck Taylor and Carl Chandler. We need to have a word. It's important." Buck heard the chain come off the door and the door opened. Kenny, in a white hotel robe, raised his finger to his lips. "Kids are still sleeping." He stepped into the hallway and partially closed the door. "Has something happened?"

"We should speak to your sister as well, sir," said Buck.

"It's early, Agent Taylor, please say what you need to say, and I will fill her in."

"Your father was killed last night; I'm very sorry for your loss." Buck never got used to this part of the job, but his voice never wavered.

Kenny was stunned. "We were with him last night. Did he have an accident? He was wasted when he left us, but he was with Uncle Bob. Is he okay?"

"Yes, Bob is fine. Your dad was shot by a sniper early this morning. He died instantly."

"Oh, my god," said Kenny. "How? Why?" Tears formed in his eyes.

Buck gave him a rundown of what happened during the early morning hours. Kenny was shaken. He thanked Buck and told him he would talk to the rest of the family. Buck and Carl left the hotel. As he got to the Jeep, his phone rang. He listened for a minute.

"Thanks, Sheriff." Buck turned to Carl. "Bob McBride did not return to the ranch last night. The sheriff issued an all-points bulletin. We need to head up there and go through his apartment." They jumped into the car and Buck headed back to Highway 9 and turned north.

Chapter Thirty-Two

"What the fuck did you do? I had it all set up. You didn't have to kill him."

The voice on the other end of the call was cold as ice. "Do not ever raise your voice to me."

"I'm sorry, sir. I don't understand. I told you I would take care of it and there wouldn't be a problem."

"There is no problem, now. I told you when we last spoke that we would deal with it in our own way. Because you cannot follow orders, we needed to respond, before this became an issue."

"I had it all set up. Everything was in place to make it look like he was involved up to his eyeballs. As soon as the investigation broke open, everything would lead the investigator back to him."

The voice cut him off. "You may think you had it all under control, but we were informed this morning that our name came up as part of the investigation. Our friends have attempted to put an end to any inquiries that might lead in our direction, but the one thing you were supposed to prevent from happening, happened. Our members are not going to be pleased when they find out. We have a tremendous amount to lose if this goes sideways and we have invested a great deal of money in your plan."

"Look, this is just a minor setback. We could have handled the investigation into her death, but now two murders and you tried to destroy her car. That is not going to sit well with the investigators. We need to make smart moves from here on out."

"It seems to me you have overestimated your value to this program. You did a great job in setting up the program so it would run with almost minimal outside interference, and it works as promised."

He didn't like the way this conversation was heading, so he decided to throw out something that maybe the cold voice hadn't heard yet.

"Your sniper was killed this morning. So much for your smooth way of handling this."

"Your smugness is unbecoming. I was aware of his death. He knew the risks, and so did the members we spoke with. The decision to move forward was ours and ours alone."

There were muted voices in the background and he wondered who else was in the room. He had never met any of them. All he knew was they were powerful people who shared the same affliction he did. They liked young children. He also knew now that they were not afraid to use violence to keep their secret safe. He wondered what that meant for him?

He thought back to when they had first approached him about setting up the subscription service. They wanted it set up like a club. There would be a steep initiation fee and then an equally steep monthly fee. The great thing was that after they paid the fees, they never had to purchase anything again, ever. Everything—the videos, the magazines, the exclusive picture portfolios—would all be uploaded to a secure location where only the member would have access. The materials would never be saved to the individuals' computers, so even if they were investigated, which was unlikely, their digital world would be clean.

He had worked long and hard putting together the code and the protocols to protect the members, and now they had gone and done something stupid. He didn't like killing the reporter, but somehow, she was getting too close; but killing her husband was plain stupid. The big question on his mind now was, "Am I next?"

The cold voice came back on the line. "We have discussed this, and we are going to give you a chance to redeem yourself. We want you to implement the final phase of the program. We have deposited the rest of your payment in the account as indicated. Please complete the protocols and then destroy all your records."

He thought about the request for a minute and agreed. All the coding was complete, and the beta tests were hugely successful. Everything was ready. It would take a few hours to upload the final code and then the members would have full control of the system.

Before he could respond, the other end of the call went dead. He realized the conversation was over. He sat back and wiped the sweat off his brow.

He didn't trust them, and now he was worried that, with his role complete, there would be no reason to keep him alive. He was now a liability.

He thought back to the conversation surrounding the final phase. At the time the request seemed a little unusual, but he hadn't thought any more about it until the beta test started. The system was designed to be totally anonymous so that none of the members could ever be exposed, but in the final phase, the cold voice had requested that he and five other members be given access to a hidden file that kept track of the access and viewing patterns of specific members, members they chose.

At the time, he wondered why they would need to have this as part of a program that guaranteed anonymity, but they were willing to pay for it, and they offered him stupid money to make it happen. During the beta test, the access protocols for several members were denied and then eliminated from the server. However, their monthly payments continued. The odd thing was, the denials occurred around the same time there was a huge scandal in two small African nations that forced several of the country's leaders to resign. The news accounts were vague and stated only that it involved a sexual scandal. He sat back and rubbed his head.

He wondered if he needed to set up a protection protocol, in case something happened to him or another person close to him. He knew these people did not tolerate failure, but this most recent murder had shaken him. He pulled out his laptop, called up the final phase program and started typing.

Chapter Thirty-Three

Buck turned his Jeep off the highway and onto the ranch road. He had to use his horn to clear a path through all the reporters and the cameramen, all of whom were yelling questions at him as he drove forward. The deputies at the barricade moved it aside so he could drive through, and he parked in front of the house. He was getting his backpack out of the back when his phone rang.

"Hey, Bax."

"Buck, did you resend the VIN request for the Dodge Dart?"

"Yeah, we didn't seem to be getting anywhere in state, so I decided to send it to all the states. Why?"

"We got a hit. Just got the notification."

"Local or out of state?"

"Kansas. A little town called Luray. There's no street address, just a post office box number. I called the Russell County Sheriff's Office and asked them for an assist. They're going to see if they can find out who owns the PO box and try to track the car for us."

"Nice job, Bax. Keep me posted."

"Hey, Buck, before you go. Melanie wants to see you when you get back this way. George and I are tracking the calls from both Jim's and Bob's cell phones. We'll have a list waiting for you."

Buck thanked her, signed in with the deputy at the door and he and Carl walked into the entry foyer. It was hard to believe it was only four days since they first walked through this door and stood and watched the search and rescue teams, working on search patterns to try to find Barb McBride. A lot had happened in a short period of time. It made Buck feel old.

Dr. Worth had removed the bodies, and they were now on their way to Golden for the autopsies. It was more of a formality than anything else. All they needed were the bullets from the victims. There was no mystery in how either one died.

Buck stepped into the office. The picture window was now boarded up, and the room was much darker and more unpleasant than it had been just a day before. He stepped behind the desk and spotted the thickening puddle of blood that was pooled under the chair. "Jim McBride didn't stand a chance," he said.

Carl agreed. "Hell of a shot. Can't wait to see the shooter's biography."

A deputy appeared in the doorway, holding a key in her hand. "Carl, we found a key to the apartment on a hook in the kitchen closet."

Carl thanked her and asked her to lead the way. They passed through the kitchen and went out the back door. Buck stood for a minute and his eyes focused on the spot across the river where the sniper died. He scratched his head. He turned back towards the corner of the house where he had fired from and back to the spot past the river. "That could have turned out a lot different," he thought. He stepped off the deck and followed Carl and the deputy as they entered the barn.

The staircase leading to the apartment was inside the barn. Wearing nitrile gloves, the deputy unlocked the door and stepped inside, followed by Carl and Buck. The apartment was a small space but was neat and clean. If they didn't know better, they would have thought it hadn't been occupied for a while. Bob McBride was very meticulous. They fanned out and worked their way through the two rooms and the bathroom. The most notable thing was the absence of anything personal. There were no pictures, no mail, and no clothes in the closet.

Buck stood next to the small kitchen counter. Carl and the deputy walked up next to him.

"It doesn't look like anyone lives here," said the deputy.

"Yeah," said Buck. "I wonder what that's all about?"

They left the apartment as they found it and headed back to the house. Buck pulled out his phone and dialed the CBI office in Denver and requested the forensics team. He told the dispatcher he wanted the house, the barn and the apartment gone through with a fine-tooth comb.

"What are you hoping to find?" asked Carl, as Buck hung up his phone.

"Probably nothing, but there is a reason Bob McBride was using the apartment, and it was not for living in. Deputy, when the forensics team arrives, have them tear apart the office, Barb McBride's office, the barn and the apartment."

Buck and Carl headed for the front door, signed out with the deputy at the door, climbed into Buck's Jeep and headed back down the ranch road, through the mass of reporters, and turned south on Highway 9 and headed back to Breckenridge.

The conference room at the sheriff's office was a beehive of activity when Buck and Carl walked in. Bax was talking on her phone and was typing away on her laptop. George and Melanie were having a conversation while looking at George's laptop, and the printer seemed to be working overtime. Melanie spotted Buck and called him over, just as one of the sheriff's clerks walked through the door and handed Buck a sheet of paper. He read it and gave it to Carl.

"What's a red flag file?" asked Carl.

"It means we aren't getting any information on our shooter. His file has been flagged by some government agency, which means it is off-limits to everyone except the agency that closed it."

"So, we have a name and his prints, and that's it?"

"Yeah. That's it."

Buck rolled the paper into a ball and threw it into the trash. He had encountered this before on several cases, but most notably, when a deputy ran his friend PIS's prints during a case they were working in Aspen, many years ago. After all these years, Buck still had no idea who had flagged PIS's prints. It was one more enigma regarding a guy whose help had been invaluable over the years.

Buck smiled, thinking about the character he called his friend, then he walked over to George and Melanie.

George, looking up from the laptop he was working on, had a big smile on his face.

"You got something, George?"

"Do I ever. Son of a bitch thought he was smart, but he's not as smart as he thinks he is."

Buck sat down next to George. "Okay, let's have it."

"First things first. I figured out why the car stopped. Buried deep in the deleted files of Bob McBride's phone was a program designed for one purpose. To stop the Range Rover. It works like OnStar. The Range Rover program does not have that capability, but he was able to hack in through the information system and link up with the electronic system that controls everything that happens in the car.

"Once the car reached the location where he wanted the car to stop, he pushed a button on a digital dashboard on his phone, and he shut down the car. No lights, no fuel, and the windows were locked out. That's why she unbuckled her seat belt and opened the door."

"Makes sense," said Buck. "How'd you find this if it was deleted on his phone?"

"Nothing is ever truly deleted unless you use an NSA-grade deletion program. He wasn't worried because he didn't think we would ever find it. The hard drive is built into the car, but because of the information system, everything that happens in the car is captured on a cloud server. This way, the company knows when it's time to recommend an oil change, or the technician in the shop can diagnose a problem from miles away and suggest what needs to happen."

"The tech guys at Range Rover were a huge help. They found the code he had written into the system, and we were able to backtrack it to the program on his phone. He did a hell of a job trying to hide it, but he wasn't quite good enough. The tech guys at Range Rover were amazed because he was able to bypass all their security protocols. They are tearing apart his code as we speak so they can create countermeasures."

"How was he able to move the car if everything was shut down?" asked Carl.

"That was the easy part. The program indicates the car was shut down at eight fifty-seven p.m. and the car was reactivated at nine ten p.m. He must have been right behind her when he shut it down. The other thing his program did was jam her phone. She was a sitting duck out there on the highway with no way to communicate with anyone. Probably scared the shit out of her until a Good Samaritan pulled up behind her, and when she saw who it was, she thought she was safe. Best guess is, he knocked her out, restarted the car, put it in gear and pushed it to the edge of the cliff. The car was running, according to the hard drive, when it hit the ice below. The airbags deployed when she hit the ice, and the car died for the last time at nine twenty-five p.m."

Buck sat back in the chair. "Fuck. She could have been alive for almost fifteen minutes as the car filled up with water. I hope she was unconscious till the end. No one should die like that. What else have you got?"

"Computer programmers, particularly hackers, leave little trails when they enter codes. Sometimes it's on purpose, like bread crumbs, so they can find their way back to where they were in the program, but a lot of the time the tells are subconscious, and they don't even realize they are doing it. Now that we figured out what to look for, I have been following his little tells. I can track where he's been, I'm just not quite sure why he's been there."

"All right," said Buck. "Can you put it up on the big screen and walk us through it?"

Chapter Thirty-Four

Bob McBride was parked across the street from the hotel in Frisco his relatives were staying at when he saw Buck pull into the parking lot. He watched as Buck and Carl walked into the hotel. He was afraid of being spotted. His old pickup truck was sitting along an old dirt trail leading to an abandoned mine up near Shrine Pass. By now it was a smoldering shell, and even if someone found it, it would take them a while to identify it as his.

The new silver Ford F-150 he was now sitting in had been stashed at the house he owned in Vail. A house only a select group of friends was even aware of. The deed would have to be traced back through five or six shell companies before anyone would get close to figuring out who the owner was.

He'd already planned to close up shop and move on when he received the news that his brother had been shot and killed sitting in his office. That information came from the same source that told him about the explosion at the CDOT shop that destroyed Barb's car, and that Buck Taylor killed the sniper who took out his brother.

He'd known when he made the phone call early this morning that his involvement in this project was rapidly coming to an end and decided then to implement his exit plan.

The first thing he did was check his account and make sure the money he was owed had been deposited into the account. He understood that just because they paid him was no reason to believe they wouldn't send someone to kill him. These people had long arms and long memories.

Once the deposit was confirmed, he spent the next several hours finishing up the programming for phase two of the project. He still had no idea what they intended to do with the information that would be available to them, and he didn't care. Once he uploaded the program, his work was finished.

Of course, he spent time revising the program with a way for him to access the information if needed, and a way to send the information to specific people who might have an interest in what these guys might be up to. Whatever they were involved in would be up to someone else to figure out.

He finished uploading the program and then left his house in his old pickup truck. He drove to the top of Vail Pass on I-70, turned at the exit for the rest area and continued along the road leading to Shrine Pass. Once he torched the truck, he walked back to the rest area, where he had arranged for a friend to pick him up.

A few minutes after Buck and Carl entered the hotel, they came back out to the Jeep they'd arrived in. He watched as Buck spoke on his phone and then jumped in the Jeep and took off out of the parking lot heading towards Silverthorne and

Highway 9. Since he assumed they were heading back to the ranch, he followed at a safe distance and parked well clear of the ranch road and the mass of reporters and cameramen standing at the entrance.

He pulled out a pair of binoculars and watched Buck and Carl enter the house and a few minutes later walk out through the kitchen door and enter the barn. They were all wearing blue gloves, and he started to panic. It was apparent they were looking for him, but why? He was certain he'd covered his tracks or had he missed something? There was nothing he was aware of that could connect him to Barb's death, so what happened?

He started to think back on everything he had done during the past couple of weeks and especially since Barb went missing, and then a strange thought hit him. What if his clients—the guys who'd directed him to kill Barb and went behind his back and killed his brother—what if they'd somehow turned on him? He didn't like the idea of being killed by these people, but he liked the idea of going to prison even less.

He decided now was the time to go, so he turned the truck around and headed south on Highway 9. He knew he could hide out at the house in Vail for a couple days, but he was afraid any time he wasted would give Buck Taylor and his people time to block his exit routes.

He drove straight back to the house in Vail and parked in the garage. Walking up the stairs from the garage, he entered the great room and stood for a minute. He loved this house. He hoped someday he would be able to come back to it, but for now, he needed to disappear.

He walked into his room and loaded up one small carry-on suitcase. He only needed clothes for a couple days. Once he got out of the country, to his other safe house in Costa Rica, he would have everything he needed. He sat down at his desk, started his laptop and opened the airline website. He discovered that flights direct to Costa Rica were limited, and the earliest flight he could get on was the next afternoon. He booked that flight and an earlier flight out of the Eagle County Regional Airport that would take him to Denver International Airport. He would have a three-hour layover in Denver before leaving for Costa Rica.

Walking over to the wall by the office fireplace, he opened the safe that was hidden behind the bookshelf and removed several sets of travel documents in different names and different nationalities. He found the set he needed and placed the rest in his suitcase.

He returned to his desk and opened the phase two program. He clicked a couple of keys and a screen popped up that he sat and laughed at. The screen showed the control panel of a high-tech spaceship, and below the picture was a countdown timer. He checked his watch and set the timer. He set it so an hour after he arrived in Costa Rica, a file would be sent to a select group of people and then the program would self-destruct. He closed his laptop, walked out of his office and settled in for the long wait until he needed to be at the airport. His new life was about to begin.

Chapter Thirty-Five

George attached the laptop to the conference room's sixty-inch monitor. Buck and Melanie watched as he brought up the startup screen. The image on the monitor was huge. Paul walked into the room and grabbed a seat next to Buck.

"Okay," said George. "This is the startup screen from Jim McBride's laptop."

He clicked a few keys, and a picture of a half-naked teenager appeared on the screen. With a couple clicks on the keyboard, he was able to blur the image.

"This is one of several hundred pictures we recovered from his deleted folder. I will tell you that this is one of the milder pictures. Most of them are, well, disturbing would best describe them." The embarrassment showed on his face.

"There are also numerous videos, many of which appear to have been made without the knowledge of the child, at least I hope that's the case."

"The office is running the pictures, using facial recognition software. They have already identified two of the adults from our pervert files. As they identify them, we will file for arrest warrants, and when you tell us to go, we will distribute those to the appropriate municipalities and make the arrests."

Buck nodded his approval and George continued. "Now we get to the best part. I will save you all the tech mumbo jumbo and will give it to you as simply as I can. These pictures may be on Jim McBride's computer, but he didn't put them there. We believe they were put there by Bob McBride."

George clicked a few keys, and long lines of code appeared on a dark blue screen. He scrolled through the list until he stopped at a line of code he had highlighted in red.

"Remember I said earlier that hackers and coders leave certain tells? This is one right here."

Buck leaned forward in his chair and stared at the line of code. He didn't see any difference between it and anything else on the screen. He seemed perplexed.

George could see the confusion in his eyes. "This is a simple photo storage application. The kind you would find on every computer and cell phone out there. We checked the program code with the creator, and he confirmed our findings. This was not part of the original code but was hacked into the program. The tell is in the way it was written: the sequence is identical to the kind of sequencing Bob McBride used in the Range Rover. In simple terms, this is his signature."

"What the program does is go through the internet and the dark web and download all the sexual images of children and teens it finds. Each time Jim McBride opened his laptop, his photo storage folder filled up with these images."

"Couldn't he just delete them?" asked the sheriff, who had walked in and was standing behind Buck.

"That's the beauty of the hack. Bob McBride set up a cloud storage system, unbeknownst to his brother, and every time Jim deleted the pictures, they moved to another storage area. What was left on Jim's laptop was a digital trail that led back to these photos. Anyone who would have investigated Jim's laptop would have been led right to the pictures. The second part of the hack was more diabolical. Each time Jim deleted the photos, the trail led back to an upload code that would show that the pictures came from a search done with this laptop. Now it's going to get complicated, so I'm going to try to describe how this would work because the next two parts are going to be confusing."

"Barb McBride receives a series of photos that appear to have come from Jim's laptop. She confronts Jim about the pictures, and he denies they came from his computer, only she doesn't believe him. By the way, the picture of the teenager in Barb's bed was photoshopped, but whoever did it really knew their stuff."

"Jim checks his laptop after she walks out and finds a ton of these pictures on it, so he does what any normal person would do, and he deletes them. They now go into another file that's hidden from Jim but would be easy for the computer techs to find. Jim thinks his laptop is clean, but running in the background is this program that keeps finding pictures on the internet."

The information on the screen did nothing but confuse Buck. "Let me see if I understand this so far. Jim had no idea this program was running in the background on his laptop, looking like he was searching all over the internet for dirty pictures of kids. His wife walks out because she is doing a major story on a pervert ring and she can't believe her husband might be involved. He dumps the pictures and thinks he's in the clear, but the program keeps running. We are called in to search for his wife, and one of the things we will do when we come to the realization that foul play is involved is to grab his laptop because most of these types of crimes are committed by the husband. He denies any involvement and acts upset, but our techs, you and Melanie, come in, go through his laptop and find all the dirty pictures and the search program. We arrest him for being a pervert and to sweat him about his wife's disappearance, and all he does is continue to deny any involvement. Do I have this right so far?"

"So far, so good, Buck. Now, the best part. As we were searching his laptop, we also found a hidden folder containing the program code to cause the Range Rover to shut down, including the coordinates for the exact location it stopped running, and a scheduling program that laid out the entire plot to murder Barb McBride, in chronological order. Case closed."

Carl whistled. "This poor son of a bitch goes to jail for murdering his wife, and there's no way to defend against it because his laptop is his accuser. Holy shit."

"Exactly," said Melanie. "And not to criticize the sheriff or his people, but if the governor hadn't asked us to help, because of her celebrity, Carl would have investigated this as a local missing person case. He would have had one of the sheriff's tech people look at the computer. They would have found all the background files and would probably not have dug any deeper. That would have only happened if they found the car and the body. Without the body, Barb McBride would be considered a runaway, and her husband would have gone to jail as a pervert, and the story would end there."

"Okay," said Buck. "Why are we certain that's not what happened?"

"It's the tells," said George. "We have the coder's signature, and with the signature, we can trace back how the code got into Jim's laptop, and the tells led us back to Bob McBride's laptop. Because we have his laptop files uploaded to our computer, we can follow the path the code took. He was smart, and he's a damn good coder, but he made mistakes along the way, and we found the mistakes. If we didn't have his laptop, we would not have been able to make the connection and be able to tie the Range Rover program back to his phone."

"He killed Barb McBride and then set up his

brother to look like the murderer. His mistake was thinking he had stopped the documentary from being made. He had no idea how security conscious Barb was, and even her death would not stop the video from being shown."

"So, he didn't know about the post-production company and has no idea the video is almost complete?" asked Bax.

"That would be our guess," said George. "The question is: did he do this all by himself, or is he working for someone else? Barb McBride named several names in the documentary, powerful people, but not him. My guess, she had no idea what he was doing, and he was right under her nose the entire time."

Buck stood up and walked around the table. "Have we been able to get into the cloud storage where she kept her evidence? Right now, what we think happened is her husband was running a child porn ring, his wife found out, and he killed her to stop her documentary. Our only real proof about Bob McBride's involvement depends on people like me understanding the computer science behind all this. That's a stretch. The only evidence we have against Bob McBride that people will understand is his fingerprints on the car door frame, and a defense attorney can beat that to death."

The entire team seemed beaten down. They'd found great evidence that Buck just shot to hell.

"What we need is a confession," said Paul.

"Correct," said Buck. "But we need to find the fucker first. You guys did great work. Let's not give up now. George, we need access to the cloud storage. Let's focus on that."

Melanie picked some papers up from the desk and handed them to Buck. "Phones are clean. We were able to ID all but a handful of Jim McBride's calls. We're still working them. Bob's phone was almost empty except for a couple calls to some burner phones. We tried to chase them down, but as close as we can get is that they were bought in a gas station store in Newcastle, Colorado. I asked the office to send someone to follow up and see if they had video, but we can't tell anything from the video. Too fuzzy. We tried the phone, and it just rings."

"Thanks, Mel."

He was about to step away to get a Coke out of the refrigerator in the break room when his phone rang.

"Taylor."

"Hey, Buck. It's Jerry Harcourt."

"Hi, Jerry. Anything at the house?"

"Yes, sir. We found two small spy cameras, one in Jim's office and one in Barb's office. Whoever set them up had a great view of both offices."

"Do you think we can trace them back to the source?"

"Nah. These are cheap, short-range models. Whoever installed them would have to be within a couple hundred feet."

"Thanks, Jerry. Call me if you find anything else."

Buck hung up the phone and thought for a

minute. He stepped back into the conference room. "I know why Bob McBride was staying in the apartment over the barn."

Everyone stopped and listened. "Forensics found two spy cameras, one in each office. According to Jerry, they have limited range, no more than a couple hundred feet. Bob McBride was using the apartment to spy on Barb and Jim. That's how he knew about the fight and about her walking out."

Buck noticed how tired his people were, yet they kept plugging along. No one had slept much the past couple days, and he was worried it might be starting to impact their jobs.

"Hey, guys. Listen up. We've been busting our asses for the past couple days, and I can't speak for you, but I'm beat. Let's shut everything down and call it a night. Dinner is on me at O'Toole's, and then get some rest. Be back at seven in the morning, and we'll hit it again. We made some progress today, but we need something to break."

Buck turned and headed out the door. The bug in his head was telling him they were close. He just didn't know how close.

Chapter Thirty-Six

By the time dinner arrived, the entire team was looking like they needed some time off. They ate their dinners, talked about the case, talked about other cases and, once coffee was served, they each gathered up their gear and headed for the hotel. Buck sat at the table with Ryker, who appeared dejected.

"This was a good idea," he said. "I think you kind of crushed their spirits tonight."

"Yeah. We don't have enough to convict Bob McBride of murder. The laptop as accuser was dead on. We would have no problem convicting Jim McBride of the murder of his wife, based on the evidence we found in the computer, and would have no luck convicting Bob McBride of the same crime based on the evidence in the computer."

"Do you think a jury wouldn't understand the computer science?"

Buck thought for a minute. "I guess I shouldn't base my opinion on just me. People in the office tell me I'm a dinosaur when it comes to technology. Did you understand most of what George was saying? I mean understand it enough that you could convict a man of murder, based on that understanding?"

Now it was Ryker who thought for a minute. "I

can't say I could, Buck. Maybe we're both too old for this job. The technology is getting way ahead of us. The bad guys are getting smarter, and we keep plodding along. I still think we should bring him in based on the original arrest warrant and see if we can pressure him. Of course, as you said, we have to find the fucker first."

Buck laughed and finished his glass of Coke, paid the bill and wished Ryker a good night. They walked out the door and each headed in a different direction. It was a beautiful starlit night, and Buck decided to take a walk along the Blue River Trail, which runs through the middle of Breckenridge. If he was so inclined, he could have walked all the way to Frisco, about nine miles north.

Buck headed north, away from the restaurant, passing a lot of visitors and locals who had the same idea. He walked about two blocks, found a wooden bench and sat down. He stared at the water as he thought about the world around him.

He closed his eyes and pictured Lucy, not like she was at the end with the bald head she was so proud of, but the incredible woman she was when the kids were born. She was the most beautiful woman he had ever seen, with her flawless olive complexion and jet-black hair.

He was the luckiest man alive, and even after her death, he still believed that. Lucy would know what to say right now. She always seemed to know what to say. She would have told him that what you have is what you have, and you need to work with that.

Buck opened his eyes and smiled, wiping away

the moisture from his eyes. She was right. They needed to make the case from what they had, and he needed to have faith they could present a case to a jury that would be understood. He pulled out his phone and speed-dialed a number. The director answered right away.

"Sorry to call so late, sir. I wanted to give you an update. We made some progress today."

Buck filled him in on the spy cameras and the computer information they had been able to find so far. As he spoke, he sounded more confident in what he was saying. Granted, he couldn't get down to the nitty-gritty as far as the computer science was concerned, but he thought he did a good job explaining their case.

The director listened to what he said, and when Buck finished, he said, "So, Bob McBride killed Barb by infecting her car and her phone. His prints indicate he pushed the car off the cliff and the computer program is on his phone. He also filled his brother's computer with filth and installed a program that made it look like everything that happened was Jim McBride's doing. If George is right, this guy is clever, but not clever enough to hide from George."

"That's about right, sir."

"If you can access her cloud storage, will that help convict Bob?"

"No, sir. Paul and Melanie watched the documentary, and although she mentions a lot of people by name, she never mentions her brother-in-law. So, the question is, how does Bob McBride fit into this whole scheme? Is he running the show or is he working for someone else?"

"Okay, Buck. So, what do we need to prove one or the other, short of a confession?"

Buck thought for a minute. "We need to find the weakest link. We've been avoiding the porn ring, to concentrate on the murder, but one is the cause of the other. We've solved the murder, but we still can't say who ordered the murder. Now we need to concentrate on the child porn ring. If we do that, we may find the evidence we need to convict Bob McBride and whoever ordered the murder. We need to find out how many of the men Barb McBride mentioned in the video live in Colorado, and then we need to find the one man with the most to lose."

Buck thanked the director and hung up his phone. He sat back on the bench and closed his eyes. They hadn't gone after any of the men named in the video, because they hadn't found Barb McBride's evidence yet, but the men named in the video didn't know that. A new strategy began to take shape in his head, and for a minute the little bug in his brain was silent. He stood up and headed for the hotel. He had some work to do, and he didn't want to wake the team. They needed to sleep.

Chapter Thirty-Seven

Buck finished his breakfast in the restaurant attached to the hotel and then drove to the sheriff's office. He walked into the conference room at a little past seven and found his team already hard at work.

Bax met him at the door. "I got a call back last night from the Russell County detective in Kansas. The man who rented the post office box was a sharecropper and lived on a small truck farm about five miles out of Luray. He died about four years back, but the neighbors remembered him as being a real prick. The car was not registered to him, but the guy who owned the farm down the road remembered selling him the car. Told the detective that the guy would buy crap cars from folks, never register them and when they broke down, he would take the plates off and leave it where it stopped. He'd then buy another piece of junk and put the old plates on it."

"The neighbors also remembered that he was abusive to his wife. One woman they talked to said his son was born with a neurological disease and was a cripple—her word, not mine—and he blamed his wife. She said she often saw the wife with bruises on her arms. She told the detective that sometimes months would go by without anyone seeing the woman or the child and then one day, the neighbors realized they hadn't been seen for a long time. She was never reported as missing, but the neighbors feared the worst, but no one did anything about it because they all feared the farmer."

"So, what do you think?" asked Buck.

"I think she grabbed the kid, ran away and ended up here. I'd like to keep working this. The woman would be somewhere in her sixties. She might still be alive. I'd like to find her and find out what happened to the kid."

"Did they give you her name or the kid's name?"

"Yeah, Stoneman, her first name was Edith. The kid was Gerald. The detective could not find any living relatives we could get DNA from."

"Okay, it's someplace to start. Follow up with Max on the kid's DNA. Maybe the woman or a relative took a DNA test, and they're in the system. It's worth a shot."

Bax thanked him, pulled her phone and headed for a quiet corner of the conference room. Buck walked to the front of the room.

"Okay, folks, stop what you're doing."

Everyone stopped clicking keys on their laptops. Bax walked back and joined the rest of the team at the table, and the sheriff stepped into the doorway and leaned against the wall.

"We have been busting our asses trying to solve a murder we already solved. We've figured out how Bob McBride killed Barb and set his brother up to take the fall. The problem we have is, we can't prove it without a lot of computer science, which

scares me, but I'm old, and that's just me."
Everyone laughed.

"One of the questions we still need to answer: is Bob McBride in charge of the porn ring or is he just an underling? We've been dancing around the porn ring because we can't access the evidence Barb hid in the cloud, but we don't need the evidence from the cloud. We have the names of two dozen men from the video, who have no idea we know about them and who don't know we don't have any evidence against them. It's time to find the weakest link in that group."

They were all focused on what Buck had just said, and he continued. "We need to break the ring. Last night I ran a quick background check on each name to see how many of these men live in Colorado. Just being associated with child porn is a crime in this state, and every name on this list came up during our murder investigation, and that gives us the justification to go after these guys. Of the two dozen names on the list, seven of them live in the state. What we need to do is switch gears." Buck gave each person a copy of the list he'd printed that morning in the hotel business center.

"I want deep background on each name on this list. We need to look at everything: family, business ties, friends, relatives, arrest records, asset searches, phone records, the whole nine yards. We need to look into their souls if we have to, and then we are going to figure out which one has the most to lose, and we are going to threaten to make his life a living hell. We have the best tool at our disposal:

the threat of public exposure. Every man on this list is a pervert with something to lose. We are going to make that person believe his world is coming to an end, and we will keep working down the list until we find one who cracks."

The team went back to their computers and phones, and Buck walked to the door where Ryker was standing.

He smiled at Buck. "Must have been a hell of a walk you took last night. You have a religious experience or something?"

Buck laughed. "Maybe so. It occurred to me while I was talking to the director that we had two crimes that went hand in hand, and we have been avoiding the porn part, trying to access Barb's evidence when we were within our rights to work that crime as well."

Ryker leaned forward. "I like that kind of thinking. You break one of these guys, and I have ten deputies ready to kick down some doors. To paraphrase what you said last night, let's get these fuckers."

George walked up as Ryker stepped away. "I was running that discreet search for anything associated with Skylark Holdings like you asked, and I found something interesting."

"Go ahead."

"The algorithm I used follows layers of corporate information, tracking one corporation to another to another. I can go as deep as I want. What used to take weeks of digging through paper, we can now do in a matter of hours. Well, this morning when I checked the results, I found a reference to Skylark Holdings. I had to go down five levels, but I found a house in Vail that is connected. The deed is registered to Five Star Investments, Limited. They are a Delaware corporation. They are a subsidiary of another corporation and so on and so on. Skylark is at the bottom of the list."

"Great work, George. Text me the address. Bax, grab your gear. You're with me."

Buck grabbed his backpack, and he and Bax headed out the door. Buck explained, when they got into his car, what George had told him. He planned to knock on the door and see who lived in the house. What George described made it sound like someone had gone through a lot of trouble to hide the actual ownership of the house. That intrigued Buck.

Buck checked his phone and plugged the address for the house on Mill Creek Circle that George had sent him into the GPS. It was about a forty-five-minute drive, and once he got onto I-70, he hit the flashers. He made the drive in a little over thirty minutes. He pulled onto Mill Creek Circle, found the address and parked across the street. They sat and watched the house for a few minutes.

"I don't see any lights on inside," said Bax.

Buck checked his phone. "I don't think it's too early to be calling on people, do you?"

Bax smiled. "Let's see if anyone is home."

They slid out of the car, crossed the street and walked up the steps. The house was a huge modern mountain mini mansion with lots of wood and stones on the exterior. From the front door, they had a great view of the ski area.

Buck rang the doorbell and then knocked. He tried to see through the stained-glass window in the door, but nothing was visible.

"No one seems to be home. Let's see if the neighbors can tell us who lives here."

They walked back down the steps, and Buck turned right, and Bax turned left. After about twenty minutes they met back at the front steps.

Bax said, "Mrs. Iverson, an amiable, talkative woman two doors down, said the owner was a younger single man who seemed to travel a lot on business. She said his name was Roger, but when I showed her Bob McBride's picture, she said it did look something like Roger. Did you have any luck?"

"Yeah," said Buck. "I got the same Roger story from Mr. Slavic, next door, but he positively identified Bob McBride. I called Paul, and he is putting together a search warrant application, and Ryker is calling his favorite judge. Should have something in about a half hour." They walked back to Buck's Jeep and settled in to wait for the warrant. Things were starting to break loose.

Chapter Thirty-Eight

The Vail Police car pulled to a stop opposite Buck's Jeep, and a young blond officer stepped out of the car. "Agent Taylor?" Buck nodded. The officer approached with his hand extended. "Officer Tim Martin, sir. The chief asked me to bring you this warrant and to see if you need any additional assistance. He also asked if you need a locksmith?" Buck and Bax both smiled.

"That won't be necessary, Officer. If you would care to stick around, we might need your help inside," she said.

They all headed up the front steps, and Bax pulled a small leather pouch out of her pocket, pulled out two tools and knelt in front of the door.

The young officer watched her work on the lock. "May I ask why you have a lockpick set?"

Bax and Buck smiled at the officer and responded in unison. "In case we lose our house keys."

The officer gave a little nervous laugh, and Bax and Buck pulled their weapons. She pushed open the door.

"Police, we have a warrant," she yelled, and they entered the front foyer, Buck moving left and Bax right. The officer, unsure of what to do, pulled his service weapon and stood outside the front door.

Bax glanced back at the officer. "Officer, please stay right where you are. No one in or out."

They worked their way through the lower level, clearing each room as they went, and then they moved up the stairs to the second floor. After several minutes Buck yelled, "All clear," and they came back down the stairs. Everyone holstered their weapons. The house was immaculate inside and didn't look like anyone lived there.

Buck called the young officer inside while Bax said she was going to look for a basement entrance. He told the officer that they were investigating a pornography ring and asked him to search the rooms upstairs for anything that might look like it was related to porn. He was not to touch anything he found but was to call for Buck. The officer headed upstairs while Buck started in the front room.

"Buck. Found the basement," Bax said, from what Buck assumed was the kitchen. He followed her voice to where she was standing. She had her hand on the doorknob and her pistol in her right hand. Buck drew his pistol and nodded. Bax opened the door and hit the light switch on the side wall, and they headed down the stairs.

The first thing they noticed was all the digital equipment and the server bank that sat humming along against one entire wall. Buck was lost when it came to this kind of technology, but he knew this was huge. He thought he was staring at the console of a starship, and it all appeared to be fully automated.

Bax stood with a stunned look on her face, as did Officer Martin, who was now standing behind them on the stairs. "Holy crap," he said.

Bax walked over to the console and turned on one of the monitors. The video that came up made her jump back and raise her hands to her mouth. "Oh, my god." She reached down and turned off the monitor. Her face was pale. "That's disgusting. How can anyone look at that?"

Officer Martin, regaining his composure after seeing the video, took a deep breath. "Sir, I didn't find anything that seemed related to porn, but in the master bedroom, there are a lot of clothes and personal items, but there are also several hangers lying on the bed. It's possible someone packed a suitcase."

"He's running," said Buck.

Buck had no idea what all the equipment in the room was for. He knew he was going to need help. This was way out of their league. He pulled his phone, took a video of the equipment and called the director.

"Sir," he said when the director answered. "I think we hit the mother lode. I'm sending you a video. We are going to need help with this." He sent the video and waited.

"Fuck," said the director. "We're gonna have to call in the Feds. Do you want to make the call?"

"Yes, sir. We think McBride is running."

"Okay, Buck. You let me know what you need, and you got it."

Buck hung up his phone. "We think he's

running. We're sitting on I-70, west is Salt Lake, east is Denver. He could be heading for Denver International, or is he driving to Salt Lake?"

"Sir," said Officer Martin. "What about Eagle County Regional Airport?"

"Good thought, Officer. Can you check with the neighbors and see if any of them know what kind of car he drives and if they have seen it in the past couple hours?" Officer Martin headed up the stairs.

Bax said, "I'll call the airport and see what flights are leaving this morning." She pulled her phone and found the number on Google.

Buck opened his phone, typed a quick message attached to the video and hit send. He waited. Two minutes later, his phone rang. He answered.

"Fuck, Buck. What the hell is all that?"

"Morning, Hank. Thought you might be interested in what we found?"

Hank Clancy was silent for a moment. "My first question is, does this have anything to do with Skylark Holdings? We told you to stand down."

Buck thought about how to answer. He thought the simplest answer would be best. "We discovered evidence during our investigation into the murder of Barb McBride that led us to a house in Vail owned by Bob McBride, her brother-in-law. We followed our evidence, and here we are."

"You should have been a politician, Buck. Okay, what do you need?"

"This is way out of our league. We are going to need full cyber forensics. Once they can determine what all this stuff does, we can figure out the next step. Also, we think Bob McBride is running; can you send his description to TSA and have someone see if he has more than one passport?"

"Can do. Send me the address and lock the place down. I'll text you when we're en route. And Buck, nice job." Hank hung up.

Officer Martin came running down the stairs, out of breath. "Sir, the neighbor next door says he drives a new silver F-150. His wife saw it pull out of the garage at about eight o'clock."

Buck checked his phone. It was now nine fifteen. Bax, who was still on the phone, said, "Deputy, can you hold on for a minute?" She put the phone to her chest. "First flight out to DIA was at eight ten, next flight is at ten forty."

"Let's take the shot," said Buck.

"Deputy, we are on our way. We'll meet you at the front entrance. Let's not attract a lot of attention, we don't think he's armed, but anything's possible." She hung up.

"Officer Martin," said Buck. "I need you to lock up the house and wait outside until the FBI arrives. Call your chief and clear it with him." He raced up the stairs after Bax, and they ran through the house, down the stairs and climbed into his Jeep. Buck waited until he merged onto I-70, then he hit his lights and siren. Bax called Paul and filled him in and then hung up and held on.

Buck made the thirty-five-mile drive from Vail to the airport in Gypsum in just over twenty minutes. He killed the lights and siren as he exited I-70 and followed the signs to the main terminal.

He pulled up out front, and they climbed out of the car. Eagle County Deputy Trujillo, a short, middle-aged Hispanic man, with dark curly hair and a mustache, was standing outside the main entrance with the senior TSA officer. He introduced himself as Bob Hellerman. Buck didn't think he was old enough to shave, but then Buck felt like everyone was younger than him.

"So far we haven't seen anyone who matches your guy's description," said Trujillo. "Are you sure he is here?"

Bax answered. "We can't say for sure. This is a long shot. What I'd like to do is have the four of us spread out on the departure side of the terminal and see if he shows up. We don't need to be discreet, since he's seen both Agent Taylor and me."

Officer Hellerman led the way, and they badged their way through security and spread out at the gates. The departure announcement for the next Denver flight came over the loudspeakers, and the passengers started to line up in front of the door at gate two. Buck and Trujillo stood along the walkway and watched the passengers. Officer Hellerman stood near the security checkpoint to check any last-minute passengers coming through the line, and Bax positioned herself down by the restrooms. The gate agent was about to open the door to the plane when Buck's phone chirped. He pulled it out and checked the message. "Restroom, coming your way."

He turned towards the restrooms and spotted Bob McBride walking away from the restrooms towards the gate. Bob McBride spotted Buck at about the same time and turned back the way he had come. He spotted Bax coming from that direction, stopped, searched for a way out, and then bolted for the exit door at gate four. He dropped his carry-on bag, hit the exit door and slammed it open, setting off the alarm. He ran across the tarmac, with Bax hot on his heels. She passed through the exit door, dodged a luggage cart and hit the gas.

Buck watched her run out the door followed by two TSA officers and was about to give chase when Trujillo whistled. Buck turned, and Trujillo pointed towards the side exit door. Buck spotted the Eagle County Sheriff's SUV parked outside, and he followed Trujillo as he punched in his security code and opened the exit. They jumped into the SUV and Trujillo hit the lights and sirens as they drove across the ramp area.

They spotted Bax about a hundred yards across the field running across the taxiway. She was gaining on McBride, which didn't surprise Buck at all. Bax ran with the grace and speed of a gazelle. What McBride had no way of knowing was that Bax ran track in high school and college, and she still ran one or two marathons a year with her dad.

McBride glanced back over his shoulder, stumbled over the edge of the grass and Bax hit him like she was a linebacker for the Denver Broncos. They both went down in a heap, and she jumped up and pounced again as he tried to stand up. McBride tried to punch her in the head, but she blocked the poorly thrown punch and, with a closed fist, punched him right in the nose. All the fight left him, and by the time the two TSA officers got to her, she had flipped the bleeding McBride over onto his stomach and was applying her handcuffs.

"You're under arrest," she said, as Buck and Trujillo pulled up. While Trujillo loaded him in the back of the SUV, Buck made sure Bax was okay.

They drove around to the front of the building, transferred McBride to Buck's Jeep and Buck thanked Trujillo and Hellerman for their help, while Bax caught her breath. They pulled out of the parking lot and headed back to Summit County.

Chapter Thirty-Nine

Buck left Bob McBride with the sheriff's booking officer and headed for the conference room. The rest of the team were busy at work, and he scanned the three whiteboards that hung on the walls. Each board was covered with information about the men Buck had identified as living in Colorado. He stood looking over the boards when Paul walked over.

"Heard about the excitement. Sounds like we hit pay dirt." Buck was focused on the lists under each name and nodded. "We have a good grasp of who these guys are," said Paul, "and we're ready to narrow down our choices."

He called over George and Melanie, and Bax grabbed a chair behind them.

Paul began. "Of the seven names you gave us, five still live either full or part-time in the state. One moved out of state, and one passed away about six weeks ago. We tore into these guys like you asked. We have two judges, one congressman, and two businessmen. All of them are married and have children. Only one has children younger than twenty."

Over the next two hours, Paul, George and Melanie walked through each man's life. They covered their friends, coworkers, and neighbors.

One lived in the house next to the Governor's Mansion in Denver. They reviewed their financials, their assets, their social statuses and they walked through their businesses. One of the things that surprised them was that many of them had large debts, and two had outstanding warrants for failure to pay child support. They were a real mixed bag.

They finished their presentation, and Buck sat back and took a long sip of his Coke.

"Great job, guys. Now, who has the most to lose?"

Melanie answered for the group. "We think it's Congressman David Kowalski."

"He's not one of ours, what's his deal?"

"He's a congressman from Arkansas. His family owns a house in Steamboat Springs, which they have had for several years. Besides being a congressman, he is also a preacher and runs an evangelical church in his hometown. He's been in Congress for almost thirty years and is highly respected. After this past election, he was appointed to the Ways and Means Committee and is the chairman of several subcommittees, two of which deal with children's rights and health. His wife is on the board of six different charities, and they host a huge Christmas party each year, for all the underprivileged kids in his district."

"What are you not telling me?" asked Buck.

George took over. "He's a close friend of the president, and he's a former marine colonel. He may be tough to crack, but we think he is the one who would be damaged most by any allegations of child pornography. We still have the offices in Grand Junction and Denver working on more background, but we think this is enough to get you going."

"Anything new on getting into Barb McBride's cloud files?"

"No luck yet. We can't crack the password. We've tried everything, and nothing works. It should be simple, but it's not. Maybe the FBI will find what we need from the house in Vail."

"Okay. Are we confident the congressman is at the house in Steamboat?"

"Yes. There is a high dollar benefit dinner tonight for one of his wife's local charities. I will send you his address," said George.

"Excellent work, guys. Let's upload all this to the investigation file and then call it a day. Paul, you feel up to a drive to Steamboat later tonight?"

Paul nodded, and Buck walked out of the conference room. It was time to have a sit-down with Bob McBride.

The sheriff met Buck in the hall outside the interrogation room. Carl stood next to him holding a file folder.

"We found a burned-out truck on an old mining road up on Shrine Pass. We only were able to retrieve the last five numbers from the VIN, but it's registered to Bob McBride. You guys need anything before you go in there?"

Buck shook his head. "No, we're good. Oh, do me a favor and swing by the conference room and ask George to come here. We may need him."

The sheriff walked away, and Buck nodded to Carl, and they entered the interrogation room. Bob McBride sat there with a bloody bandage on his nose. He sat up when Buck walked into the room and said, "Call my lawyer." He checked his watch, which Buck noticed he'd done several times earlier in the day.

"You got a hot date?" Buck asked.

"Why would you ask me that?" he said.

"You keep checking your watch. You've already missed your plane to Costa Rica, and we have all your passport and ID packages. I don't think you're going anywhere for a while."

"You think you have all the answers, but you've got nothing," said Bob McBride.

"The FBI cyber people are tearing apart your basement as we speak," said Buck.

"Nothing to find. It's my cable TV system."

Buck laughed. Bob checked his watch again.

Someone tapped on the window glass and Buck waved his hand to enter. George walked in and pulled up a chair.

"That's not my lawyer."

"Yeah. He's coming. In the meantime, I wanted George—he's one of our cyber guys—to fill Carl in on how we got into your system. It's fascinating stuff if you understand all the technological mumbo jumbo."

"You can't do that. I said I want my lawyer and I'm not answering any of your questions."

"That's okay, Bob. You see, we aren't interested

in asking you any questions, so we're not violating your rights."

Bob checked his watch again.

Buck got up and walked out of the interrogation room, leaving George and Carl to talk tech. He stood outside the window and watched as their conversation progressed. There was some seriousness and a couple times some laughter, and for two hours Bob sat there stone-faced, looking like he wanted to explode. Buck had no idea what Carl and George were talking about, but George kept laying it on thicker and thicker as the time went on.

After three hours, Ryker walked up and stood next to Buck. "How long are you going to let this go on? The guy looks like he wants to strangle someone."

"George should be about ready to wrap it up. Did you call his lawyer?"

"Yeah. He'll be here in a couple hours. We had trouble getting through to the lawyer, so McBride won't be arraigned until tomorrow."

Buck watched Bob through the window.

"What are you thinking?" asked Ryker.

"I wish I knew why he keeps checking his watch. He's been doing that since we hauled him back here. Something's up, but I don't know what."

George and Carl stood up, they laughed at something Carl said and they walked out of the room.

"Well, what do you think?" said Buck.

"I think we got to him," said George. "I could

see it in his eyes. He knows we got him and it's burning him up inside. He thought he was the smartest person in the room. Now he's not so sure."

Buck thanked George and Carl and told them to wrap up for the evening. He wished Ryker a good evening and went to find Paul.

Chapter Forty

Buck and Paul headed up Highway 9 and turned onto Highway 40 at Kremmling. The GPS showed about an hour and twelve minutes until they reached the congressman's house.

Darkness settled across the road, and the last rays of the sun were disappearing behind the mountains, giving the world around them a strange golden glow that would soon give way to black.

As they passed the McBride ranch, they noticed that the media vans were no longer parked along the road and the deputies had removed the barricade. The house was dark, and Buck thought about what a terrible waste had occurred in such a pristine location.

Barb McBride died doing a job she loved. She spent a lifetime trying to right the wrongs she saw around her, and it cost her her life. Her husband died for no other reason than he was expendable. He was a convenient tool for someone, namely his brother, to use as a patsy in his wife's murder. What happened next was still speculation. Bob denied ordering the hit on his brother, but when you consider he was the one who set him up to take the fall for his wife's murder, it was hard to believe him. But if he didn't do it, then who?

Buck believed that Bob had lost control of the

situation and someone he worked either with or for had set up the murder of Jim to protect someone else. Bob was now expendable, and Buck was counting on the fact that Bob would have trouble knowing who to trust. He figured the escape to Costa Rica was Bob's way out, to protect himself. He thought back to watching Bob in the interrogation room. He was annoyed with the story George was telling; it was clear to everyone, but why did he keep looking at his watch? He was waiting for something to happen, but what?

Buck slowed down on a dark curve, just as he started the climb up Rabbit Ear's Pass, so he could keep an eye on the herd of elk grazing along the shoulder of the highway. Hitting an elk was like running your car into a tree. If you survived the encounter, the damage could be significant. He picked up speed once he was certain they were well past the herd.

Buck was hoping their visit to the congressman might give him some of the missing answers. He believed Bob McBride was not the top person in this porn ring. Bob had the computer skills to set this up, of that there was no doubt. The death of Jim made that clear in his mind. Someone higher up made that call, and that's why Bob rabbited. He needed to find out who that person was.

It was possible the information was in Barb McBride's files, but the little bug that went away when they decided to look at some of the men named in the video was back. He wondered if there was someone involved in all this that they weren't aware of yet.

Buck slowed as he made the last downhill curve heading into Steamboat. He turned onto State Highway 131 at the Haymaker Golf Course, turned onto County Route 14 and followed it to Agate Creek Road, where he turned into the fourth driveway on the left. He parked in front of the door, and they both stepped out of the car.

Buck rang the bell and waited. A young man in a dark blue suit answered the door.

"May I help you?"

Buck held up his ID. "Agents Taylor and Webber, Colorado Bureau of Investigation. We'd like to see the congressman, please."

"May I ask what this is about? The congressman is very busy."

Buck stared at him. "Who might you be, sir?"

The young man puffed out his chest. "I'm Jake Parker, the congressman's chief of staff. Now may I ask what this is all about?"

"No, Jake. You may not ask what this is all about."

"I'm sorry, gentlemen, but the congressman is busy. You will have to make an appointment." He attempted to close the door, but Paul reached out his huge arm and pushed the door back.

The young man started to object when a voice came from behind him. "Jake, please show the officers in."

Congressman Kowalski was of average height and in great shape for someone who had been in

Congress for thirty years. He wore his hair in a gray crew cut and spoke with a deep Southern accent.

As Buck and Paul stepped into the foyer, he reached out his hand. "Gentlemen, David Kowalski. How can I help you?"

Buck introduced himself and Paul again. "Congressman, we need a few minutes in private to discuss a sensitive matter," said Buck.

A slender woman with grayish-blond hair wearing a dark blue cocktail dress stepped into the foyer. "David, is everything all right?" She glanced at Buck and Paul.

"Everything is fine, Liz. Gentlemen, why don't we step into my office."

He led the way down the hallway, and they entered another dark wood man's office. Jake tried to follow them in, but Buck put his hand against his chest to stop him and then he reached around and closed the door.

"Now, gentlemen. What's this all about?" He sat in the leather chair behind the desk.

"Congressman," said Buck. "Your name came up during an investigation, and we wanted to ask you a few questions, just to clear you from our list."

The congressman seemed confused. "What sort of investigation?" His Southern accent was getting a little thicker.

"Child pornography, sir."

The congressman had picked up a glass of water to take a drink, and he almost dropped the glass.

"What? That can't be right. I've never . . ."

It was too late; Buck caught the fear in his eyes, and he knew he was on the right track.

"Sir, we are investigating a pornography ring that is responsible for three murders we are aware of to cover up the child porn. Your name came up in a video, set to air on NBC next month. The investigative journalist was murdered a week ago, but the network has the video and all the evidence she collected. Your name is one of several that will be broadcast nationwide. We are here tonight to give you a chance to come clean and try to get ahead of this."

Buck stopped talking to give the congressman a chance to refill his glass and take a long drink.

"I have no idea . . ."

"Sir, before you start lying to us, I have to warn you the evidence is compelling. You will most likely lose your seat in Congress, and you will definitely be going to jail."

The congressman tried to regain a little of his composure. "How dare you come into my house in the middle of the night and threaten me with this vile filth? I will be calling your governor, and I will have your jobs."

Buck held up his phone. "I have the governor right here on speed dial. Would you like me to connect you?"

The congressman sat back in his chair, picked up a decanter of brown liquid that was sitting on the corner of his desk and poured himself a full glass. He drank half the glass in one gulp. Buck decided to push a little more.

"Sir, what can you tell us about Skylark Holdings?"

The congressman dropped the glass, which spilled on the carpet under the desk, and his face turned white as a ghost. He stared at Buck with his mouth half open. His chief of staff knocked on the door. Paul opened the door and told him that the congressman had dropped a glass, and everything was fine. He closed the door.

"No. I can't help you. I want you to leave."

"What are you afraid of, Congressman?" asked Buck.

"I want you out of my house." There were tears in his eyes.

Buck was tired of trying to be nice. He reached across the desk and grabbed him by the front of his shirt. "Now you listen to me, you slimy little pervert. Your career is toast. When your family finds out you like to look at little kids being fucked, your marriage will be toast. If you don't want to spend the rest of your life in jail, getting butt-fucked by everybody on the cell block, then you better talk to us, because we are the only hope you have. You've got one chance here, don't blow it."

Buck shoved his business card into the congressman's shirt pocket. "You've got one fucking chance. If you try to run, I will track you down, and your life won't be worth shit. There is nothing worse in this world than a pervert who gets off on little kids. So, you can count on the fact that I will hound your ass till the end of time, and I will make you suffer, so you better think hard about your next move."

He shoved the congressman back into his seat.

"You have till noon tomorrow, or I will be back with a warrant, and I swear to God I will burn you down."

Buck walked towards the door. "By the way. We arrested Bob McBride today. You may not know who he is, but someone you know does. I'm going to break him, and when I'm done, I will know more about what's going on in your world than you could ever imagine. When I'm done with you, you will have told me everything, you can count on that, but with or without you, I'm going to destroy your little pervert ring."

Tears flowed down the congressman's face, and Buck could see the fear in his eyes.

He opened the door and walked out. Paul was right behind him. He left the door to the office open. Jake ran into the office. "Congressman, are you all right?" The last thing they heard before they walked out the door was the congressman telling Jake to get the fuck out of his office. They walked out the front door, slid into the Jeep and Buck pulled out of the driveway. He drove around the corner and pulled to the side of the road. His hands were shaking.

"You okay, Buck?"

Buck sat there for a minute and calmed his breathing. "Yeah, I'm okay. I hate people who hurt kids more than anything in this world. I wanted to rip his fucking heart out and feed it to him."

"Well, I think you got your point across. It's up to him now."

Buck pulled the car out and headed back towards Breckenridge.

Chapter Forty-One

Buck and Paul were halfway back to Breckenridge when his phone rang. He recognized the number and answered the phone.

"Hank, what's up?"

"The whole damn thing disappeared."

"What are you talking about? What whole thing?"

"The entire computer system self-destructed. Everything. It's all gone. Get here as soon as you can." He hung up.

Buck didn't know what happened, but he knew it wasn't good. He checked the clock on the dashboard. "I don't think we're getting any sleep tonight."

Buck stepped on the gas and headed for Vail.

****

Mill Creek Circle was a beehive of activity as Buck turned onto the street. He couldn't park in front of the house, so he pulled to the curb a couple houses away, and they walked to McBride's house. They walked up the steps to the open front door and walked in. Buck wasn't sure what was going on, but there were a lot of long faces and raised voices, and they walked down the stairs into the basement. Buck found Hank Clancy standing by the console having a loud conversation. He stopped talking to the tech as Buck walked up. Buck had never seen Hank look so frustrated.

"What happened, Hank?"

"We can't say for sure. One minute the tech guys are downloading information from the servers and the next minute, all the little lights go out, and the system is completely dead."

Paul directed his question to the tech standing next to Hank. "Did you guys trip a booby trap?"

"No idea. We can't even bring the servers back online. The whole thing is dead. I've never seen anything like it."

"What about the data? Is it still there?"

The tech shook his head. "We have no way to access it." He walked away with one of the other techs. Paul walked over to see if he could help them. Buck asked Hank how much data they had been able to retrieve, and Hank told him they had just gotten started downloading the data when the end came. Buck sat down in one of the chairs at the console.

"I called Washington, and the NSA is flying in a couple of their techs to help us out, but they won't be here till the morning. Fuck, this is unbelievable."

Buck could sense the frustration. "I will take another stab at McBride in the morning and see if I can find out what he did to crash the system, otherwise our entire case may evaporate."

Buck stood up. Paul told him he was going to stay and see if he could help. Buck climbed the stairs and left the house. He walked to his car, slid in and headed for the hotel. He needed sleep before he forgot what sleep was.

He pulled into the hotel parking lot, grabbed his backpack and headed up to his room. He dropped his backpack on the floor, sat on the bed to take off his shoes and fell fast asleep.

The alarm clock on Buck's phone woke him up at dawn. This was the first night in a while he had gotten any sleep, and he felt worse than he had the past couple days. He shook the grogginess out of his head, showered, found a somewhat clean shirt and got dressed. He clipped his gun and badge to his belt, grabbed his backpack and walked out the door. The first task on his agenda was breakfast, so he stopped at the hotel restaurant and enjoyed his eggs, steak and toast. He washed it down with his first Coke of the day.

He spotted the black FBI SUV as he pulled into the parking lot. He wondered if Hank was inside having a conversation with Bob McBride. The fiasco at the Mill Creek Circle house the night before was not going to sit well with his bosses at Justice. He felt bad for Hank. They had become good friends over the years, and Buck hated to see anyone's career hurt.

He did feel good though. They'd caught their murderer and could close that portion of the case. The porn stuff, from what he could see, was going to end up as a national story if they were able to find the evidence they needed, and he figured the FBI would take the case over anyway, and his team would be out of it. If he only knew how wrong he would be.

Buck checked in with the deputy at the front desk and was buzzed through the security door. He was heading back to the conference room to check in with his team when he ran into Ryker.

"Morning, Sheriff. I see the FBI has arrived, huh?"

Ryker smiled. "They are getting nowhere with Bob McBride. They've been at it two hours, and he hasn't said a word, just keeps telling them he wants his attorney. By the way, he spent three hours with his attorney last night."

"What time is his arraignment?"

"Judge called this morning and wants to do it at two p.m. You want another crack at him when the Feds are done?"

"Yeah, but let me check in with my team, first."

Buck walked down the hall to the conference room and stepped inside. Bax was the first one to meet him at the door.

"Don't you answer your phone anymore? I've been calling since four."

He pulled out his phone and opened the missed call log. Sure enough, he'd slept through five calls, three from Bax and two from Paul.

"Any idea what Paul wanted?"

"Yeah," she said. "He wanted to tell you, they had no luck last night with the data, and he was going to get some sleep before they took another crack at it today."

"Okay. Now, what did you need?"

"First, Paul told me about the meeting with the congressman. Are you okay? He said you were pretty heated."

"Yeah, I'm fine. We definitely rattled his cage; I hope it was enough. He almost shit himself when I told him we arrested Bob McBride. I think he knows more than we thought, but he's probably halfway to Brazil by now. I gave him till noon to call me. We'll see."

"Max sent me a text last night. They got a hit on the DNA from one of the DNA testing companies. It's only a partial match, a half-sibling or cousin, but according to the text, her people felt it was a decent lead. I need to go to Salt Lake City."

Buck scanned the room. George and Melanie were still typing away on their laptops, and Carl was reading through a pile of documents that were sitting on the table. "I think we can spare you. Have you contacted Salt Lake PD?"

"Yeah, I'm meeting a Detective Yolanda Diego. She's running some background for me as we speak. I've got a flight out of Eagle County in two hours."

"Okay, Bax. Go find out why that little boy died. And Bax, be careful."

Bax thanked him, grabbed her backpack and raced out the door. He liked when Bax got excited. She made shit happen.

Melanie glanced up from her laptop. She didn't look like she'd slept much the night before.

"Hey, Buck. Paul said you had an interesting evening. Wish I could have been there. He asked us to work with the Feds, trying to recover the data from the Vail house. Whoever set this system up was unbelievably sophisticated. This is the kind of fail-safe you find in the military or the NSA. So far, we've been able to help them bring a couple of the servers back up, but we have no idea where the data went. Couple NSA guys showed up about an hour ago, and they headed over to the Vail house."

"Any luck getting into Barb McBride's cloud account?"

George was not happy. "I'll tell you, Buck; I've never had this much trouble cracking a password. I'm giving it one more shot."

"Let me ask you this. Her production guy told you guys that when the show is broadcast, she sends the evidence to the particular jurisdiction with authority over whatever she investigated. Do you think she could have a backup plan in case something happened to her? She seems to have backup plans for everything; otherwise, how would she be able to send the evidence to the correct authority?"

George sat back in his chair. "She would either have to have a third party who was directed to send the stuff to someone in the event something happened to her, or she would need an automatic trigger in her computer, set up to do the same thing."

Melanie said, "Her phone records. We identified most of the callers, but there were a couple we hadn't been able to track down. Could one of them be her third party?"

Buck smiled. "Let's focus on that and figure it out. George, forget about getting into the cloud. Work the phone list. We need to identify everyone on the list and call them all. We need to find out what her relationship was to each person on the list."

Carl stepped over. "I can help with that too. If you give me the list of those numbers you identified, I can start calling them."

Buck walked to the end of the table, pulled his laptop from his backpack and opened the investigation file. He spent a little while filling out the arrest report on Bob McBride. He was looking at the digital copy of his airline tickets when the little bug in his brain threw a rock at him. He checked the flight times. The wheels started to turn.

He pulled his phone and dialed Hank, but his phone went straight to voice mail. He walked over to George.

"Can you find out what time the computers shut down last night?"

George pulled out his phone and picked up a business card he had sitting on the table next to his laptop. He asked the question to the party on the other end and listened. He hung up and said, "Nine twenty-seven p.m."

"No wonder he kept watching his phone. He set the computer to delete everything one hour after he was supposed to land in Costa Rica." Buck showed him the digital ticket.

"I'll be a son of a bitch," said George. "He was closing up shop. The shutdown was deliberate."

Buck walked back to the end of the table. He sat for a minute thinking about the whole scenario. He kept coming back to why? He completed the arrest report, logged all the evidence and headed for the lunchroom for another bottle of Coke. He was taking a sip when a deputy walked in. "Agent Taylor, someone at the front desk asking for you."

Buck took his bottle back to the conference room, set it on the table and headed for the front desk. The deputy on duty pointed to a man and woman sitting on the bench on the public side of the entry. Buck froze. He asked the deputy to buzz him out, and he walked up to Congressman Kowalski and his wife.

Chapter Forty-Two

Buck led the congressman and his wife through the security door and back to an empty interrogation room. As he passed the desk, he asked the deputy to find the sheriff. They entered the room, and he asked them to have a seat. He offered them a drink, but they both refused. Neither one of them appeared to have gotten much sleep the night before.

Ryker leaned into the door, and Buck excused himself for a minute and walked out to talk to the sheriff. Buck told him what he thought was going on, and he asked him to start up the digital recorder and then join them. He walked back into the room.

The sheriff entered the room, and Buck introduced him to the congressman and his wife. Both Liz and the congressman wore casual clothes, and they had their sunglasses perched on the tops of their heads. The sheriff sat down.

"Congressman, before we begin, I'm going to read you your Miranda rights." Which he did, reading from the official Miranda Warning card he always carried in his pocket. The congressman, in a sad, tired voice, said he understood his rights. Buck asked him if he was willing to waive his right to have a lawyer present. The congressman stated his affirmation, Buck slid a copy of the waiver form to him with a pen and he signed it and slid it back. Buck thought he was going to cry.

The formalities out of the way, Buck told them the interview was being recorded, and he introduced everyone in the room. He leaned forward.

"Congressman, why don't you tell us why you are here this morning?"

Liz Kowalski spoke first. "Agent Taylor, if I may. Last night after you left our house, my husband told me and his chief of staff a whopper of a tale. After he finished, his chief of staff resigned and left our home. We spent the rest of the night talking, which is the first time that's happened in a long time. If I had the sense God gave me, I would have followed Jake out the door, but I have been married to this man for almost forty years, and I made a promise a long time ago. My husband understands he is going to prison; he also understands that this is a disease that will take a long time to cure, if ever. We will travel that path together. Three hours ago, my husband submitted his letter of resignation to the Speaker of the House and to the governor of Arkansas. He is ready to tell you everything, and he is ready to go to prison."

"I don't know what you said to him, Agent Taylor, but you might have saved his life and our marriage. We called your office this morning, and they told us you were working from here, so we drove straight over."

Mrs. Kowalski sat back in the chair and put both

of her hands in her lap. The congressman smiled at her weakly, his face full of anguish.

"I'm one of six people in the world who can tell you what Skylark Holdings does and how it operates. We started Skylark with one purpose in mind. The plan was to give like-minded men a place to exercise their proclivities in a safe and secure environment that we controlled. Then, at a select moment in time, to reveal those proclivities in order to force them either out of public office or out of specific businesses we needed to control. By forcing the right individuals out, we could replace them with people who held the same political beliefs as we did. In a short period of time, we believed we could control most of the world. Not to control the world in a mega-maniacal way but control it through government and business."

"We planned to start by removing key figures in Congress and the Supreme Court. These people would then be replaced with people we held sway over so that they could help produce the right results. We did some beta testing, and it worked very well. My wife has a list of all the people we were able to force out of office during the test phase. We did this in mostly poor African and South American nations so no one in this country would catch on. The system worked like a charm."

Buck sat up. "How were you able to make sure the right people joined you?"

"Skylark Holdings is our little secret in all of this. I said we offered men like ourselves a safe environment to practice our art. We set up a private internet club, accessible only by membership. It was not easy to find on the internet, but eventually, the same kind of people find each other. It's almost funny how that works. We wanted to keep it very exclusive, so the costs are high. One hundred thousand dollars to join. Once you paid your fee and filled out our online profile, you were given access to a secret website. This site ran video and still photos of children, twenty-four hours a day. The way we set it up, none of this content ever showed up on your personal computer. It stayed in our private cloud. You see, most pedophiles are caught because the authorities find porn on their computer or phone. With this system, the porn was viewed on a secure cloud, and nothing showed up on your computer. The charge for this service was five thousand dollars a month, and we guaranteed the content would always be new."

"How many members do you have on this site?"

"Well, sheriff, at last count we had over ten thousand members. Does that surprise you?"

The sheriff didn't answer, and Buck continued. "How did the blackmail piece work?"

"That was the beauty of the system. When we identified a person who was not of the same political persuasion and who was in the right position, our system would track their viewing habits. We would then either expose that information to the person and force them to resign, or we would send the information to a news outlet and have them forced out of office. We would then work with the local government to install a person in that position who was more to our liking."

Mrs. Kowalski pulled a couple sheets of paper out of her handbag and passed them to Buck, who read them and handed them to Ryker.

"So, the membership was unaware this was happening until it was too late, and only those people involved in Skylark Holdings knew about this."

"Correct. We were wrapping up the beta testing and were ready to roll it out full time. It was around the same time we began the beta testing that we found out Barb McBride was working on her next documentary, which was going to focus on child pornography. Mr. McBride was a friend of the head of our group, and we tasked him with keeping an eye on her, to make sure she didn't get too close. He reported back to us that she was in production and had enough evidence to name names. We had no idea if she only knew about the club or if she knew about Skylark, but we couldn't take the chance, so we had Mr. McBride take care of this."

"Who hired Mr. McBride to kill her?"

"We all agreed it was necessary. The problems started when we were unable to access her laptop to see what information she had. The body we thought would never be found was discovered by accident, and you got involved. We were fine when it was a missing person case being investigated by the local authorities—no offense, sheriff—but once you and your team arrived, we had to take stronger measures."

"Who decided to kill Jim McBride?"

The congressman sat back in his chair and closed his eyes. He opened them and said, "We were not aware of that until after it had taken place. The same thing with the bombing of the CDOT facility. We grew even more concerned when we found out that the man who was hired was also killed. Things seemed to be spiraling out of hand."

Buck slid a piece of paper out of his folder and handed it to the congressman. "Sir, can you tell us who the other members of Skylark are?"

The congressman read down the list. He took the pen Buck offered and circled three names and slid back the list.

"There are only three names circled," said Buck. "Who are the other two members?"

The congressman hesitated before turning to his wife, and she nodded. He took back the list and the pen and wrote two names down. He slid the list back to Buck, who read the names and slid it over to Ryker. He stared at the congressman.

"Everett James Randolph, as in retired Supreme Court Chief Justice Everett James Randolph?"

"Yes, Everett was a friend of my dad when he was in the Senate. They discovered they liked the same things. Skylark was Everett's idea. I guess he never got used to the fact that twice he lost the primary fight to become our party's nominee for president after he retired from the Supreme Court. He had unfinished business, and he didn't like the direction the country was moving in."

"Did Everett Randolph order the death of Barb McBride and her husband, Jim?"

The congressman said, "Yes."

Mrs. Kowalski removed a computer disc and a stack of papers and slid them across to Buck. He picked up the papers.

"What are these?"

"Those are transcripts of all the cell phone conversations we had, along with the digital recordings. I've highlighted the ones where Everett discussed killing the reporter and her husband."

The questioning went on for several more hours, and the congressman answered every question they asked. Things started to slow down, and Buck was running out of questions; he checked his watch and stood up. He thanked the congressman for his candor, and he thanked Mrs. Kowalski for coming with her husband. He started to walk towards the door when he stopped.

"One more question. Were you guys planning on having Bob McBride killed?"

The congressman looked at him like he had two heads. "Why? Bob McBride was a nobody in our organization."

Buck seemed perplexed. "He was important enough to have him kill Barb McBride?"

The congressman laughed for the first time all day. "Bob McBride didn't kill the journalist; Jim McBride took care of that. Bob McBride was hired by his brother to run the programming. He was a nobody."

It seemed the congressman was not as well

informed as he believed he was. Up to this point, he seemed to be part of the program, but Buck wondered if things were happening in the background that he was not a part of.

Chapter Forty-Three

Buck and the sheriff walked out of the interrogation room, and the sheriff directed Carl to place the congressman under arrest and process him. Hank, who was standing in the hallway looking pissed, said, "What the fuck, Buck? What was that all about, and what the hell is this about Everett Randolph and Bob McBride?"

Buck was about to answer when four guys in trench coats and dark suits walked into the hall, followed by a distinguished-looking older gray-haired man and a younger Hispanic-looking man in a three-piece suit.

"Perhaps I can answer that, Special Agent Clancy."

Hank stared at the two men in disbelief. The older man walked up to Buck and Ryker and shook their hands. He said, "Agent Taylor, Sheriff Morgan, I presume. Walter Armitage, attorney general." He motioned towards the other gentleman. "This is Hector Olivetti, director of the Costa Rican DIS. Is there a conference room we can use?"

The sheriff led the way, and Melanie and George stood up when the party entered. They started to move towards the door when Buck said, "You guys stay."

Hank's frustration was beginning to show. "Mr. Attorney General, what's going on, sir?"

"Please, everyone take a seat." The attorney general directed his next statement to the four men who accompanied them and said, "Gentlemen, no one in or out."

Two of the men remained inside the conference room while the other two stepped outside and closed the door. The United States Attorney General took off his coat and laid it over a chair.

"Good afternoon, everyone. I would like to keep this short and sweet because we still have a lot of work to do and we are running out of time. Mr. Olivetti here is the director of the DIS. This is Costa Rica's version of the FBI. Most people have never heard of his organization. Three years ago, an agent in his organization spotted a pattern while investigating a series of child abductions. What he discovered was an increase in the amount of child pornography that was showing up on the internet and the dark web. The trail he followed eventually led to the United States, and Mr. Olivetti brought it to our attention. We knew the organization responsible was huge and had an entirely new way of dealing with the many problems associated with accessing porn. We were also not sure who in our country could be trusted.

"The investigator, who had incredible computer skills that we taught him, recognized a pattern in the programming and requested the opportunity to go undercover to expose the bad guys. It wasn't until he was able to embed himself in the organization that we realized how large the enterprise was. To say we were stunned would be an understatement. With the help of our insider, the DIS assembled a list of members throughout Central America. They were prepared to start making arrests, but six months ago something changed. Two government officials in Ecuador and Nicaragua were exposed as pedophiles and forced to resign. They were replaced with, shall we say, extremely right-wing people."

"DIS investigated this and discovered several similar cases in several other countries in South America and Africa. It was like someone was systematically eliminating certain politicians. Mr. Olivetti alerted me to the situation. The problem was, we had no way of knowing why this was happening or who was responsible."

Everyone in the room sat quietly, staring at the attorney general.

"That brings us up to the past week. You are all aware of what's been happening this week, but what you are not aware of is that you and your investigations have gotten us closer than ever before to getting to the bottom of this. When you mentioned Everett Randolph, we knew we hit pay dirt. For several months, we have believed that Randolph was plotting to slowly overthrow several governments, but we had no idea he was involved with child porn. Now we think we have a good idea of how he planned to do it."

Hank seemed confused. "Excuse me, sir, but

how do you know what we have been working on? Even we're not sure."

"That's very simple. Last night, I received a call from Bob McBride's lawyer, and he filled me in."

Everyone at the table now seemed confused, and a low murmur took over the room.

"Folks, what you are unaware of," the attorney general said. "Bob McBride works for us—well, technically he works for DIS. He used to work for us."

The group sat in stunned silence.

Buck broke the ice and asked, "Why didn't he say something?"

Mr. Olivetti stood up. "Bob McBride was deep undercover. We still don't have any idea who we can trust or who is involved in this terrible thing. When we found out his brother had been murdered, I ordered Bob to suspend his operation and catch the next flight back to Costa Rica. That's what he was attempting to do when you arrested him, Agent Taylor. We had no idea if he was compromised or not, but he was ordered to destroy his computers and bug out. We were going to continue the operation, long distance. Last night, that changed."

"How so?" asked Ryker.

"Mr. McBride's lawyer called to tell me that Bob had been arrested and he believed he had found a group of people we could trust to put the final pieces together and wrap this up. That group sits in this room. Whatever you guys have been doing convinced Bob that you were the right people for the job. Hell, you almost solved this without any of our help. Arresting Congressman Kowalski was a huge break. We are here now to offer you the help or the encouragement you need to finish this."

Everyone sat in stunned silence, and the low murmur turned into a loud conversation as questions and comments started flowing. Buck cut everyone off. "Okay, quiet down. We still have a lot to do. One question, sir. Bob deleted all his files from the servers at the house he was living in. We need a way to retrieve that information. That is going to hamstring our investigation. Did Bob have a way to retrieve the files?"

Now it was the attorney general who seemed confused. "You have the files."

"No, sir. With all due respect, he crashed his servers. You can ask Hank. The FBI couldn't retrieve anything. That information could be critical."

"Agent Taylor, have you checked your email lately? Bob sent you a link to the files before he headed to the airport."

Buck realized he hadn't even opened his email since yesterday afternoon. He pulled it from his backpack and opened his email. Sure enough, halfway down the page was an email from anonymous.net. He clicked on the link, and the entire child porn world opened up to him. He had access to everything the members had, but there was something else. He clicked on the next link, and the phase two program opened. He opened the page, and in front of him was a complete list of everyone who had been targeted and a full list with links of the pages they were viewing, and as he watched, he noted it was all in real time.

He flipped back to the original page and clicked on the admin tab. When the tab opened, Buck had access to a complete list of the members, along with their profiles.

Buck was stunned and annoyed. He had been driving all over Colorado with the very thing they were looking for sitting in his email folder.

Mr. Olivetti made a coughing noise. "We did not know who we could trust with this program. Jim McBride was the one who created it, but he couldn't work the bugs out of it. That's when he reached out to his brother. He knew Bob had worked for the Defense Intelligence Agency many years back and was amazing when it came to computer programming. He had no idea he was working for us. Bob agreed to work with them, and while he was debugging the code, he created an admin program so he could monitor what was going on. He was never told what the phase two program was for, but he knew it was strange. On his own, he's been trying to identify the ten thousand members of this sick club."

Buck tapped Hank on the shoulder. "You may want to pull your people off the house. We have a shitload of work for them to do here."

"How do we go after Everett and the other people involved with Skylark?" asked the attorney general.

Buck pulled the disc and the transcripts out of his backpack. "It seems the congressman didn't know who to trust either. He gave me this list and the disc this afternoon. It is transcripts and audio of his conversation with Everett and the other owners of Skylark. If what he says is true, then on here is the evidence we need to go after the five remaining members of Skylark."

He slid them over to Melanie. "Can you go through these and see if what we need is here? If it is, then write up the warrant applications for the three members that live in Colorado. The out-of-town members will be up to Hank and his people. Sheriff, I think we need to get Bob McBride out of lockup."

The sheriff stood up, the attorney general signaled to his guy by the door, and Ryker left the room.

Chapter Forty-Four

Buck was sitting in a cubicle in the bull pen going through his investigation file on Barb McBride when a shadow crossed the cubicle doorway. Bob McBride stood in the doorway looking at him.

"Agent Taylor, didn't mean to disturb you, but I think I owe you an explanation."

Buck pointed towards the guest chair opposite the desk, and Bob McBride sat down. Buck closed the cover on his laptop.

"We've been through a lot the last couple days, and I apologize for not being able to tell you about it," said Bob. "We really had no idea who we could trust. When I first got into this, I was stunned at the number of people who get off on little kids. It made me sick to my stomach, knowing my brother was one of them."

He appeared sad and distant for a minute. "After watching you and your team work this case, I realized you were people I might be able to trust. That's why I sent you the link to the websites. Yesterday at the airport I started to have doubts. I didn't know how you found me as fast as you did, and when you put me in your car instead of taking me to the Eagle County Sheriff's Office, I wasn't sure what to think. The whole time we were driving, I kept waiting for you to turn off the highway and onto some out-of-the-way forest service road, where you would put a bullet in my head."

He stopped talking for a minute. "I was never that scared in my life. You have no idea how relieved I was when we pulled in here. I knew then I was right about your team. I wanted you to know that."

He stood up and walked out of the cubicle. Buck smiled and went back to his computer. He completed reading through the McBride file and opened the file on the six-year-old boy. He read the DNA report that Bax had told him about and hoped the tentative match was truly a relative of some kind. No one should die without family around. He closed his laptop and sat for a minute. The bull pen was empty since the night shift had started their patrols, and he sat and enjoyed the quiet.

The conference room was a buzz of activity now that they had the files to work with. Hank had his entire team working on identifying the members of the club. These people were located all around the world, and this was a massive undertaking. It would be fun to bust every one of them, but that was too much to ask for.

He was starting to shut down when George walked into the cubicle and sat down.

"Mel, Carl and I have identified almost everyone on Barb McBride's phone log." He handed Buck the list. "We've got about a dozen numbers that could be sources or informants, so the phones are probably burners, but we noted in what locations they were purchased." He sat back and closed his eyes as Buck read down the list.

There were some famous and infamous people on her call log, most of whom worked in the TV industry. It was quite a list. He got down to the bottom of the list to the unknown numbers. He read the list once and then backed up and reread it. "Son of a bitch," he said.

George opened his eyes. "Did we miss something?"

"One of these phones was purchased in Steamboat Springs."

"Yeah. Is that significant?"

"Barb McBride's sister lives in Steamboat. Her husband is a retired attorney. Who better to keep the evidence than family, especially if that family member is an attorney?"

"Could it be that simple?"

Buck thought for a minute. "Yeah, maybe it could be."

He stood up and put his laptop in his bag. "Anyone looking for me, tell them I'm on my way to Steamboat, but don't tell them why until we are sure."

He grabbed his jacket off the back of the chair and headed out the door.

He arrived in Steamboat just as the last rays of the sun disappeared behind the mountains. He always liked the northern part of the state, especially during summer. The farther north you went, the longer the sun stayed out. He thought about the trips they had taken as a family when the kids were younger and Lucy was healthy. Those were great memories that didn't make him sad when he thought about them. He wondered why that was, until his GPS told him to make a right at the light. He turned onto Eleventh Street, turned right on Crawford and pulled to the curb.

The house was a modest home that sat on a larger lot than he had seen in Steamboat before. He slid out of the car, walked up the driveway to the front door and rang the bell.

Elizabeth Grainger answered the door.

"Agent Taylor, this is a surprise. Please come in. Let me take your coat."

Buck shrugged off his coat, and Mrs. Grainger hung it in the closet.

"What brings you out this way? Is there news about Barb's killer?"

"There have been some developments, but unfortunately I can't go into those. I'm here to speak with your husband."

"Why on earth would you need to talk to Harold?"

"Is he here, ma'am? It's kind of important."

Mrs. Grainger seemed suspicious, but she called her husband. Harold walked into the room carrying the TV remote. He was tall and thin with balding white hair, and he walked with a little bit of a slouch. Mrs. Grainger introduced him to Buck, and they shook hands.

"Mr. Grainger, is there someplace we can talk in private?"

Harold started to say something, and Mrs. Grainger cut him off. "Agent Taylor, if this concerns my sister, I have a right to hear what you have to discuss with my husband."

Buck thought for a minute. "You're right, Mrs. Grainger. Please accept my apologies. It's been a long week."

She invited him to sit down in the living room, and they sat together on the couch.

"Mr. Grainger, do you own a burner phone?"

Mrs. Grainger was appalled. "What are you suggesting, Agent Taylor, that my husband is some kind of criminal? Does he look like a gangbanger to you?"

"No, ma'am. We found a number in your sister's call log that we determined to be a burner phone that was purchased here in Steamboat."

Mrs. Grainger was about to object when her husband squeezed her hand. "Elizabeth, stop."

She sat there with her mouth open, but no words came out. Mrs. Grainger glared at Buck.

"Yes, it's my phone." His wife stared at him in disbelief. "Harold?" was all she said.

"Sir, does this have anything to do with your sister-in-law's work?"

Mr. Grainger thought for a long minute before responding.

"Barb purchased the phone so we could have private conversations about her projects. Periodically she would need to cross the line that separates legal from not so much. I was her sounding board."

"Sir, did she leave her evidence packages with you to distribute once her report aired on TV?"

"Yes, Agent Taylor, she did. I never knew what was in the files, unless she had a particular legal question about something she had obtained. Otherwise, it was just a file she would email me with instruction for the distribution, with names and dates. Why do you ask?"

"Harold, why didn't you ever tell me?" asked Mrs. Grainger, looking on in disbelief.

"It was just business, Elizabeth."

"Mr. Grainger, we have been looking all over for her evidence files for her most recent projects. Why didn't you come forward after she died?"

"No one ever asked me for them. Once I received them, I would upload the distribution notes into my calendar and then forget about them until it was time to send them. To be perfectly honest with you, I forgot about them, what with worrying about Elizabeth."

"Mr. Grainger, as her legal representative, would you be allowed to let me see the files?"

Mr. Grainger stood up and walked out of the room and returned carrying his laptop. He sat back down on the couch, opened the laptop and pulled up the files. He handed Buck his laptop.

Buck spent the next hour reading the files, while Mrs. Grainger prepared tea for her and her husband and offered Buck a bottle of water, which he accepted. He stopped reading and handed the laptop back to Mr. Grainger.

"Sir, can you send me this file?"

"I don't see why not? I have her power of attorney. This was meant to be sent to the authorities, and it seems to me, Agent Taylor, that you are the authorities, so I see no harm in emailing this to you."

Buck gave him his email address and watched as the file was sent. He stood up, thanked Mr. and Mrs. Grainger and walked back to his Jeep. Today was a good day.

Chapter Forty-Five

Buck and Paul spent most of the next day typing up arrest warrant applications on their laptops and preparing the files they'd obtained from Mr. Grainger, along with the information they were able to get from the congressman's transcriptions.

Early in the afternoon, they sat in the conference room with the county judge, the Colorado Attorney General, the U.S. Attorney General, the sheriff, and Hank Clancy. They walked through the entire case and presented their evidence. The judge and the attorney general listened to the cases, discussed the merits of the evidence and the judge decided they had enough evidence to move forward with the arrests.

The FBI would handle the arrests of the people from Barb McBride's list that lived in Colorado with the help of local police and additional CBI agents. The high-priced targets, the three remaining people who made up the ownership of Skylark Holdings, LLC, would be arrested by Buck and his team.

The teams met in the sheriff's conference room. The U.S. Attorney General suggested that, for this first round of arrests, it might be best to keep using the Summit County Sheriff's Office as their base of operations. It was out of the way, and it was easy to control access. They all agreed.

Buck handed out the warrants to his team. With Bax still in Salt Lake City, he brought in several additional agents from the Denver office. The director volunteered to lead the arrest of Stanley Barkley, one of the names the congressman had circled on the list as being part of Skylark Holdings. He was the CEO of a Denver-based aerospace company and lived in a penthouse apartment across the street from Coors Field.

Paul and George would handle the arrest of Adam Kinkade, a federal district court judge who lived in Fort Collins, another name on the list.

Buck drew the short straw. He and Melanie would arrest Everett James Randolph, the retired chief justice of the United States Supreme Court. Randolph lived in Beaver Creek, west of Vail. He was the big prize.

Hank handed out the warrants to his teams. They would hit the rest of the local names on Barb McBride's list at the same time the other arrests were taking place. Once the arrests were under way, Hank had a team of trusted agents and clerks back in Washington, DC, preparing arrest documents for the rest of the two dozen out-of-state names on Barb McBride's documentary list. After that, it would be a long slog to identify members of the porn club and arrest them as well. That part of the operation would involve Interpol and a whole slew of federal, state and foreign governments and would take years.

Bob McBride thought he had the best job of all. While his colleagues at the DIS and the Public Police Force were preparing to arrest the pedophiles in Costa Rica and coordinating the arrests in seven other Central and South American countries, he would be pulling the plug on the child porn network. He sat in the conference room and watched as the team departed.

Ryker and Carl sat with him and wished the teams luck as they left. Since the arrests were out of their jurisdiction, their work was finished. Earlier in the day, they had arraigned the congressman, who was remanded without bail. He was now on his way to the state penitentiary in Canon City, where he would remain until his trial.

At seven p.m., with all the teams checking in, the word was given, and teams proceeded with the arrests. The arrests went like clockwork, and the news media was having a field day with all the information they were receiving.

Two of the men being arrested by the FBI chose a different route and committed suicide as the agents entered their homes. One was found hanging from the rafters in his garage, and the other blew his brains out in his master bathroom.

Buck and Melanie badged their way through the gate in Beaver Creek. They left an Eagle County deputy at the gate to make sure the security guard did not alert the chief justice. They pulled into the large circular driveway and parked behind a dozen cars that Buck only wished he could afford. Accompanied by two additional Eagle County deputies, they walked up the steps and rang the front doorbell. A woman in a black maid's outfit answered the door, and Buck could hear a party going on somewhere deeper in the house.

Buck, wearing his badge around his neck outside his ballistic vest, said, "Police, Judge Randolph, please." The maid, seeing four police officers all wearing ballistic vests, turned and headed towards the noise, and she walked through an archway with Buck and team right on her heels. She entered the room, and the noise stopped.

A short, gray-haired man wearing a suit jacket and no tie walked towards the group. "Gabriella, who are these people?"

Buck stepped forward and unfolded a piece of paper.

"Mr. Randolph, Buck Taylor, Colorado Bureau of Investigation. I have a warrant for your arrest."

Melanie stepped behind the judge and pulled out her handcuffs.

"On what charge?" He started to resist Melanie applying the cuffs until one of the deputies stepped up and grabbed his arm.

"You are being charged with the murders of Barb McBride and Jim McBride, as well as the production and distribution of child pornography."

Melanie snapped on the cuffs, and she led him away. The entire time he was screaming at the top of his voice, "Do you know who I am? I was the chief justice of the United States Supreme Court."

Buck stopped in front of him, turned around and got right in his face. "Maybe once you were someone important, but not today. Today you are just an old pedophile, and you are mine." He grabbed him by the other arm and walked him past his stunned guests.

In the conference room, Ryker answered his phone, listened and hung up.

"It's time, Bob."

Bob McBride opened his laptop and clicked on the URL he had waiting on the search bar. When the administrative website opened, he started entering a series of codes. One by one, the porn sites that were attached to the website shut down. In half an hour, he shut down all the sites. All around the world, pedophiles lost access to their web content.

Bob sat back in his chair and smiled. Three years of his life had been devoted to destroying these people, and now it was all over. He could go back to Costa Rica, hold his head up high and resume his job at the DIS. He thought about all the needless costs. His sister-in-law Barb was gone, and the world would be worse off without her in it. She had spent her entire life working for the oppressed and the downtrodden, and she had so much more to give.

His brother was gone as well, and even though he felt little remorse, he felt responsible in some small way. His brother was a talented individual who had lost focus and used his talents for all the wrong reasons. He wished he could have done something to save him, but that ship had sailed. He was grateful that his brother's legacy would no longer hurt children. Deep inside, he knew that what they did here today was only a drop in the bucket in the war on child pornography, but he could always hope that it made a difference.

He closed his laptop and sat back in his chair. Ryker stood up, patted him on the shoulder and said, "Nice job, Bob. Thanks." He walked out the door and left Bob McBride alone with his thoughts.

Chapter Forty-Six

Bax landed at Salt Lake City International Airport, stood in line for twenty minutes to get her rental car and drove past all the construction. Salt Lake was building a new terminal and parking garage, and the roads were a bit confusing. She found her way to the airport exit and headed downtown to Salt Lake City Police Headquarters.

She walked up to the desk and told the desk officer she had an appointment with Detective Yolanda Diego. She was escorted back to the detective's office on the fourth floor. Yolanda was waiting for her. Bax stepped into her office, and the detective stood up and shook her hand. Yolanda was of African and Mexican descent, with dark skin and short shoulder-length straight dark hair. She wore dark slacks and a medium-blue blouse.

"Hi, Agent Baxter, pleased to meet you. Please call me Yo."

"Thanks, Yo. Call me Bax, everyone does."

They talked small talk for a few minutes, and Yo asked Bax to tell her about the case. One of Detective Diego's duties was cold cases, and she was fascinated by this case. Bax explained about the car and how they came to find it. She kept the details about the child porn case light as she described the condition of the car and the autopsy results of the body.

Yo said, "I did some digging into the family information you sent me from the DNA site, and here's what I've been able to glean. The name you provided is a young woman about twenty-five years old, so I doubt she is directly related to your victim. Her family consists of her mother, father, three brothers and two sisters. She is the oldest of the siblings. The family has lived in Salt Lake since the early nineties, so the dates work out with your victim. I didn't interview the daughter because I didn't want to spook anyone."

Bax read the file. "If I had to bet, I would say the mother is probably in the right age range. She would have been in her mid twenties, early thirties at the time the body was dumped."

Yo nodded in agreement. "That's what I thought too. Why don't we grab a quick lunch and then head to the house and see if we can solve this? There's a great Italian place down the street."

Bax told her Italian was perfect, and they headed out the door.

Finished with lunch, Yo offered to drive, so they found her unmarked car in the police parking lot and headed out. Bax was glad she hadn't driven, because the streets in Salt Lake always drove her crazy. She knew the street numbers all started from Temple Square, but the use of coordinates instead of street names always confused her, so she sat back and let Yo navigate the streets.

After twenty minutes, Yo pulled to the curb and

turned off the car. She pointed to the house across the street, a modest mid-century ranch house with an immaculately landscaped front yard. She grabbed her rover, her portable radio, off the dash, and she and Bax exited the car.

They walked up the sidewalk to the front door, and Yo rang the bell. A middle-aged woman with long gray hair wearing jeans, a flowered shirt and no shoes answered the door, wiping her hands on a small checkered dish towel. "May I help you?"

"Mrs. Anderson, I'm Detective Yolanda Diego with the Salt Lake City Police Department, and this is Agent Ashley Baxter of the Colorado Bureau of Investigation." They flashed their badges.

Mrs. Anderson stared at Bax. "Oh, my god, you found Gerald." She sat down on a chair that was standing next to the door and started to cry. Her husband, a brown-haired man of medium height with thick glasses, walked into the room and saw her crying.

"Hon, what's the matter? Are you all right?"

Wiping the tears from her eyes with the kitchen towel, she said, "She's from Colorado." He focused on Bax.

"Mark Anderson," he said by way of introduction. "Perhaps you should come in." He stepped to the side and rested his hand on his wife's shoulder. Bax closed the door, and Mark Anderson led them into the living room. He offered them seats and then sat on the couch next to his wife, who was still in tears. He held her hand.

"We knew this day would come, but over the

years, life goes on, and you soon lose track of time," he said.

Bax reached into her shirt pocket. "Before we begin, I'm going to read the Miranda Warning to your wife. Mrs. Anderson, would that be okay?"

Mrs. Anderson wiped her eyes with the towel she was still holding and nodded. Bax read her rights off the card. "Mrs. Anderson, do you understand your rights?" Mrs. Anderson nodded and said, "Yes," in a soft voice.

"And do you waive your right to have an attorney present?" Again, a nod followed by, "Yes."

Bax reached into her backpack, pulled out a waiver form and a pen and slid it across the coffee table to Mrs. Anderson. She signed it, barely reading it. Bax pulled out her phone and turned on the voice recorder.

Formalities out of the way, Bax said, "Mrs. Anderson, why don't you tell us about Gerald and the day he died?"

Mrs. Anderson gathered her thoughts and wiped her eyes.

"Gerald was my son. He was born with a terrible muscular disease, and he almost didn't survive his birth. My husband at the time and me, we were very religious, and I kept praying for a miracle. My husband, on the other hand, lost all faith in God and blamed me for having a crippled kid. He grew to hate Gerald like it was an assault on his manhood. We were dirt-poor at the time, and after three years, Gerald developed diabetes. The cost of the insulin made my husband crazy. That's when he started drinking, and the drinking led to beatings. Several times, while he was drunk, he put a gun to Gerald's head and threatened to kill him. I was afraid, I had no idea what to do."

She stopped and took a breath. Her husband stood up, walked into the next room and came back with a glass of water. She took a sip and composed herself.

"One day, after a nasty beating, I'd had enough. While my husband was working in the next field, I took our old car, loaded up Gerald and took off. I had no idea where to go, so when I got to I-70, I turned west and just drove. We ended up in a small town in Colorado. I think it was called Dillon. I found a spot outside of town that was isolated, so I pulled in and went to sleep. I was exhausted. Sometime during the night, Gerald had a seizure. I never heard him."

The tears began to flow, and her husband pulled her close. Bax gave her a minute.

"I'm sorry," she said. "Even after all this time, I miss him so much. When I woke up, he wasn't breathing. I didn't know what to do so I grabbed his insulin and gave him a shot in the thigh. But it didn't help. My baby was finally at peace. I just sat there and held him for the longest time. I didn't know what to do, but I was afraid I would be arrested. I was twenty-five at the time, and I was just plain scared. I put Gerald in the back seat, covered him with a blanket and drove into town. I found a hardware store and bought some black plastic, tape and a shovel. I was going to find an out-of-the-way place to bury him. On the way out of the store, I saw some flowers, and I bought a small bouquet with the little money I had left. And then I just drove."

"The car had been giving me trouble all along. It was an old junker, and when we started to climb up the road past a big lake, it started making a lot of noise. I pulled over, and where I stopped the view was amazing. I knew this was where God wanted Gerald to be. I found the perfect spot and tried to dig a hole, but the ground was so rocky, I couldn't. That was when I decided to put him in the trunk. I wrapped his frail little body in the plastic and placed the bouquet in with him. I pulled the license plates, and with everything I had, I pushed the car off the road and into the canyon. I had never known such sadness until that day. I found a rock and sat there for hours, praying. As it got dark, I threw the plates into the lake and hitchhiked back to Dillon. A trucker was heading to Salt Lake, and he offered me a ride. I met Mark while we were working in a department store and told him the story. We drove to Reno one weekend so I could get a divorce, and then while we were there Mark proposed, and we got married the next day."

She stopped talking. Her husband asked, "What happens now?"

"Based on what you have told me, you violated Colorado Statute 18-8-610.5, tampering with a deceased human body. But the charge will be up to the DA to decide. Right now, we are going to arrest you, and you will be extradited back to Colorado to stand trial unless you try to fight the extradition."

Her husband walked to the closet and brought out her coat, and Bax turned off her recorder.

"Mrs. Anderson, I'm sorry we have to do this, but there is no other way. Based on the life you have lived so far, the DA might be lenient. I hope so, and I will do all I can to persuade him."

Bax and Yo led Mrs. Anderson to Yo's car, and they headed for the city jail to process her and prepare her for transport back to Colorado.

The following day, Yo dropped them off at the fixed base operator at the airport, and she and Mrs. Anderson walked onto a small Learjet and headed for Colorado.

Chapter Forty-Seven

Buck drove his Jeep up to the front entrance of the Eagle County Regional Airport and pulled to the curb. Bob McBride sat in the passenger seat and unbuckled his seat belt. The drive from Breckenridge had been pleasant. They talked about fishing, which was also Bob's favorite thing to do, and they talked about Costa Rica. Buck and Lucy had always talked about traveling there when the kids were grown, but it never seemed to happen. The way Bob spoke about the country and the people, Buck decided that someday he would get there.

Bob told him he would always be welcome and to just give him a call. He reached for the door handle.

"You know, Bob, I never got to ask you a question that's been bugging me."

"No problem, Buck, ask away."

"I'm curious. How did your prints end up in Barb's car?"

Bob answered right away. "A couple days before she walked out, she was pulling out of the barn, heading to town for groceries. I was walking down the road, and I waved her down. She rolled down her window, and I leaned in the driver's side and asked her to pick me up a couple things. When I stood up, I rested my hand on the door. It's that simple."

Bob thanked Buck and reached for the door handle.

"That makes sense, Bob, but why were your prints and a perfect clear palm print on the back hatch of her car?"

Buck knew he had him when his face turned white as a ghost. The forensics report he had been shown during his debrief never mentioned his prints being found on the trunk. Buck had held that information back since the little bug was still running around in his brain. Bob put his hand on the door handle.

Someone walked up to the passenger door and tapped on the window. Bob knew his life was over, and he turned towards the window. Bax leaned down, smiled and then waved her handcuffs in front of the window. Standing behind her were Eagle County Deputy Trujillo and two other deputies.

Epilogue

Buck stood in the quiet solitude of the Gunnison River and played the large cutthroat trout he had on the end of his line. The sun was setting over the hills to the west, and the rain that had threatened all day never materialized. He released his fish and faced upriver. Twenty yards away, his daughter Cassie was landing a fourteen-inch brown trout.

The day had turned out perfect. The entire town, it seemed, had turned out for the dedication of the newly completed Lucy Taylor Memorial Riverwalk, and the trail was getting plenty of use. Hardy Braxton, his brother-in-law, and his wife, Rachel, Lucy's younger sister, played host and hostess and organized the big event. There were speeches, food, games and activities for all ages.

The riverwalk was Hardy and Rachel's gift to the town of Gunnison to honor Lucy. He'd bought the one-mile strip of land along the Gunnison River, hired Jason, Buck's younger son, to work on the design for the various pavilions and shelters along the walk and hired the best biologists and fishery people he could find to improve the habitat in the river. The fishing, which was already first class, was now something special, and Buck spent as much time as he could fishing this stretch of the river.

He stood for a minute and watched Cassie cast. She was a top-notch fisherwoman, and even in high school she would run casting clinics for the younger kids in town that wanted to learn to fly-cast. She waved to her dad and then hooked into another fish. Buck waved back. He was glad she'd come home to spend some time with her dad.

He thought about the last month. He'd attended the funerals for the two Grand Junction police officers that were killed in the line of duty. He'd attended the memorial service for Barb McBride and was amazed at the huge turnout.

He'd testified at the trial of Bob McBride and was pleased when he was found guilty for his part in the murder of Barb McBride and his brother, Jim. He was now awaiting trial on the child pornography charges.

The lawyers for the retired chief justice of the United States Supreme Court, Everett Randolph, were filing motion after motion to delay his trial on murder and child pornography charges. Rumor had it, his mental faculties were slipping. The others arrested that night and in the following weeks were all awaiting trial. The FBI was in the process of identifying the other members of the porn club, and several members had been arrested in several countries and in the United States.

Mrs. Anderson, the mother of six-year-old Gerald, plead guilty to the lesser crime of tampering with evidence. Based on the mitigating circumstances and her exemplary life since then, the judge sentenced her to one thousand hours of community service. She was released to go back to her family in Salt Lake. The family buried Gerald in a private ceremony near their home. Bax had testified on her behalf at the trial. It had been a busy month.

Buck had even managed to find the little girl in the sniper's picture. She lived out of state, so he tracked down a number and called her. Her mother answered the phone, and he identified himself and told her what happened and where she could claim the body. She allowed him to talk to the young girl, and he gave her the message from her father. The mother came back on the line and he asked her if there was anything he could do to help with arrangements to get the body. All she said was, "No thanks," and she hung up the phone.

Buck spent some of his downtime, after the conclusion of the investigation, following up on reports of murders in Florida that had similarities to the murders they knew were committed by Alicia Hawkins. He'd contacted several of the municipalities that had murders identified by the FBI as possible Alicia Hawkins killings and was in the process of going over the police reports and autopsies. What concerned him the most was she was becoming much more proficient at killing and was honing her craft.

Buck walked to the riverbank, climbed out and set his fly rod down next to his cooler and pulled out a bottle of Coke. He was about to take a sip when his phone chirped with an incoming text message.

He undid his waders and dug his phone out of his pants pocket and checked the number. He wondered why Hank Clancy was sending a text instead of calling. He opened the text, read it and stood dumbfounded.

"She's out of Florida, task force heading to Mississippi."

Acknowledgments

A special thank you to my daughter Christina J. Morgan, my unofficial editor-in-chief. She devoted a significant amount of time making sure the book was presented as perfectly as possible.

Thanks to my editor, Laura Dragonette, whose efforts helped turn my manuscript into a polished novel. Her help is greatly appreciated. Any mistakes the reader may find are solely the responsibility of the author.

Also, I would like to thank my family for all of their encouragement. I have been telling them stories since they were little, and I always told them that someone should be writing this stuff down. I decided to write it down myself.

I want to thank my closest friend, Trish Moakler-Herud. She has been encouraging me for years to write my stories down. I hope this will make her proud.

A special thanks to my late wife, Jane. She pushed me for years to become a writer, and my biggest regret is that she didn't live long enough to see it happen. I love her with all my heart and miss her every day. I think she would be pleased.

Finally, thanks to the readers. Without you, none of this would be important.

About the Author

Chuck Morgan attended Seton Hall University and Regis College and spent thirty-five years as a construction project manager. He is an avid outdoorsman, an Eagle Scout, and a licensed private pilot. He enjoys camping, hiking, mountain biking and fly-fishing.

He is the author of the Crime series, featuring Colorado Bureau of Investigation agent Buck Taylor. The series includes *Crime Interrupted*, *Crime Delayed*, and *Crime Unsolved*.

He is also the author of *Her Name Was Jane*, a memoir about his late wife's nine-year battle with breast cancer. He has three children, three grandchildren and two dogs. He resides in Lone Tree, Colorado.

Other Books by the Author

"*Crime Interrupted: A Buck Taylor Novel* by Chuck Morgan is a gripping, edge-of-the-seat novel. Right from page one, the action kicks off and never stops, gaining pace as each chapter passes." Reviewed by Anne-Marie Reynolds for Readers' Favorite.

"This crime novel reads like a great thriller. The writing is atmospheric, laced with vivid descriptions that capture the setting in great detail while allowing readers to follow the intensity of the action and the emotional and psychological depth of the story." Reviewed by Divine Zape for Readers' Favorite.

"Professionally written in the style of a best-selling crime novelist, such as Tom Clancy, *Crime Unsolved: A Buck Taylor Novel* by Chuck Morgan is a spellbinding suspense novel with an environmental flair. Intriguing subplots of fraud, survivalist paranoia, and murder weave their way through the fabric of the plot, creating a dynamic story. This is an action-filled, stimulating tale which contains fascinating details that are relevant in our present climate." Reviewed by Susan Sewell for Reader's Favorite.